Forkpoints

Advance Praise for Forkpoints

"Good reading for our hard times. These are stories of opportunities unseen, glimpsed, suddenly brought into focus—maybe to slip away, or be refused, or maybe just delayed. There's a gentleness to them, a melancholy, that sets off the glints of new possibilities and hope. The last story gives us a child's-eye view of the Blitz so clear and detailed—readers who loved Michael Ondaatje's Warlight should have a look here."

Suzy McKee Charnas, author of The Holdfast Chronicles
and *The Vampire Tapestry*

"Sheila Finch is one of the treasures of modern science fiction. She's literate, imaginative, and deeply insightful. Her contributions to the field include not only specific, awesomely good works, but her careful attention to how language shapes story structure and flow. Her short fiction works are like polished gemstones, with each facet reflecting and informing the central theme. Here is a collection of such jewels, each speaking to the profound transformative power of human understanding. We are more than our circumstances, these stories say, we have the ability to shift our perspective, to look and feel more deeply, and thereby to shift entire realities. From an elderly music teacher who could also have been an iconic physicist to an extraordinary communication across species to a time-traveler visiting his own ancestor during the World War II London bombings, each tale reaches deep into the mind of the reader, inviting us with Finch's characteristically gentle wisdom to see the universe and ourselves in a revolutionary light."

Deborah Ross, author of *Collaborators* and
The Seven-Petaled Shield fantasy series

For the Asilomar Writers Consortium

FORKPOINTS

Stories of Decisions Made and Roads Not Taken

by Sheila Finch

Aqueduct Press
PO Box 95787
Seattle, Washington 98145-2787
www.aqueductpress.com

Library of Congress Control Number: 2021970085

ISBN: 978-1-61976-218-3
First Edition, First Printing, June 2022
10 9 8 7 6 5 4 3 2 1

Cover Illustration courtesy Kenn Brown
http://www.mondolithic.com/

Printed in the USA by McNaughton & Gunn

Prior Publication Acknowledgments

"The Old Man and C," *Amazing Stories*, November 1989

"Field Studies," *Asimov's Science Fiction*, May/June 2017

"The Persistence of Butterflies," *2020 Visions*, M-Brane Press 2010

"Madonna of the Chromosomes," First publication in this volume

"Forkpoints," *The Magazine of Fantasy and Science Fiction*, February 2002

"Miles to Go," *The Magazine of Fantasy and Science Fiction*, June 2002

"Where Two or Three," *Is Anybody Out There?* Daw, 2010

"Reach," *The Magazine of Fantasy and Science Fiction*, February 2003

"A Very Small Dispensation," *Asimov's Science Fiction*, October/November 2013

"Czerny at Midnight," *Asimov's Science Fiction*, Nov/Dec 2021

"Sequoia Dreams," *Amazing Stories*, July 1990

"Not This Tide," *Asimov's Science Fiction*, January/February 2019

Contents

THE OLD MAN AND C

LIGHT sprang to the wall when his wife opened the casement window to let in a little breeze from the lake. It shattered, sparkling over bookshelves and wallpaper, as his young student's bow scraped across the E string, and the fingers of her left hand searched for high C. She still could not seem to get it right. The note must sing, not screech!

He had shown Rosa over and over, patiently correcting her fingering, the pressure of the bow across the string, explaining to her how the sound was produced in the hope that if she understood perhaps she could improve. She was so brilliant in every other respect.

"*Kaffee*, Papa?" his wife whispered in his ear.

He shook his head.

"Don't lose sight of the time. Eddie comes this afternoon. And Lisl will want to go with her Opa on the boat!"

Rosa had progressed to the arabesque, a passage she played excellently, her fingers flying like the scintillating reflection of water on the wall. His wife left him to his pupil and the music lesson, closing the music room door quietly behind her. He gazed at Rosa. Eyes closed, she bit her lower lip in concentration. Wisps of fair hair escaped from braids trailing over her shoulders. She was a good girl, the best student he had ever had. If she mastered this one note, she should easily take the gold medal—perhaps the last he would see a pupil take. She had more natural talent than any of his previous medalists.

1

But the other students in the competition, children who came from the wealthy suburbs of Zurich where they had *Waschmaschinen* and *Fernsehapparaten*, they could afford to spend all day practicing, whereas Rosa got up at first light and helped her father milk the cows. Time for the violin had to be sandwiched between farm chores and schoolwork. Now she was approaching sixteen; her father had begun to think of the day she would marry a solid farm lad and give him one less mouth to feed. This was her last chance, too. He had worked hard with Rosa, giving long lessons and extra lessons that her family had paid for with cream and eggs. Who could say if it would be enough?

Rosa finished the piece with a flourish, the notes sparkling almost visibly in the air between them.

"So, Herr Professor, are you pleased?" Triumph shining on her round face showed what answer she expected.

"I'm very pleased," he agreed.

"We're going to win the medal," she promised.

It was important to him that this little farm girl take the very last gold medal. Yet he knew he should not allow his own sense of self-worth to become bound to a pupil's performance in a competition. How had it happened? When one is young, he thought, how many choices lie at one's fingertips? How many roads beckon the eager traveler? Time spreads out before the young man like a map of a marvelous sunlit country. He knows he can write symphonies, build castles, discover the secrets of the universe—which will it be? He does not know (for God is merciful) that the choice of one road shuts out the possibility of another. Who can guarantee which is right to take? His mother had always wanted him to play the violin. And he had been an indifferent scholar in school.

"Herr Einstein?" Rosa said, her young face creased in a frown. "Aren't you well?"

He discovered that he was sweating and took out a linen handkerchief to mop his brow. "I'm well, Rosa. It's hot today, that's all. What else should we expect of July?"

"If I get my chores done early enough, my mother says I can take my little brothers swimming." She looked up at him, blue eyes innocent as infinity. "Do you wish me to play something else, Herr Professor?"

He patted her hand. "Enough for today, *Liebchen*. Enjoy the lake!" And the light, he thought, the vast potential of the realms of light.

Rosa put the violin away in its case, gathered up her music, dropped him a hasty curtsy, and scurried from the room. The dancing light, fragmented by her departure, gathered itself together again, settling back on the walls and the Turkish rug and the dark wood of the grand piano.

The day's post lay on the floor by the armchair under the open window, where he had left it at the beginning of Rosa's lesson. Sunshine fell on the fat pile, a correspondence he carried on with old friends, poets, pacifists, and Zionists, people he had met all over Europe when he had still been touring with the orchestra. They sent letters full of music and philosophy and grand theory, wonderful talk. It was like a rich, festive meal that today he did not feel like eating. He set most of the letters aside, unopened. There had been a time when he had shared his friends' sense of the universe in the palm of his hand, a gift of a benign God who revealed His existence in the harmony of His creation. He shook his head mutely. It was a young man's belief. The world had fought two terrible wars

3

since then. Now it was enough to sit quietly and look at what had become of the promises.

He was so tired today.

One letter was from his widowed cousin Elsa, full of news about her daughters, no doubt; he had always liked Elsa. He tore the stamps off the envelope carefully, saving them for his granddaughter, Lisl.

"Papa?" His wife appeared in the doorway, her hands still floury from making *Dampfnudeln*. "Are you coming to lunch?"

"Ah, Millie," he said. "I'm getting old."

"Seventy-five isn't old!"

"And what have I accomplished?"

Millie spread her arms wide. "This house—two fine sons—your sailboat down there on the lake—your pupils—perhaps Rosa gets the gold this year. How many will that make for you? And you ask what you've accomplished?"

He was silent, looking at the shimmering light from the lake that shot its arrows into his soul.

"Besides," his wife said. "Lisl adores you. That must be worth something."

But the sense that there might have been more gnawed at him.

Later, with his son and granddaughter, he took the sailboat far out on Lake Zurich, tilting gently in a mild breeze and grand weather, sailing under the lee of slopes covered with ripening vineyards, presided over by the hump of the Albishorn. Millie was right, he thought, all the tiny joys had to add up to something.

"I picked up a translation of a new thing that came out last year from this American writer, Hemingway," Eddie said, as Lisl trailed fingers in the cold, clear water, shattering the drowned light in its depths into diamond fragments. "It's about an old man fishing, and sharks."

"I don't like to fish."

"You'd like this story!"

He gazed at his younger son, a banker, already thickening into comfortable middle age. "I don't have as much time to read as you, apparently."

"Nonsense! You read the wrong things—about wars and terrible things like that. You should read fiction."

"So many wars. Where will it all end?"

"Pfft!" Eddie made a derisive sound. "These Asians are all alike. The Koreans will run out of steam just as the Japanese did in 1947. You'll see. The Americans hate to do anything violent. They'll make another treaty."

"Opa," Lisl interrupted, hanging over the low side of the boat, brown hair trailing through sun-spangled water. "Are there sharks in this lake? May I go swimming?"

"Careful!" Eddie warned. "You'll fall in fully clothed, and then your grandmother will scold."

The sun's slanting radiance scattered from the child's flowing hair. He stared at it, fascinated. The play of light had always obsessed him.

"Opa?" Lisl urged.

"A man should leave a mark," he said, watching the flash and dazzle in the lake. "It's not enough just to have lived."

"Exactly the point of the Hemingway story I referred to," his son said with obvious satisfaction. "I took the liberty of putting my copy on your desk, Papa."

The child began to cry.

Venus, the evening star, was already burning in the western sky. They heeled over and brought the sailboat swooping back to the dock.

The map does not indicate which is the best road, only that more than one possibility exists. One afternoon many years ago (perhaps early May, for he remembered the cuckoo's melancholy call outside), he had been at his desk in the patent office in Bern. Splinters of sunlight fell through green branches onto the papers he was reading. The work was sterile, soul-killing. He lived for the evenings when the street lamps were lit; then he walked under pale yellow flowers of the linden trees to the back room of a small *Gasthaus*. There, he joined a string quartet, exploring their way across Beethoven's stark territory, the rich jungles of Brahms, the tidy gardens of Johann Sebastian Bach. He had just recently graduated from the Polytechnic Academy, where he'd studied mathematics. But music had proved to be his Lorelei.

That particular day, he remembered, he had trouble chaining his mind to the endless march of dull papers across his desk, while outside the marvelous vernal light called to him. Instead he played with numbers (the abstract language of music, he had always thought) that combined and recombined in mysterious ways, numbers like the swarming stars that dazzled overhead in the clear Alpine night.

"Ho, Jew-boy!" The supervisor, a spindly little man with a receding hairline who had taken an instant dislike to the new employee, stopped by his desk.

He hastily slid a pile of half-finished forms over the mathematical doodlings. The supervisor leered over the desk, hoping to catch him in blatant error so there would be cause to fire him.

"Is the report ready, young genius? Or have you been too busy to bother?"

"I'll have it done on time."

"You certainly will—or you'll look elsewhere for employment."

He was not born to work behind a desk, filling out forms, following someone else's orders. But he also was not capable of ignoring a challenge. For two hours he worked without stopping till the report was done, far more thoroughly than even the thin supervisor had a right to expect.

That evening at music practice, a warm spring breeze blowing, full of starshine and promises, he received his first request to give tuition on the violin to the child of the *Gasthaus* keeper. The next morning he gave notice at the patent office.

Rosa worked the bow smoothly across her instrument, moving through the difficult passage that led inexorably up the scale to high C, her nemesis. He leaned back in the armchair, eyes closed, evaluating, trying to hear the Rachmaninoff the way the judges would. Rain spattered the closed window, and Millie had lit the lamps in the middle of the afternoon. One week to go, he thought. One week to make a mark, to change the path of the stars that told man's fate, to mold the universe to one old man's will. He was tired all the time now. The Earth under his feet tugged at him, bending him out of shape.

Then she faltered once again on the high note, and he leaped up from his chair, forgetful of stiff joints.

"'No! No! No!" He seized the instrument from her hands. "What have I told you? You aren't milking cows here. You must glide up the notes like a fish swimming in a river. Like this." He ran the bow smoothly up and down the scale, arthritic fingers for once remembering how they had moved in their youth when he had been the soloist with the orchestra in Paris and Vienna and at the Albert Hall.

Rosa lowered blond lashes over her ruddy cheeks, and he caught the gleam of tears in the glow of the lamps.

He relented. "All right now. We've worked hard enough for one lesson. Perhaps it'll go better tomorrow, or the next day."

"I'm sorry, Herr Professor. I don't wish to let you down."

But perhaps he had let himself down? Perhaps if he had stayed longer in the patent office, used the time to think about numbers?

"Let me try it again," she pleaded. "I will get it right."

He gave her back the violin, thinking about possibilities and life that had a habit of squeezing them down.

His Uncle Jakob had urged something else, but Mama had her heart set on music. And music had been good to him, he could not deny that. He had moved back to Zurich, married his university sweetheart and raised two young sons in relative comfort. In his orchestra days, he had seen something of the world. He had books and music and friends around the globe who wrote to him and came to visit. He'd had good students—more silvers and bronzes than any other teacher in the canton, and a respectable number of golds. One had even gone on to world-class competition—he remembered a brief, breathtaking visit to New York. And now he was at home with the lake and the boat and the crisp Alpine light sculpting the mountains.

If he had been someone like Van Gogh, he would have painted that light. Sometimes he thought about the incandescent heart of distant galaxies, spewing brightness through the universe to break at last under its own weight on the shores of Lake Zurich. It made his heart ache to think of it.

Rosa tried the passage again. This time he did not have to wince as she reached high C.

That evening, drinking his coffee with whipped cream and chocolate, sitting beside Millie, hand in hand on the balcony, watching the moon come and go in the scudding clouds over the lake, he thought about the mystery of roads where one made decisions in darkness.

"Do you never wonder, Millie, if your life might have been different?"

"How so, different?" she asked suspiciously.

"Do you never entertain the idea that perhaps you might have done something else with your time, something you might have been better at?"

"No," Millie said.

He sighed. "We could have traveled. We could have seen more of America…."

"We could have had problems and divorced!" she said sourly.

He patted her hand. "Never."

The ache persisted, nevertheless.

The next morning, Hans Albert telephoned from Berlin, where he was a professor of physics.

"Have you read the newspaper, Papa?"

Behind the telephone in the hall, the wallpaper—Millie's favorite pattern, clumps of creamy roses festooned with little pink ribbons—glowed in warm sunshine. He stared, imagining the artist making the very first drawing from a real vase of roses, the blooms illuminated by a ray of sunlight falling like a benediction on the studio. In some sense, it was all happening now: the painter, the roses blooming in the garden before somebody cut them, the old violin teacher gazing at wallpaper. The past, like the future, was only a stubborn linguistic illusion.

"Papa?"

"Ah. What should I have read?"

"The war, of course. Don't you always read about the war in Korea?"

Yes, the war. The strangeness of the place-names, *Seoul, Pyongyang, Pusan*. And the stupidity of young boys killing other young boys in jungles and rice paddies where light slanted through palm trees and bamboo thickets, light that had crossed the darkness of space from a distant star to illuminate a scene for painters.

"They're still fighting?"

"Papa!" Then another idea seemed to occur to his son. "Are you feeling well?"

"You're going to tell me that the American airplanes dropped a most peculiar bomb on a Korean town with a name as singular as roses. Isn't this so?"

"Yes—but, roses? Anyway, let me tell you about this weapon, Papa. A great advance—the future beckoning! You see what they've proved? A particle of matter can be converted into enormous outbursts of energy. This is something we've been working on here at the university, splitting uranium atoms."

"Light," he said. "It travels so fast. No time at all, really, from our point of view."

Hans Albert was silent. After a while he said casually, "Is Mutti there? Let me speak to her."

The afternoon was quite warm, but Millie insisted he wear his hat, anyway. He had the impression if he had argued, she would have dragged out muffler and gloves too. *Stop at the barber's on your way*, she had ordered. *Your hair is all over the place again.*

He descended the narrow street that took him from his house, built during Zwingli's Protestant Reformation in the sixteenth century, to the violin-maker's shop on Bahnhofstrasse in the center of the modern tourist district. Strange, the road that unwound in time from one to the other, and he too trudging down it. A Mercedes-Benz with German license plates blared at him as he stepped off a curb without looking. A donkey cart clopped by in the opposite direction, its driver wearing a peasant smock that Zwingli might have recognized. There was no such thing as past or future. It all happened at once in the wonderful, brimming light. He felt the weight of it, soft as petals on his face and hands.

The shop was cool and dim inside until his eyes adjusted. Sawdust muffled his footsteps. His nose filled with the scent of pine and ebony, maple and resin. Unstrung instruments hung on the wall like dreaming angels, waiting to wake and sing. He would not—could not—deny he loved music. He ran his fingers over wood like satin and velvet.

"Stradivari's design remains the standard of excellence, even today."

He glanced up at the speaker, a pale, stooped young man who carried on his father's and grandfather's business of making some of the best violins in Europe.

"That's my latest copy you're holding."

The young man took the instrument from his hands, tightened pegs, plucked strings, then took a bow and drew from the instrument a cascade of sound so rich it was like listening to a river of radiance pour down from the sky.

"High C," he said. "Let me hear it."

The young man demonstrated a pure, singing note.

He nodded. "Ah. And it lies easily under the fingers?"

"Very much so," the young man agreed. "But why does that concern you, my friend, expert musician that you are?"

"I have a student with a great deal of talent and a small hand."

The instrument maker glanced quizzically at him. They were after all speaking of violins, not pianos.

"And a present might give her the confidence she needs to take the gold."

"I see." The young man laid the violin in its case and closed the lid. "On your account?"

"On my account, thank you."

And if it had not been music, he thought as he was leaving the shop, his gift in his hand, what then? What grand enterprise would have filled his life? Whatever might have been, surely it would have been sufficient. God was subtle, but he was not malicious.

One time, when he had been perhaps eleven or twelve, there had been a conversation around the kitchen table in his parents' home in Munich. An early snow sifted down outside, and his mother pulled heavy velvet curtains across the windows. In his memory, the kitchen was hazy with blue-gray smoke from his uncle's pipe, like a stage scene painted on gauze.

"Another poor report!" his father said, his hand over his eyes as if the mellow amber glow of the table lamp was too much for him. "I don't see why you don't just leave school now and come and join your uncle and me in the factory, instead of wasting your time and my money in the classroom."

"It was just low marks in history and geography, Hermann," his mother pointed out. She stood with his father's *bierkrug* in her hand, on the way to the cellar to refill it. "It said nothing about other subjects."

"Ah, leave the boy alone," Uncle Jakob counseled. "He's a slow learner, but he's capable of good things."

"You say so?" his father asked. "Well, I don't see it."

A small fire chuckled to itself behind the glass doors of the potbellied stove; it was not yet cold enough in the room to open the doors.

"Sometimes…" he began hesitantly, not because he was afraid of his father but because he was not sure himself what he wanted to say. "Sometimes I think there's some great work for me to do."

His father forked up a slice of cold meat and added it to a hunk of dark bread and cheese he had been preparing before the subject of young Albert's bad marks came up. "Electrical engineering is great work, lad. It's the future."

"He's good at mathematics, a natural," Uncle Jakob said thoughtfully. "Too good to be just an engineer, like you and me, Hermann."

"Music is like mathematics, isn't it?" his mother asked, coming back into the room with a full *krug*. Foam leaked out from under the pewter lid.

"Then let him be a civil servant," his father said. "But this schooling is a waste."

"There's something I have to do," he insisted. "I think there's a plan to my life. A riddle I have to solve."

"So good at words, and yet he can't pass his composition test!" his father mocked.

His mother smoothed his hair—even as a young boy it had been unruly. "There's always more than one way, *Liebchen.*"

"Life's a great game of chance," Uncle Jakob said. He leaned back from the table and re-lit his pipe. "An uncertain ride on a merry-go-round at the Oktoberfest."

"But Uncle, that's like saying God is a gambler, throwing the dice for our lives."

"The dice tell me you are no good in school!" his father roared. "I don't need God to advise me not to spend more money on a poor scholar."

His mother pulled him to her, pressing his face against her starched apron. "Don't worry, *Liebchen.* I have money for music lessons. My money. Neither God nor your father shall have any say in how I spend it. I'll buy you a new violin."

"Come, Papa. You haven't even tasted your champagne."

Millie linked her arm through his and drew him through the crowded living room, past the neighbors, the friends from their musical circle, the rabbi and the priest of the local Catholic church deep in a discussion of the world soccer cup, past his sons who were arguing over the Korean bomb.

"This atom they've split has unleashed a terrible demon in our world," Eddie said.

Hans Albert had made the trip unexpectedly from Berlin on the *Schnellzug.* "You don't understand. When the governments of the world are aware of the power of the atom, they'll finally make peace."

He was not fooled. One more gold medal was hardly cause enough for his oldest son's visit. They worried about his health.

Strange, for he did not worry about it himself. Rosa, flushed and shining in a new dress, stood by the refreshment table that Millie and the housekeeper had worked all afternoon to set up with Millie's heirloom silver and best china. The gold medal flamed like a sun on Rosa's chest. Her parents stood with her, thick-bodied, slow-thinking. They were good people from the farm, not quite sure they understood why all these elegant folk in silk and velvet and glittering rings had come in taxis to kiss their little Rosa on both cheeks and shake her father's hand. The future unfolded before them like a rose petal uncurling, and they did not have the wit to know it.

"Herr Einstein," Rosa called. "Thank you!"

She blew him a kiss with her fingertips that had so flawlessly reached high C. Then she turned to the young man beside her—a cousin, he knew, a farm lad—and tucked the hand with the gifted fingers in his.

Millie herded her husband to an armchair from which he could see everybody in the room. He sank into it, feeling for a moment like the apple whose falling to Earth had demonstrated gravity. Lisl promptly climbed into his lap, spilling champagne over the new gray trousers Millie had made him wear. His daughter-in-law retrieved the child and took her away to bed; her own cheeks were as rosy from champagne as the child's were from summer sun. Across the room, he caught sight of his oldest grandchild, a serious boy, much too old now to sit on a grandparent's knee. He showed signs of following his uncle into the sciences.

Hans Albert, still glowering from the argument with his brother, came to sit in the chair beside him.

"Grand theories are in the air now," Hans Albert said. "Wonderful ideas about extending the Poincaré theory of dynamics to include gravitation. But some fools oppose the work."

"Ah. Who invents this?"

"Papa, physicists don't invent. They're not engineers. They propose theories and test them. Anyway, the ideas come from some Americans, Dyson and Feynman. And from our own Heisenberg too, of course."

"Light," he said, gazing at the warm play of candlelight on silver.

Hans Albert nodded impatiently. "Of course. The role of light, following an innate curve made by matter, that's in the theory. And space and time too, threaded together and warped by matter. The equations describing this reduce to Newton's familiar prescriptions in the limit of essentially flat geometries. That's what's so exciting. I wish I could make you understand. You see—"

"How heavy it is."

"What is?" His son frowned at the interruption.

"Each ray as subtle as a rose petal," he said dreamily, "bending down to the Earth."

"Something like that," the younger man said carefully.

"And everywhere it bends. If we go far enough away, does the light streaming out from the stars seem to curve?"

"Well, I don't—"

"Even to the end of things? Mustn't light bend then, at least?"

Hans Albert stared at him. "No disrespect, Papa, but you're certainly not a physicist."

When Millie's back was turned, he slipped out of the crowded room. The balcony was dark and empty, and the air rising off the lake was fresh. Overhead, a huge tapestry of stars blazed, a panoply of light streaking outward to the far horizons of the universe. It was a time to see not just backwards but forwards too. Someday, he thought, man would follow the elusive light of the stars, sailing out into the far reaches of space. Hans Albert could have told him how this would be done, but he already knew the truth of it in his heart.

He had the sense again tonight of endings, of a wave that had traveled so far finally curving on a distant shore. So be it. He was ready for it; there were few things to regret. All in all, it had been a good life.

Rosa had reached her C.

And yet—and yet.

The book Eddie had left for him was wrong in one respect. The sharks who snatch away the victory were not external. They swam in the dark waters of the soul. The trick was not to let them.

He gazed up into the sky at the great gorgeous light.

FIELD STUDIES

MARLY brought out the bag of apples from the Ralph's dumpster, passed it around. Bruised. It was fucking disgraceful what people threw away. Big Mo took three. That was okay. She couldn't eat more than a couple of bites anyway. Indigestion been bothering her for days.

"Teeth hurtin' again, chica?" Marly asked. "Not that you got many left!"

Pat ignored it. Marly had her back when she needed it. She threw another chunk of damp wood on the sputtering fire. Lots of junk wood under the railroad trestles. All of it damp from a puny rain that hung around all day. Nothing but a tease.

Marly and Big Mo chewed loudly.

"Slobs," she told them. "No manners."

"Don't need manners in country," Big Mo said.

Marly's eyes flashed in the firelight. "You was never there, Vietnam."

"Fucker! You don't know nothin'—"

She held up her hand. They'd both hit the Fireball hard. "Not tonight, kids."

The fire popped. Rain dripped off the tarp Marly had rigged over them. She folded her arms over her belly and rocked. Sound of freeway traffic was kind of soothing, like the nearby river should sound but didn't.

Marly rustled something, crouched over his hands. Hard to see what he was doing without glasses. She'd put them down beside her to rub sweat off her nose two days ago, and Big Mo stepped on them. Nothing wrong with her ears though. Marly was rolling a joint.

Big Mo stared at him. "Gonna share that?"

"When don' I?"

Marly stuck the thin joint between his lips, took a burning stick from the fire and sucked. The end of the joint glowed. Big Mo never took his eyes off it. Something bad wrong with that one, like you could smell it.

Marly passed the joint, and she took a hit. Weak stuff, hardly made a difference. Might settle her gut though. She took another.

"Hey!" Big Mo leaned over and snatched the joint out of her fingers. "Goddamn it. Gone out!"

Big Mo jammed the whole thing into his mouth and swallowed.

Marly scrambled to his feet. "What the fuck you do that for, mano? You loco?"

Big Mo got up too. He was a good foot taller than Marly—which didn't mean much with Marly being such a little cabrón. They hit and kicked each other like a couple kids on the school playground.

She pulled her blanket around her shoulders, headed for the LA River. Just a trickle this year. Full of trash from the cities upstream. The sky was half-covered in cloud, the moon a splinter. Behind her, thuds and cussing. Big Mo and Marly pounding each other. Both too drunk to do much damage. They should keep it down or the cops would come. Always cops snooping about down here. Getting meaner every time. Life on the street.

She saw the cigarette first, a glow in the shadows under the trestles. Tall guy. Slim. She squinted. Looked like he was wearing sweats.

"Evening," he said.

Stupid runner. Clueless. The jogging path the city made such a fuss about was higher up the bank, not down here near the river. She tried to pass him.

"Pat," he said.

That stopped her. "You a cop?"

"No."

Couldn't hear Marly and Big Mo fighting now. In the silence, the faint gurgle of river over some junk in its path. Grocery cart maybe. Plenty of them in the water.

"St Mary's soup kitchen," he said. "Yesterday."

She did sorta remember him. Blue cook's apron behind the trestle table with a couple other volunteers. Ladling cream of broccoli and cheddar soup into paper cups. Telling people to help themselves to crackers, hard-boiled eggs.

"What you want with me?"

He tossed the cigarette at the river. "I have something for you."

"Better be good!"

"Here."

A pair of glasses on his palm. Two unbroken lenses catching a bit of light.

"Why you showing me these?"

"I thought someone stepped on yours and broke them."

She hadn't said anything about her glasses in the soup line. And Marly kept warning her not to tell strangers where they camped. So how did he find her? Her skin crawled.

"What's it to you?"

"I didn't mean to scare you."

"You some kind of social worker?" They were the worst. Snooping around. Prying into folks' business. Them and the census takers. "Trying to get me into a shelter or something?"

"Would that be so bad? Take the glasses. They were in the donation bin."

She snatched them off his palm. No way she was going to say thanks to a creep who followed her around!

"What did you do, before you were homeless?"

"What's it to you?"

"I think you were somebody, once," he said.

The starving dog lunged at the half sandwich she'd just pulled from the trash and swallowed it whole. Damn thing been following her all morning. No energy to get mad. Hotter than hell today, and summer just starting. Yesterday's rain tease long gone. Pain shot through her gut, part hunger, part something else. Didn't want to think about it.

Cars slid by on Ocean Boulevard, an endless stream. Kind of like trash on the river. No trees along this section of the Bluff. Concrete burning through the soles of her shoes. Cart had a bad wheel. Everything she owned in it. Couldn't leave it. Big Mo'd steal it if the city didn't clean it up.

A flash of black and neon yellow almost knocked her over. Cyclist. Damn fool supposed to be on the bike path down on the beach.

His voice hit her like a gloved fist. "Outta the way!"

She raised her own fist at his back. Too tired this morning to curse. Better not to draw attention anyway.

Water fountain ahead. Two levels, one for her, one for the dog. Both not working. Empty coke bottle in her cart. She needed to fill the bottle with water soon.

Stone bench ahead, still no shade. She pushed the cart beside the bench, plopped down, felt a touch. The dog leaning against her leg.

Marly and Big Mo were snoring when she got back to camp last night. She could've told Marly about the guy who'd ladled soup at St Mary's, but she already knew what he'd say. *Some guy lookin' for a quick poke, chica. Not too choosey, some. Long as it's cheap.*

The Pacific was flat, a few kids, seagulls. The sand looked hot. The new glasses let her make out striped towels, a beach bag. An island took shape off shore. The glasses might even be better than the ones that got broken.

The ache in her belly wore her out. The heat made her sleepy. The dog sighed and settled against her ankles. A seagull swooped past, screaming. She dozed.

"Get a job, you lazy slut!"

Middle-aged woman with short yellow hair done up in a red sweatband. Yelling in her face. The dog ran off. There were words in her mouth, but no use letting them out. Only make it worse.

The woman waved a cell phone. "This bench is for people who pay taxes. You're making it filthy. Go on, go! Before I call the police!"

Pat put her hands on the bench, pushed herself up. Hate and the hot sun pushed back. Her gut clenched. The woman walked away, talking on her cell. Nothing new here. Happened every day. Just life.

Had there been a time when it didn't happen? She thought about it. Must've been a kid once. Must've been nice. School. Clean clothes. Dinner on the table?

She couldn't remember.

The dog came slinking back. They walked, the cart wobbling and pulling. Two more litter bins, both empty. Endless stream of cars. Some kid had left a towel on the railing. Mermaids and seashells. She took it, wiped sweat off her face, draped it over her head.

Way down the path—long way down—the new glasses showed a familiar sign. Jack-in-the-Box.

Joint like Jack's meant people with more food than they could eat. She didn't beg. Big Mo teased her for that. She never asked, but sometimes the older ones—the social insecurity crowd, Marly called them—felt generous. Or guilty. She walked. The dog followed.

Couple of metal tables outside, in the parking lot. No shade. She pushed the cart to the one nearest the door and slumped onto hot metal. Pain in her belly doubled her over for a minute.

Group of teens in beach shorts and flip-flops came out. Laughing. Clutching paper bags. Trailing the smell of hamburgers and fries. Sun block. Walked right past, not seeing. She could wait. She did waiting well. The pain in her gut settled into an ache.

Two cars headed for the drive through. Then nothing. Too late for lunch. Too early for dinner. Everybody else in this town too well fed today.

She was so tired. Maybe she'd just close her eyes for a minute. Not be too obvious or the manager'd come roaring out, chase her away.

"Here."

She tried to scramble out of the seat. He put a hand on her arm.

"I bought you a hamburger."

Him again. Weird guy. Long, odd looking face like it never grew a beard. But not a young face. He wasn't wearing the tracksuit today. Shirt with collar, jeans. Something off about the cut and color. Like he was trying not to stand out and not doing too well.

The dog had gone again.

He sat down opposite her. "Eat the hamburger."

Hunger lifted her hand to take the packet from him. She almost fainted at the smell. One of Marly's little apples yesterday—not much else.

"I didn't get pickles," he said.

"I like 'em plain."

"And I have a bottle of water here." He pulled the bottle out of his pocket and placed it in front of her. "You don't want to get dehydrated."

He watched her eat. It was like he didn't miss anything—the size of the pieces she bit off, the way she chewed, the meat juice that dribbled out of the corner of her mouth. He took a paper napkin off a stack and handed it to her to wipe her chin.

That annoyed her. "You get your kicks watching the animals eat?"

"I suppose it does look like that."

"Bet your life it does! I could report you for being a pervert."

Not that the cops would listen to a street person. But maybe he didn't know protection was only for taxpayers like the woman in the red sweatband.

She was getting ready to say something that would really cut him when a wave of pain and nausea came boiling up. She had just enough time to bend over, aim the vomit away from him.

When she straightened up, mouth full of acid, he was pouring water from the plastic bottle onto a napkin. He held it out.

"You need to get help with that problem."

She took the wet paper and dabbed her chin. "Know better than to gulp food down like that."

"Are you sure that's all it is?"

She knew it! One of those do-gooders who'd try to shut her up in County General—for her own good. Lucky to come out alive from those places, Marly said. Or at least, not the same as you went in. "Leave me alone! Going home in a minute."

"Let me call a taxi—"

"I look like the Queen of Sheba to you?"

She pushed herself out of the metal chair and reached for her cart. He didn't move. Lucky for him, or she might've hit him, she was that mad.

He sighed. "I'm not handling this very well. I apologize."

"Damn right!" She pushed the cart away from Jack's parking lot.

He followed, a couple of steps behind. "Can I at least walk with you, see you get back okay?"

She stared at him. "A bit far for you, innit?"

The road past Jack-in-the-Box was still full of cars. Hot exhaust streamed after them. At the stoplight on the corner of Ocean, she bumped the cart over the curb.

Didn't see the car running a red until too late.

She woke up to darkness and a splitting headache. In a bed somewhere. Cold feel of clean sheets. Left arm tangled in something. Tubes. And she recognized that smell—disinfectant and rubber. Hint of urine. Hospital.

She made an effort to sit up, got caught in the sheet tucked in too tight.

"Hold on. You don't want to pull that out."

A shaded light came on in a corner of the room. She squinted—her glasses had gone missing again. A blur. But she knew it was him. The man with the odd face. This time he was wearing a doc's white coat.

"What happened to me?"

"You walked in front of a car. The paramedics brought you here."

Three other patients in the room, curtains pulled around them. "County?"

He nodded. "Nothing broken, but you have a concussion."

"You a doc now?"

The door opened. A Filipino nurse came in, handed her a pill, plastic cup with a straw, took her pulse. Her gut cramped as the water hit it. She kept waiting for the guy to say something. The nurse ignored him like he wasn't there. So, not a doc. The nurse made a note on a pad, went out. A patient in one of the other beds moaned.

"I gotta get outta here. Marly'll worry about me."

"You should stay another night. They need to come up with something for your problem."

"Who says I have a problem?"

He didn't answer.

"County don't care about stuff like that. Get 'em out fast as possible and collect the money from the government. Fall down dead on the street, not their problem."

"That's exactly what could happen," he said.

"Indigestion. Comes from eating at all those high class eateries on the Bluff."

"Are you sure about that?"

What was she supposed to do anyway? What if they thought she needed surgery? The thought of going under the knife at County gave her the shakes.

"Like hell!" She closed her eyes, felt drowsy. Like she could just slip away anytime she wanted. Go back to the time with dinner on the table.

"You need to get help. There are things they can do."

"Ah, give it a rest." No use anyway. Only putting off what was going to happen someday.

A memory surfaced. Her Gran, talking to "angels" in the room. Just before she passed.

"You the Angel of Death or something?"

She heard him laugh. Heard the door click.

Marly shook out the pills they'd given her in a little plastic bottle and counted them with a finger. The fire crackled with dry wood Big Mo had found somewhere. He'd set a pot on it and was boiling coffee grounds. The river ran quiet under the setting sun.

"Enough for a month if you take two a day."

She pulled her blanket around her. Still felt cold. "Two months if I only take one."

"Not thinkin' straight, chica,."

"What they suppose to do?" Big Mo asked.

"For belly ache, mano."

"Maybe they're worth somethin'? We could sell 'em."

She wished they'd stop talking. She hadn't given it much attention when the nurse gave her the pills because what was the point? Indigestion wasn't the problem right now—County shot her up with drugs before they discharged her. But her head still hurt from the concussion.

They had a bigger problem. County found a social worker to drive her here when they let her out. That meant the city knew where the camp was now. The cops would come and clear them out. They'd been real nasty about it lately. How long could she expect the guys to let her tag along to find another spot if she was sick? When she'd first met up with them, she'd figured she didn't need them. Managed just fine on her own. Now, not so much.

"Thing is," Marly began.

Here it came. She waited. He tossed a piece of trash onto the fire. It burned fast and bright with oily smoke. Couldn't see his face without the glasses.

"Thing is, chica…"

"You've messed up," Big Mo finished. "Gonna have to move on now."

"Not so quick, mano," Marly said. He didn't go on.

They all knew what the thing was, anyway.

"Been thinking about striking out on my own," she said.

"Good thinkin'," Big Mo nodded at her.

Marly didn't say anything. So yeah, that was the way it would be.

"Tomorrow then," she said.

Marly shared out the coffee. Tasted like shit, but maybe that was the drugs.

They left camp well before the sun came up. The fire still smoldered—Big Mo wanted to kick it back to life, start a real fire under the trestles. Marly wouldn't let him.

"Don' need cops comin' any faster than they gonna anyway."

"You gonna need all those pills?" Big Mo asked.

The pills were beside the backpack she'd have to use now she'd lost the cart.

"Not giving them to you, you lunatic!"

Marly fidgeted with his backpack. "Well, probably see you in line sometime, chica."

"Soup's good at St Mary's," she said. "See ya."

The men headed upriver.

She watched them go for a minute, waiting for her indigestion to settle back down. It was back today, biting like it had teeth. They were all the family she had. Funny, that. Wasn't good luck to make a fuss of goodbye. Even though they'd been together—what?—a year now. That was the street.

She rolled the blanket, tied it under the backpack. Struck out to familiar territory along the Bluff. Neck and shoulders hurt too. Must've slept odd.

The city was still deep in shadow. Crows about the only living things awake. She put one foot in front of the other, then another, heading east. Didn't feel like the feet belonged to her. After a bit, the sky ahead turned pink.

Big old tree by the path. Bronze notice on the trunk stating it was for somebody's memory. Somebody who paid taxes. Too fucking tired to go on. She dropped the backpack. Slumped on the bench under the tree. Flock of birds flew over, heading out to sea. Not making any noise. A rat rustled in the ivy supposed to stop the cliff from tumbling onto the beach. Rats, feral cats, and birds. No people.

And no pills because she'd left them at the camp. Getting harder to remember things all the time.

He sat down beside her, saying nothing. She wasn't surprised this time. They watched the orange flame come up over Huntington Beach down the coast.

"Gonna be a hot one," she said. Then she laughed. "Ain't they all!"

"Pat," he said. Wearing jeans and a gray sweatshirt today. Long face serious in the slanting light.

"You know my name. Don't know yours."

He held up a hand.

She thought about it. Something not normal about him. "You could help if you set your mind to it, am I right?"

"I've already done more than I was supposed to."

"What was that?"

He pressed his lips together. Like he was afraid words might fall out. Dangerous words.

"Can't tell me where you come from neither, right?"

He let it go, answer too obvious maybe. She watched the sky for a while. More birds headed out to sea, this lot squawking and crying like somebody was murdering them.

"I ain't that old, you know," she said. "Don't wanna die yet."

He turned his head away from her, quickly, like she'd smacked him. Her gut hit her with a wave of fire like punishment.

She said softly, "This life ain't so bad. I'm used to it."

He stood up. "I have to go."

"While I was in County, I thought you was the Angel of Death my Gran talked about. But you ain't, right?"

"You don't believe in angels."

"Got that right."

Sweat on her face. Under her arms. Something brushed against her. The stray dog was back, rubbing her ankles. She touched its head. Felt the bones of its skull.

"At least say why you was following me around?"

He hesitated. "I'm an anthropologist."

She looked down at the dog like maybe it knew that word. It looked back at her with wise eyes. A crow landed on the railing. Stared at her. Cars started the day on Ocean Boulevard.

No sense looking back at him. She knew he was gone.

THE PERSISTENCE OF BUTTERFLIES

Toward midnight, the woman died.

Matt watched the woman's brother fetch a tarp from the dormant Tesla VT6. A waning moon low in the cloudless desert sky sent the man's shadow crawling like a spider over the rocky ground. Her father, who hadn't come out of the plane at all since she started moaning three hours before, stuck his head through the open window and made a "hurry up" gesture to the younger man.

The woman's day-old baby, lying on the other side of the small fire Matt built, had stopped its thin mewling. It would've been lying on hard ground if he hadn't wrapped it in his leather jacket with the NASA patches he'd once been so proud of. He wondered if it was dead now like its mother.

"You comin' or not?" the father shouted, his voice raspy.

"What's the hurry?" the younger man answered sullenly. "Going nowhere till the sun comes up."

The younger man's face was thin and set in hard lines. A century before, he and his father might have been Oakies escaping the Dust Bowl. Drought turned to blizzard, but desperate folks still struggled to reach the west coast. He'd run into them just outside Knoxville. They'd agreed to take him with them in the crowded four-seater because they needed his engineering skill to patch the old craft's solar skin. He assumed they'd probably stolen it. Lots of abandoned equipment out there, rotting in the mud.

By day the younger man had flown the plane along Interstate 40, but the Tesla's solar batteries didn't hold much power, and they hadn't been able to find fuel for the hybrid engine. Forced to stop every night when the sun went down, father and son had become increasingly ill-tempered. Then the woman had gone suddenly into labor just as the anemic trickle of the Colorado River came into view.

Matt shrugged. "I'm an engineer, not a magician. You need sunlight or fuel. Right now you've got neither."

The brother walked away. After a while, he came back, hunched over. He had made a carrier of his jacket to hold a quantity of rocks. "Wanna help?" he asked.

Together they mounded stones over the tarp-shrouded body, forming a crude cairn. Matt doubted it would be enough to keep the coyotes off. Afterward, the younger man curled up by the fire, and the father finally slept, his snores rumbling out of the Tesla's open window. It was still a couple of hours before dawn, maybe a couple more before the solar batteries had soaked up enough power to lift the craft for the final leg of its flight to the coast.

Matt gazed at the huddled mountains to the west. Between them and where he stood, the Mojave Desert waited.

He hadn't had much choice.

"I'm leaving," Karen had said a month ago.

Her words had barely registered. The data onscreen showed him what he'd looked at a thousand times: something kept the solar shades from deploying properly in all the test flights NASA had undertaken. The tiny spacecraft made of transparent film were supposed to orbit a thousand kilometers above the Earth, deflecting the sun's punishing radiation, slowing global warming, buying time. But they didn't. There had to be a fix—he was an engineer; he believed in fixes. Not so NASA; the space agency was about to pull the plug on the project. Already they were gutting the east coast team, and his job was next in line.

The screen blinked. Came back again.

"Did you hear what I said, Matt?"

It was taking too long to reduce greenhouse gas emissions. The climate crisis was cumulative. Glaciers rapidly disappearing. Low-lying islands flooding world-wide. Harvests failing. The planet's own long range cycles against them too. The solar shades had to work; it was humanity's best chance to bring the problem under control.

"You said you're leaving. Going shopping?"

Karen laughed, a brittle sound. "Shopping for a better life!"

He turned from the screen and gazed at her. Burnished blonde hair swinging over the shoulders of her elegant snow jacket. She'd never wanted children, and he'd been too busy, but he'd thought they were a team.

"You're leaving me?"

"Oh my. The signal finally got through."

Behind her, blades of cold light through long windows sliced the room. He heard the strangled wheeze of the automatic snowplough at work in drifts deeper than it was intended to clear. Severe winter storms on the east coast were just one symptom of weather systems out of whack. The world's economies, barely recovering from the market collapses of the previous decades, teetered on the edge of failure again. On-screen, a rolling wave of interference dissolved his data into sparkling points.

"If you can tear yourself away from your work for a few minutes, you'll see what I've tried to tell you, over and over again. Everybody with a grain of sense is leaving Maryland."

"I'm working on a solution, Karen. I'm so close—"

"You're a dreamer!"

The door slammed behind her, shaking loose a waterfall of snow that blanked the window. The screen blacked out as the system went down again. This time, he had the feeling it would be down for a very long time.

"Her own fault she got pregnant."

Matt opened his eyes and saw the old man sitting on a boulder, staring at the cairn. The brother was still asleep on the other side of the dead fire, the collar of his jacket turned up over his ears. The sun was little more than a handsbreadth above the eastern horizon. He sat up.

The father stood up and aimed a kick at his son.

"What're we going to do about the kid?" The younger man's voice was still thick with sleep.

"Leave it with Teela. She wanted it."

The rising sun splashed rivers of gold over the western mountains. Matt got up and stepped over the ashes of last night's fire. The infant wrapped in his jacket hadn't stirred. Dark eyes, huge in their bony sockets, stared up at the sky through the spindly branches of a half-dead cottonwood. Breathing, though he couldn't imagine how.

"It's still alive," the brother said.

"Not for long."

Matt's dislike of the old man rose in his throat. His hand moved to touch the gun he'd shoved into his pocket before leaving home. Karen had made him get it, afraid of the looters who increasingly prowled the dying cities of the Beltway.

The kid didn't stand a chance anyway. And he needed the ride to the west coast. As he'd expected, NASA had shut down the east coast lab. Matt hadn't had the seniority or the prestige to convince them otherwise. But Walter Chen in Pasadena was still managing to keep his lab operating, last Matt had heard. The only option he could see was to go west, join Chen's team, keep working, not give up. *Go down trying,* his dad had always said.

"Get aboard if you're going." The younger man climbed into the pilot's seat.

There'd be just enough power in the Tesla's batteries by now to get the craft airborne; then the blazing sun of the Mojave would see them through till they reached the coast. All they had to do was follow the track of Interstate 40 till they reached hit Los Angeles.

"Last time I'm telling you!" the father shouted.

Matt stood, one hand on the Tesla's door. "Goddamn it! We can't just leave the baby—"

The door slammed, spinning him backwards. The Tesla took off straight up.

So much for the dream of getting to Pasadena. He'd be lucky to survive more than a couple of days out here.

The baby lay as he'd left it in the meager shade of the cottonwood. He thought of the shepherd pups he'd raised as a kid, how it had been a kindness to the mother, and the pup too, to take the weakest, the runt, and put it out of its misery. He fingered the gun, warm with his body heat, and looked at the baby.

He couldn't do it.

He dropped the backpack on the sand and lifted the infant. There was a small dark stain on the lining of his leather jacket where it had been lying; he wrapped the jacket loosely around the thin body. Cradling the tiny bundle in the crook of one arm, he took his canteen out of the backpack and unscrewed the cap that made a small cup. He stared at the cup and the canteen's opening and the child's small face, then tipped the canteen and dipped a finger in the water. Awkwardly, he brought the wet finger to the child's mouth. It didn't seem to know how to suck.

"Come on, kid," he said. "That's supposed to be an instinct."

The child stared unblinking at him, its eyes all dark pupil. But when his finger touched its mouth this time, he saw a tiny movement and was encouraged. On the second try, he managed to make a drop of water slide between the lips. It dribbled uselessly out of the side of the infant's mouth. Overhead, the dry cottonwood rustled in the hot breeze.

On the third try, the infant's mouth moved to hold the water. He repeated the maneuver several times.

"That'll have to do for now."

He screwed the cup back on his canteen. Where there were cottonwoods there should be water, but last night he'd scrabbled away at the sand to a depth of a foot and not found any.

The Tesla had been forced to leave the trail marked by Interstate 40 just as it reached the California border when the woman went into labor. He figured they must've flown about two miles north looking for a site level enough to set the plane down. They'd skimmed two spiny ridges, stone fingers extended from a peak in the distance, the land between littered with boulders large enough to damage the plane, before they'd found an open patch. He needed to retrace their flight path and find the interstate, then maybe he'd get lucky and pick up another ride out to the coast. Not an easy task, even if he'd been prepared for a hike through the Mojave, but not impossible. His dad, a dedicated outdoors man, had taken Matt and his older brother out west to Death Valley one spring; they'd hiked the canyons and gazed at the stars. His love of space had begun on that trip.

Rough country between where he stood now and the interstate on the valley floor. Hampered by the baby, he'd have a hard time. He set it down and took up the backpack. It was almost empty, a water canteen, two small energy bars, a packet of raisins, an apple, an extra pair of socks. He'd been on the road more days than he cared to think about.

He arranged the things as evenly as possible on the bottom of the backpack, then carefully slid the jacket-wrapped infant on top. Once his first impulse to rescue it faded, he recognized the hopelessness of the task.

Scanning the ground as he walked south, he saw the faint line of a trail across rough sand. A coyote's path, better than nothing. He took it toward the brow of a stony hill. Sweat poured down his face and soaked his collar then dried instantly. His dad would've counseled walking at night and resting during the day, but he didn't have time for that luxury. He tried to remember the average daytime temperature of the Mojave in May. The warm incense of the desert rose up to him on the breeze, heavy with the scent of sage.

The animal track meandered between huge boulders, slowly climbing to the crest of barren hills. To the east, a slick, black slope where a volcano had long ago spewed its lava, and sheltered under an overhanging rock, the glint of a small pool of collected rainwater, left over from a desert storm that must've passed through recently. He knelt and trickled water into his almost empty canteen, allowing himself a taste from one fingertip first; the water was warm but potable.

His legs tired rapidly. No time for sleep in those last few days before he'd accepted the conclusion that he couldn't do anything by staying in Maryland. Karen, of course, had cut out long before. There was no pain in that memory. Physical exhaustion had a way of washing out emotional exhaustion, and there was something peaceful about walking through this warm, scented silence that soothed his nerves. The desert reminded him that after he and his kind had vanished, it would still be there, growing along the bleached bones of humanity's feeble attempt to survive.

In mid-afternoon, the baby's thin cry stopped him. Carefully, he eased the makeshift carrier off his shoulder and set it on the ground. He uncapped the flask and repeated the water maneuver he'd perfected earlier. After a while, he wrapped the baby in his jacket again and hoisted the backpack over his shoulder. It took him the better part of the day to reach the last line of bleak hills before the land began its descent. The sun was already searing its way down the western sky when he stopped to scan the desert floor below him. A light breeze sprang up, scouring his face with hot sand.

In the distance he saw a section of it, shimmering in the heat haze of late afternoon, a long, straight silver ribbon like the promise of life-giving water across the furnace lands of the Mojave: Interstate 40.

Encouraged, he started down the slope. Cactus spines reached for his jeans as he pushed past, and a dry tumbleweed bounced across his path. Off-balance, he stumbled, turned his ankle, and yelped in pain. He flopped heavily onto a sun-warmed boulder, and the baby whimpered, jostled in its make-shift carrier.

Damn. His dad would've reminded him: RICE. No ice to be had around here, and no time to rest or elevate. That left compress. But the baby was wrapped in his jacket, and there was nothing else he could use in the backpack. This trip west was turning out to be an exercise in futility, just as Karen would've predicted.

After a while, the pain in his ankle settled into a dull ache, and he stood cautiously, testing to see if it would carry his weight. It did. The sun slipped behind the western range, and purple shadows crept across the sand. In contrast to the heat of the day, nights were cold in the high desert, and without his jacket he started shivering. He really didn't have a choice: either go on, or both of them could die of exposure right here. He took a few slow, painful steps forward.

The coyote trail he'd been following petered out at a lime-stone outcropping.

He was almost too tired to eat but knew he needed food if he had any hope of making this journey at all. The energy bars were limp in their foil wrappers. He opened one carefully and took a small bite, chewing methodically in the gathering dusk, then took a swallow of water.

The infant's eyes were open again. It occurred to him that he might try the melted chocolate of the bar as a substitute baby food. Couldn't be any worse than letting it starve to death. He smeared a fingertip in the brown sticky mess, care-ful not to pick up any of the chopped nuts. Gently, he daubed a little on the tiny lips and was pleased to see the infant's tongue poke hesitantly out.

"That's right. Try a little for me."

The infant lay motionless, the tip of its tongue still visible. He rummaged in the backpack again as if it might magically produce a bottle of formula. His fingers found the apple. He remembered his sister-in-law feeding his little nephew apple-sauce, but that was an older child, sitting up already. He stared at the apple, wondering what to do.

Something rustled in the tumbleweeds. This was rattle-snake country. He wished he'd paid more attention to his father's camping lessons. But even Dad wouldn't know what to do with the world the way it was now. For the first time since his father's heart attack, he was glad the old man wasn't alive to see it.

He had a folding knife in his pocket; he took it out and cut the apple in wedges.

"You're not thinking of giving that baby a chunk of apple?" a voice demanded.

Startled, Matt dropped the piece he'd cut into the dirt. A figure materialized out of the darkness and seized it. A woman. He stared at her as she stuffed the apple into her mouth.

"Idiot!" she said, chewing. "How long since this kid ate?"

Silently, he handed over the canteen. She unscrewed the cup and dribbled a little water into it, then leaned over and let the mushed apple fall into the water. She rocked the cup, stirring its contents with a finger.

"And don't look at me like that. I may be female, but I don't magically produce milk. If this is thin enough, it'll do in a pinch."

She reached for the child, making cooing noises. Then she hooked her finger into the mush and did what he had done earlier, feeding the child. In the dark, he heard tiny smacking noises.

He felt foolish for not having thought of what to do with the apple himself.

After a while, she laid the infant down on the ground and unwrapped the jacket. "Yours?"

"Somebody left it to die. I picked it up."

"Bet you've never diapered a baby before."

"But you have," he guessed. He heard the sound of fabric ripping, but by now it was too dark to see what she was doing. He slumped on a boulder, resting his head on his arms, trying to ignore the ache in his ankle. After a while she put the infant in his arms.

"What she really needs is milk."

"She?"

"Didn't you even know it was a girl?"

The baby's sex hadn't registered on him. What difference did it make anyway? There was no way he could chew apples to make applesauce all the way to the coast, even if he could find any.

He looked at the woman. "What're you doing out here?"

"Same as you, probably. Waiting for the end."

Angered, he replied sharply, "I'm headed to Los Angeles."

"LA's a mess—no water. San Diego's the same. All those miles and miles of new development, dried out, abandoned. Ironic, isn't it? Too much water in the east, drought in the west. Why would you want to go to LA?"

"I'm an engineer. I'm working on global warming."

"Not doing too well, are you?" she said scornfully. "They've got water riots out there now. Water's more expensive than gold."

He thought of the thin trickle of the Colorado he'd caught sight of as the Tesla neared the state line, major water source for Southern California.

"My husband was a Riverside County Deputy Sheriff," she added. "On the Crisis Force. But they couldn't solve this one."

A cascade of disasters triggered by severe climate change. How many nights had he and his colleagues sat around discussing the possibilities, never really quite believing that time would run out before they found the solution?

She touched his arm. "There's a cave back in the rocks. Better come inside. Hungry coyote 'round here, got pups nearby."

Overhead, the Milky Way poured across the darkening sky like the torrent the Colorado had once been.

When he woke, sunlight was entering the cave's mouth. The woman lay on a camp cot, nursing the baby.

"I thought you said—"

"Right. No milk. But she needs the comfort of sucking."

He wondered which of the two needed the comfort more.

It was a good size cave, braided rug on the floor, water jug, cooking pots stacked in a corner, a sack of potatoes, another of rice, cardboard boxes proclaiming their contents: tuna, beans, sliced pears, dried milk she'd used for the baby last night. She seemed well-stocked to wait out any normal emergency.

He stood gingerly on his injured foot, found it much improved, then picked up his soiled jacket and stood blinking in the sharp morning sunlight. The cave was near the top of the ridge; the other side fell away in folds of butter-colored rock to the desert floor where he'd seen the interstate. On the spine of the ridge, he saw the coyote silhouetted against the sky like an Indian petroglyph. He should make a start now, while it was still cool.

There was a small mound of stones by the cave's entrance; he rested his foot on it and carefully tightened his boot to supply some support. It was going to be a rough trip till he reached the interstate—rough enough anyway, without this added problem.

The woman came out, carrying the baby wrapped in a blanket. She was smaller than he'd realized last night, with a sharp-boned face under a thatch of tangled red curls. She wore grubby but serviceable jeans and a long-sleeved, plaid shirt. Her eyes were wary and a very deep brown.

"You weren't thinking of leaving?" she challenged.

"No—Of course not. Just looking around." Karen would've seen right through that lie.

She held out a sun-burned hand. "Name's Persephone."

"Really?"

She grinned. "Hey! I happen to like it." Then she turned serious again. "Doesn't matter what real names are anymore, does it? But you can call me Persey."

He took her hand. "I'm Matt."

"Still planning on getting to the coast?"

"Have to. I worked on the solar shades project—"

"Heard of those. They don't work." She made a face. "You'd be better off staying right here. Couple of miles east, there's an abandoned native trading post I've been liberating. They've got everything but fresh meat."

"You didn't always live up here," he guessed.

"No. But where I used to live is getting too rough for me. After Joe got killed...." She didn't go on.

"Are there other—" he hesitated "—survivors up here?"

She shrugged. "Some of the ones that're still around, I'd sooner not meet—if you know what I mean."

"You know this territory well?"

"Joe and I used to come up here to camp. He loved the desert. Maybe you should wait till the sun goes down. Gets hot in the day, even if it is only May."

"I have to risk it." He glanced around. A sturdy-looking manzanita branch lay in a tangle of dead cactus and small twigs. Not as large as he'd like, but it would give him a little support. Persey watched him without comment.

"Well," he began, straightening up and testing the stick.

"I'll keep you company for a while." She arranged the blanket into a sling and settled the baby against her chest.

The morning was fresh, the air sparkling, and a light scent reached him like hidden flowers. He set his mind to ignoring his ankle by going over the solar shades data in his mind again. Nothing wrong with their design—they unfurled properly. But then they tanked. Dozens of tests, same dismal results. Why? He'd thought he'd glimpsed the reason during those last days in Maryland.

When it became too difficult to climb two abreast, Persey went ahead. Even carrying the infant, her movements were sure-footed. At the top she stopped and waited for him to catch up. He turned his face away from her so she wouldn't see the strain he was already feeling.

She pointed into the valley below. "There's the interstate. What's left of it."

Like a dotted line, the I 40 started and stopped in a jumble of broken concrete, a dark gash on the gold desert floor. No way anybody could follow it anywhere.

His heart pounded. "What happened?"

"Earthquake. Few days ago. What you saw must've been a heat mirage. You get used to them out here."

He turned away, embarrassed to let her see his sudden, flooding despair. No traffic would be getting through on that mess any time soon.

"I could've told you, but you wouldn't have believed me. Could be days before they get that sorted out," she said. "If they do."

"I have to find a way around it. There's got to be traffic further west—"

Persey shrugged. "Your party."

For twenty minutes she led the way over the rocks, now south, now west, uphill then down again. Then suddenly the valley floor below them was ablaze with color. A carpet of pink and red and yellow spread before him like a fallen rainbow.

"My God, it's beautiful!"

"God doesn't come around here anymore," she said fiercely. "Cactus survives on its own."

Some of the color was moving. *Butterflies?* It couldn't be. But there they were, shimmering over the field of blooming cactus. Butterflies, he thought, the sheer, incredible persistence of butterflies.

"One spring in seven, cactus really puts on a show," she said, sounding wistful.

His father had explained how caterpillars turned into butterflies when he and his brother were kids. He remembered Dad in the back yard, showing them a butterfly, damp from the cocoon, spreading its wings to dry in the sun. Something about that image—

"Did you know the mother's name?"

He glanced at the small woman cradling an infant, the sun gilding her shoulders. She was like a cactus herself, a prickly survivor.

"Teela, they called her."

"You might as well call the baby that." She brushed the top of the baby's head with her lips.

How could he plan to take the child along when he wasn't certain he could get himself through the desert? "I could leave the baby here with you—I mean—she'd be better off—"

"And how am I supposed to take care of a baby out here?" she demanded, anger rising redly into her cheeks.

He shook his head. "That was stupid of me. I'm sorry."

"Well, go ahead and leave her. She'd die for sure with an idiot like you. And when you get to LA, you'll find I'm right. It'll all have been for nothing. Nothing. All a stupid waste."

He put a hand on her shoulder, breaking into her anger.

"Damn government!" she said. "Damn weather! Damn world!"

The child's voice joined hers.

"Come with me," he urged. Maybe he was as crazy as Karen thought he was.

She jerked away. "You asking me to leave my own child?"

He realized he'd seen the small stone cairn a few paces from the cave's mouth and was ashamed he hadn't recognized what it meant. After a moment, he put his arms around both of them. Persey was rigid with resistance. The baby's light, powdery smell came to his nose.

Her voice muffled against his jacket, she said, "He wasn't much older than this one."

The desert had no mercy for those who believed in illusions, teasing them with mirages. Yesterday's exhaustion came surging back.

"I was doing okay before you showed up." She sniffed away tears. "Joe taught me how to trap jackrabbits. I'm a good desert cook. Rabbit, rat, crow, you name it."

Maybe Persey was right. She had it no worse up here than the pioneers who'd gone west in wagon trains. Maybe the solution was to make the best of it and stay right here. If he were a realist, he'd admit there was no cause for optimism, even if he made it to JPL. The solution that had eluded him in Maryland might just as well elude him in Pasadena. He hadn't been in contact with Chen for a couple of weeks now. Maybe NASA had shut him down too.

"It's all over. All the good things we took for granted. We should've known. Nothing on this Earth is guaranteed to last forever."

He glanced down at her, weighing the implication of her words as if they were an engineering problem. If nothing lasted, the rule must apply to bad as well as good. The thing about mirages was you didn't know they were until you tested them. That's what he did best, testing things to find solutions. Go down trying—not a bad motto for humans.

In the silence, he became aware of the gun in his belt. He took it out and offered it to her.

"Don't need a gun to catch jackrabbit," she said, slapping it away. "And you're making a big mistake if you think I'd use it on the baby or myself."

He laid the gun down on a boulder. "It'll keep the neighbors polite."

He touched the baby's soft cheek and set off down the slope toward the interstate. The sun hammered his bare head; the glare hurt his eyes.

"Wait."

He stopped, not turning, hearing her feet dislodge stones behind him.

"Idiot. How long you think you can keep going like this without supplies and with a gimpy foot?"

"Dreamer!" Karen's voice said in his memory. "As long as it takes," he said.

"Wait till the sun goes down. I'll find something to strap up your ankle. Gotta find some cloth to use for Teela's diapers anyway. Can't keep washing the one piece and expecting the sun to dry it in a hurry so I can put it back on."

Something rose like a sunburst in his mind. Something about the last data he'd been playing with before he left Maryland. *The problem is moisture outgassing when the sails unfurl—*

"I still know some guys on the Crisis Team. Not too far off the interstate from here."

—causing tumbling— Gotta get the gyroscopes stabilized—

"What?" He hadn't been listening, his brain spinning through remembered data. If Chen was still in business—he had to be!—they could do this. A relatively small fix and the shades would work.

"We'd have a chance of catching a ride with the sheriffs."

"But you said—" He stopped, awkward in the face of her grief.

"I couldn't save mine," she said, so softly he almost didn't catch the words. "But maybe this one—"

The baby's dark eyes were open when he looked at her. *The package needs to be dried out before it goes into the envelope.* That was it. That was what Chen needed to know.

Sunlight hazed Persey's hair into a halo of fire. Their scent was warm, familiar somehow. He gazed at her. "No illusions?"

She shook her head.

"And no guarantees the future's going to be better. At least," he amended, "not immediately."

"Beats the alternative." She made an attempt to smile at him. "Deal?"

"Deal."

He tucked her free arm under his. Funny, he thought, life doesn't make any guarantees, but when you think you've run out of options, it gives you butterfly wings and babies. And somehow, that was enough to keep going.

MADONNA OF THE CHROMOSOMES

DELGADO recognized her type as she entered his office. Callista Orlov—tall, thin, wearing a conservatively-cut black silk pant-suit that he guessed cost more than his annual property tax. Late thirties, perhaps. No jewelry—the woman didn't need diamonds to proclaim her status. She was the last person he'd expect to be interested in NovaGen's business of cloning prize farm animals. He indicated a chair in his cluttered office. Rain blowing inland from the Bay Area spattered the window. He turned on the desk lamp, a small pool of light in the December gloom and waited for her to explain her visit.

"I want you to make a clone from Damiana, Dr Delgado," she said.

Beloved pet? Cloning pets was an indulgence, a flagrant waste of money, something his company didn't promote but occasionally did.

Then he remembered recent headlines. Only child of billionaire Mikhail Orlov and his wife Callista, dead at the age of two. Nightmare accident, the headlines had called it. Grief-stricken parents. The media's coverage of the funeral at Forest Lawn had shown something else, dark-coated Mafia security types watching from a distance, vultures waiting to descend. What she was asking was unethical.

"Terrible tragedy," he said. "But NovaGen clones breeding bulls—"

She held up a black-gloved hand. "Friends used your service to reproduce a valuable racehorse."

"We don't clone humans."

"Don't tell me you haven't contemplated taking the next step."

Hardly a researcher in the field of reproductive cloning who hadn't dreamed of trying! But the ethical issues involved were overwhelming. Look what had happened to that Chinese guy who'd merely tinkered with DNA in unborn twins. He gazed at Callista Orlov. She was still young enough to conceive again. If she was having problems then there were places to go. But not here.

"It could be done, isn't that correct?"

Sad, really that he had to say no. "I'm cynical enough to think it probably has been tried already somewhere, Ms Orlov. But not in the western world. What you ask is illegal, more than my career is worth."

"Your work will remain our secret."

"Why not just have another child?"

She looked away. "Damiana was a difficult birth. There were—side effects."

He picked up a pen, spinning it between his fingers. He'd never been one to refuse a challenge. It was possible, given the money and the right person to do it. Someone as skilled as himself, because of course there'd be problems. He'd had great ambitions once, before he'd settled for the safer career of livestock cloning. The answer had to be no. Though surely it wasn't unethical to save a life or put a stop to suffering. And why should the government or some misplaced belief in a magical being in the sky stand in the way of scientific progress?

"My husband wants an heir. I have no one else to turn to for help."

"You're asking me to risk my professional reputation."

And yet—

The opportunity might never come his way again. To achieve a great advance in medical science. To have his name up there with the great ones in the halls of science. To alleviate human distress— She was very obviously in distress. This was about more than scientific advance. He studied her pale face, the dark eyes brimming with tears, and felt a disturbing urge to put his arms around her.

She placed a check on the desk in front of him. Even upside down he could read the numbers. Very large numbers. More than a small cloned herd of prime milk cows would bring in.

"A down payment. The other half when the child is born."

He couldn't do it.

Oh—he could do it all right, he was confident of that. One part of his mind already assembled strategies and outcomes. He gazed at her, motionless in the twilit room. He'd never wanted a child himself, but he'd witnessed the joy of his clients, checking out a prized newborn calf or foal. "There's one big problem, I'd need your daughter's DNA."

She pulled a box from her pocket, opened it and laid it carefully on his desk. "I imagine that should give you enough to work with."

Buried in dry ice he saw a small glass capsule.

"Cord blood. Saved at the time of the child's birth on the advice of my obstetrician. Will that do?"

He could still refuse to do it. He would be risking his career, his reputation— But if he succeeded?

She stood, her musky perfume washing over him. "My people will stay in touch."

"I can't promise this overnight."

She glanced back as she left the room, the slightest smile on her lips as if she read him very well. "I put my trust in you, Dr Delgado."

"No," Gwen Mackenzie said when he laid out his plan the next day. "Unthinkable."

She'd come with him from UC Davis, a small, slightly overweight graduate student in genetics, short on funds and prospects, grateful for the experience he offered when he founded NovaGen. She'd turned out to have a skill he lacked, and he rapidly gave her full command of the business side of his company.

"How can you even consider it?"

Delgado refilled her glass with a good California Pinot Grigio and replaced the bottle in an ice bucket on the deck. He'd waited until sunset to take advantage of the magnificent backdrop of the Sierras, knowing she was going to be difficult to persuade. Without Gwen, he couldn't pull this off. The rain had blown inland overnight, dusting the mountains with the first snow of the year, dusting the pastures and barns sheltering the valuable calves and foals his work produced. Very little opportunity for anything except unrelenting work if he wanted NovaGen to grow. And then what? Just a moderately successful startup offering livestock cloning in a field where it was no longer cutting edge.

"It's not that different from what we regularly do," he said.

But of course it was, though the difference lay elsewhere than in biology. Human cells might be more difficult to clone than bovine cells, yet surely it wasn't impossible. Medical research with animal subjects rarely translated immediately into cures for humans, but science pressed on. He'd struggled with the problem all day, shutting himself in the office and neglecting his staff's concerns to hunt through the Internet. The challenge excited him. Teams in Korea claimed to have successfully cloned an embryo in a test tube, but there was no evidence to prove it. Yet there were enough rumors and uncorroborated stories to suggest it had been done somewhere. This was cutting edge science he'd do well to get into.

"You'd risk everything. NovaGen. Your reputation—"

"Darwin's work was despised at first, Gwen. Every pioneer faces scorn and rejection."

"How will you explain this to the team?"

"I don't need to explain. They don't need to know what I'm working on. They're used to not always knowing."

She shook her head. "Don't do it, Tom. NovaGen doesn't need money. We're growing rapidly—people trust us."

Easy for her to say. Something in him yearned for more than just making farmers happy. From the barns, the mooing of a pregnant cow reached him. Feeding time. One of his employees making the rounds. A good, comforting sound, but it was time to move forward.

Her reluctance irritated him. "Just this once, Gwen. We don't need to do it again after that."

"You can retrieve the child's genes from the cord blood, but what about the donor's egg?"

"Not a big problem. Students at Davis sell blood, sperm, eggs, whatever, to pay their tuition. I have friends there— I'll make some discrete enquiries."

A cursory glance at the latest research had revealed even better solutions might be possible. He itched to get back to the computer.

"Did you explain the potential problems to her?"

"How many of our clients ever care to hear that?"

"Did you explain about the sex of a clone?"

Her resistance annoyed him. "She's a grieving mother, for godsake! She's lost her daughter. How does it help to burden her with technical details?"

Gwen set her mouth in a stubborn line. "Not like you to miss dotting the i's and crossing the t's."

"Give it a break, Gwen—"

"If she misses a child so much," she said savagely, "why doesn't she just have another?"

He was silent for a moment. Then he covered her free hand with his. "Think about us for a moment, Gwen, not just NovaGen. What it'll mean for us being the first to do this."

"But you won't be able to claim it. Don't you see? You can't admit something like that without risking everything."

"Times are changing. The peasants opposed *in vitro* fertilization at first."

She pulled her hand away and left him on the porch

The first three months, he had no luck. The dead child's umbilical cord provided mature somatic cells. He successfully retrieved their DNA and transferred it into a donor oocyte that had been stripped of its nucleus. But all the fertilized cells stopped dividing when they reached the four-cell stage. He suspected spindle proteins, damaged when the host nucleus was removed, were the cause. This preliminary process which he'd endured so many times in reproductive cloning of animals, hardly thinking about it anymore, took on a new significance now that he dealt with human cells.

An unexpected sense of dread filled him. Some nights he lay awake, listening to a heavy spring rain battering the roof, thinking. The task of creating a child for Callista had begun to seem like an illicit act of intimacy. The time might come when he'd have to explain his failure. He worked on the problem by himself, shutting himself off from his team, even Gwen.

One day, an older assistant he'd always found reliable resigned. This was a relief; the man had begun to ask awkward questions. Delgado didn't want to have to hide his project from someone who'd guess immediately what was happening. The following week, two competent but rather silent women, one middle-aged, one younger, arrived before he'd got around to a discrete hunt to fill the empty position.

"Ekaterina," the younger woman said, holding out a hand. "Kat."

The older one walked past, ignoring his outstretched hand.

He learned they'd been sent to assist. So the Orlov Mafia were keeping him under surveillance. The women moved their bags into the empty dormitory sometimes used by the field workers and began to work in the barns as if they were used to farm work. He accepted the fact that they must be reporting back to the Orlovs.

He renewed his search for reports and published papers—many later discredited—for anything to do with human cloning, searching for the clues to get him past this obstacle. Nothing new. He'd read it all before. He considered giving up. Callista would want her money back, but that would be the least of his worries.

In April, some of the dividing cells passed the stage of becoming viable in their test tubes. Inspecting them under the microscope one morning, he found that two of the experimental clusters showed signs of developing into human embryos.

"Time to stop this before it goes any further."

He hadn't heard Gwen come into the lab. He turned to her, excitement making it difficult to speak. He'd put off making plans for what came next, afraid there wasn't going to be a *next*. But now, seeing those healthy cells under the lens, he was euphoric.

"It's happening, Gwen. We're going to make history. Look here."

She ignored the microscope. "It isn't right, you know. I didn't grow up Catholic like you, but even I know there are some things we shouldn't be trying to do. Making humans in a test tube is one."

Exasperated, he said, "There was a time when you supported me, Gwen."

She sighed. "Have you ever wondered what kind of people would even want to replace a loved child with a clone?"

"We don't ask a farmer about his plans for an Angus bull. We're not responsible for the life of the animal once it leaves here."

"Maybe we should be."

The following days brought a crucial decision. The cells could not be left to go on developing in a test tube. They needed to be implanted. He reached out to shut down the microscope he'd been using but a hand closed over his, preventing him. The young woman Callista Orlov sent met his gaze.

"Now it's my turn, Doc," she said.

He processed this. Mid-twenties, he'd guessed. She radiated good health, almost as if she'd been selected. He realized now she had.

"Yes, I've done this before." She grinned at him. "Do it soon, and we'll all go home for Christmas. That would be appropriate, don't you think?"

Two days later, one of the embryos stopped developing.

He implanted the remaining embryo in Kat the next morning. That part at least was little different than what they did routinely with cows and mares. Kat recovered easily and returned to work. His task now was to monitor her progress. Worn down by the pressure of the past weeks—they were operating with a depleted staff and he hesitated to hire—he skipped his habitual glass of wine on the deck and took an early night.

Snow vanished from the mountaintops, warmer winds swept over the pastures, poppies and lupines bloomed. Not as exotic as the flowers in Callista's perfume. He pushed the thought out of his mind.

The pregnancy proceeded uneventfully. Gwen oversaw the regular part of NovaGen's operation, which he was ignoring. Ranchers came with their requests for champion stock, and his staff accommodated them as usual. On the surface, nothing had changed at NovaGen. He should have been used to this natural process by now, but he hovered over Kat like a nervous first-time mother, moving her into a more secluded part of the main building when she began to show, to avoid gossip. Summer heat set in and the smell of distant wildfires reached the deck where he sat in the evenings, wineglass in hand, waiting for Gwen who rarely spent time with him anymore.

The day he made the first ultrasound exam, Kat stretched out on the table before him, his hand shook with nervousness as it moved over her belly. How many times had he monitored bovine or equine ultrasounds? Too many to count. But this hit him harder. Gray-white swirls like clouds in the primal mud appeared on screen. He adjusted the visuals. Something took shape, amorphous, nebulous. No animal fetus could move him like this. Perhaps fatherhood felt like this.

"Everything okay, Doc?" Kat asked.

"Yes. Right. Almost done."

He dared not make the assumption that a human fetus produced in a test tube would develop like any other mammal in a healthy uterus. That was a trap he must avoid falling into, thinking of Kat as just another brood animal. He marked the progress of her swelling belly with more anxiety than he would a cow carrying a priceless calf. The way to overcome this strange state of nervousness and almost parental pride was to focus on the medical details.

The weeks passed. Heartbeat remained regular and strong. Blood panels normal for a human *multigravida*. Ultrasounds continued to look promising.

"Satisfied?" Kat asked one morning. She swung her legs over the examining table and sat up, hands folded lightly over her swollen belly.

"Quite." He turned from the autoclave where he'd been loading instruments and gazed at her. She had more experience at this point than he did. "Why are you doing this?"

She made a cartoon face at him. "Same reason you are, Doc. Money."

"I have more reasons than that."

"Oh, yes. Science. Vastly over-rated, if you ask me." She picked her scattered clothes off the floor and left the room.

He scrubbed his hands under the hot tap until they were red and sore, but the unease was slow to wash off.

The following week, he signed a contract with a pharmaceutical company to produce a line of animal clones for drug testing. He needed to be careful not to over-extend NovaGen's footprint, nothing that would draw unwanted attention, but everything must look to a curious outsider to be operating as it normally did. Afterwards, he walked over to the barns to inspect the pregnant mares. The earthy smell of dung and warm animals calmed his anxiety, anchored him to his world. He used to inspect the barns every day before Callista showed up. When this was completed—when Kat had delivered a live child—he'd consider the next stage. But it would be hard to find a project so absorbing, so fulfilling as this one. Even during the first few nervous times he'd done this with livestock, he couldn't remember being so emotionally overwrought. He hadn't had time for a family, the work always coming first. It had never seemed much of a problem before.

Perhaps it was time to think about delegating authority, stepping away as soon as this was over. Not give NovaGen's work up entirely, of course. It might be good to explore a life away from the hard work of the barns and laboratory, perhaps take up the offer UC Davis had extended for him to come back and teach. He'd enjoy that.

The child was born by C-section in late January. He didn't want to take chances with unforeseeable hazards lurking in the journey through the birth canal. Even animals ran into difficulties at times, and it wasn't unheard of to lose mother or calf during birth. Sometimes both. He didn't want to think what would happen if anything went wrong. He would've felt better with an obstetrician present, someone more used to human birth and its potential problems, but he learned now that the other woman the Orlovs had sent was trained as a midwife. Looking down at the slippery, blood-covered infant he'd just delivered, the ammonia smell of blood and amniotic fluid in his nose, he was overwhelmed by reverence. He hadn't felt awe-struck like that since his first communion. No livestock birth could produce that experience.

The midwife took the newborn baby out of his hands. She cut the cord and put it away; then she cleaned away the blood and reached for a blanket. He busied himself sewing Kat up, taking the smallest stitches he could, hands shaking with stress. It felt like a sacrament more than a medical procedure.

In the following days he hovered over the infant in a secluded part of the building converted to serve as a nursery, counting fingers and toes, then counting again to be sure, like a nervous new father, marveling at the tiny pink mouth, the delicate eyelashes, worrying over each whimper of distress. He told himself he was exercising caution, checking for problems. Nothing he wouldn't have done with a newborn animal. That was only partly true. The thin cries of the newborn brought tears. He wondered if Joseph had felt like that, gazing at the infant he hadn't fathered.

"She's not yours, you know," Gwen said.

"You think I don't understand that?"

She'd come into the makeshift nursery behind him, standing with her arms crossed over her stomach. Her animosity both bewildered and annoyed him.

"There's a lot of money hanging on the health of this child."

But it wasn't just the money, or even the fantastic achievement of the child's birth that overwhelmed him. An emotion new to him controlled his reactions.

After the day's work, he dropped into his usual chair on the deck as the sun went down and poured a single malt to ward off the cold. Gwen didn't join him. She'd come around at some point, probably when the child was gone. The thought of the child leaving jarred him.

A week later, a sleek black limousine pulled up on the driveway. The uniformed driver got out and held open the passenger door. A moment later, the midwife came out from the building carrying the baby wrapped in a bulky white shawl. Kat followed, carrying her suitcase.

"Wait." He stood outside NovaGen's front entrance. "You can't take her just like that. She's not ready to go—"

The midwife stared silently at him.

"There are examinations—tests—I need to be certain—"

Ignoring him, she allowed the driver to help her into the limousine.

Kat held out a check. "Seems our little enterprise here is ended, Doc."

The limousine moved silently down the driveway.

Gwen joined him on the deck that evening; he was grateful for her presence. It was hard to absorb the reality that all the tension, the fears and stress of the last year were finally laid to rest. He'd done what he set out to do, yet he felt strangely deflated. Maybe that was what losing a baby felt like to a parent. Emotional exhaustion brought on by the stress of the last twelve months. Nothing a good night's sleep wouldn't cure. How long had it been since he'd slept through the night?

"Now we get to think about our next step," he told Gwen. "But maybe we'll take a few days off first to recuperate."

She looked older. It had been hard on her too, he realized. He wasn't likely to find someone as reliable as Gwen, as good-hearted. As down-to-Earth. He'd never seen her in anything except jeans and boots and old sweatshirts that inevitably smelled of the stable.

"Do you suppose we can really ever be done with this?" She wasn't looking at him, staring instead over the valley to the foothills already swallowed up by the shadows of approaching night.

"What do you mean?"

"Will things go back to normal? *Can* they go back to normal?"

"You've been very valuable to me, Gwen—"

"Valuable!"

"Of course. More than that. You know what I mean. You need a break— We both do. Maybe we should take a trip. Have you ever been to Europe? I can afford London—Rome—Paris—" But it was Callista Orlov he was imagining in Europe's glitzy capitals.

"I can't help thinking there'll be consequences."

"Good consequences. We have a bright future ahead of us."

"Do we?" She turned to look at him, her expression open, vulnerable.

He hadn't treated her well. She deserved better, but not what he suspected she might be hoping. "I could even put the day-to-day operation of the company aside and take that professorship UC Davis offered."

"What would happen to NovaGen without you?"

"I'd trust the company in your hands. You could run it."

She gazed at him for a moment. "I could. But you've worked so hard. Will you be content to give it up and just teach? You won't be able to talk about your work."

Was any pioneer ever truly content being the only one to know what he'd achieved? He hadn't expected emptiness to replace euphoria quite so quickly.

"I couldn't bear to do something like this again, Tom. There's too much pain in it."

Could she even imagine the pain he'd felt when the Russian women had carried the child away? He hadn't expected that to be a greater loss than public acclaim.

"Don't think about it. I'm not going to."

"I wish I could believe that," she said.

Floodlights came on as they approached. The porch gleamed wetly in the aftermath of a late spring rain. Grass in the pastures was tall and lush, and the comforting sound of a cow lowing drifted on the evening air. They'd just returned from his interview with the dean at UC Davis. The man had been supportive of Delgado continuing with his research as well as lecturing. Delgado hadn't gone into detail about what that research might entail.

Before they could enter the building, a familiar black limousine slid up the long driveway.

"I'll deal with this," he said. "You go on to bed."

The uniformed chauffeur got out and opened the back door. His jacket bunched as he bent over. If this had been a movie, there'd have been a gun under that jacket. But this was rural Solano County, not Chicago. His muscles tensed. Callista Orlov stepped out. She was wearing a long fur coat and black veil that hid half her face, but her same dark perfume engulfed him. His heart thumped as he took her gloved hand in his. She was even more beautiful than he'd remembered, only now her face seemed lined with grief.

A second man, young and muscle-bound, took a picnic cooler out of the limo's trunk and accompanied Callista into his office.

"We had a verbal contract, Dr Delgado."

He felt on the edge of nervous laughter. "And I observed it, Callista. I can promise you the clone is all you could desire. There were no problems with this birth."

If she noticed his use of her first name, she didn't react. Baby Orlov's chromosomes had been young and strong. Premature shortening of the telomeres, as happened when the donor animal was old, led to a reduced life span in the clone. Not going to be a problem in this case. Callista's genes and his skill had made a perfect baby between them.

"You cloned a female."

"Yes. A healthy one—" He broke off. Gwen had guessed there was something he'd missed, but he hadn't listened.

"My husband desired a boy."

"I'm afraid that wasn't possible. I should've explained better. Cloning a female produces a female. It's because of the chromosomes. A male donor, with both X and Y, can be used to produce a female clone. We just remove the Y. But a female donor doesn't have a Y chromosome to begin with—"

"After Damiana's birth, there were two more. I lost them both."

"I'm sorry—"

She held up a hand. "I thought he loved her. I was mistaken."

He had an overwhelming urge to take her into his arms.

"My husband didn't want another female. He wants a son. And I can't give it to him."

"An heir."

She flicked a finger at the silent attendant. The man released the catch on the picnic cooler. Beckoned him to look.

The small body of the perfect baby he'd created, packed in dry ice. Beside it, another small glass vial. His heart jumped.

"You killed her? Our beautiful child?"

Her eyebrows lifted, she tilted her head. "Not I."

He stared at her as this sank in. "But you didn't stop him."

Wordlessly, she lifted the veil with the tip of a black-gloved finger. Her face was pale as a statue of the grieving Madonna. One eye was underlined in purple and brown as if she'd used too much makeup. His knees went weak.

"Why do you stay with him?"

She dropped the veil. "Because I love him. Now you will make a son for him."

Cold rage rose in him. "I won't do it."

She spoke as casually as if they were discussing the price of livestock "If I reveal this verbal contract, your university might not want to hire you."

"He killed the child."

"He'll kill me too, if I don't produce a son. If *we* don't produce a son. You and I."

"You ask too much of me."

She stood up, gathering the folds of her black skirt, her dark eyes gazing into his, her perfume engulfing him. "Do I, Tom?"

She left the room; the musclebound man followed.

He gazed at the little corpse, the new vial of fresh cord blood beside it, consumed by more than rage at her manipulation.

She didn't understand this was more than just a business trans-action for him.

The scientist and the Madonna.

He was already thinking how it might be done.

FORKPOINTS

THE backstage maze at the New Globe InterAct PlayHouse reeked of cannabis when Cass arrived, in spite of the director's recent lecture about what smoke did to the delicate Sonytronic rig. The head gaffer had an Aiwa negative ion pulsar going over by the mainboard in the control room. Someone had draped a plastic Christmas wreath over the fire extinguisher next to the board.

The gaffer looked up at Cass. "How's it going?"

"Not my favorite time of year."

"And Jamie?"

She shrugged.

The PlayHouse—a large, rambling, done-over art deco mansion just off Hollywood Boulevard—was almost freezing. Computers needed it cold; InterActors didn't count for much. Amazing somebody hadn't already tried to replace them with machines. Cassandra Romano, she thought, an incredibly realistic simulation of a human being. Maybe not so realistic this time of year.

She headed down a dark corridor to Wardrobe. The costumes in this show were her immediate problem. The third decade of the previous century had glorified flat, skinny women, and Cass was neither anymore. Wardrobe had wanted her in a chunky tweed suit for the first act, huge padded shoulders, ugly fur collar, the jacket belted army-style over a skirt with inverted pleats, and a sort of black fur helmet on top. She'd yelled so much they settled on an ankle length maxi coat and more fur trim.

Then Myron had added insult to damage by lecturing her on her slipping audience appeal, measured each week in the box office receipts by the number of people willing to pay to help her character make decisions in the interactive drama.

This morning the insect-squeaking voice of the scale had announced the addition of another two pounds to stuff into the costume.

Forkpoint. Why not quit now?

Because of Jamie, that was why not.

It started with the parade down Colorado Boulevard in Pasadena, a sunny, rose-scented December day twenty years into a new century. A hero's welcome home, the last of a dozen similar cavalcades across the country. Johnny in the back seat of the convertible, bronzed and athletic as she remembered him from high school playing fields, champagne glass in one hand. Later she'd learn how much NASA hated that champagne glass, and how they would come to hide behind it.

But for now, Johnny Romano was the first astronaut to set foot on an asteroid, and that counted for something. She could never remember which one it had been.

Seeing her face in the crowd, he stopped his driver and pulled her aboard. "Marry me!" he shouted in her ear over the roar of the crowd as the parade passed the Norton Simon Museum. His fingers tangled in her long, dark hair. He was so drunk. "Sure," she said, because his face had been on all the nets for days and hadn't she just about always known him?

Minor actresses never had too many options. Yet there had been choices, a show in Cincinnati, a little theater production in Des Moines. They glimmered at the back of her mind, shut out by the glamour spotlight of Johnny's triumphal tour, and were abandoned in that moment under the flags, the scent of rose petals, and the deafening cheers. She was an actress; she lived for attention.

They were a media creation: space hero weds sexy actress, high school sweethearts. They married in Hollywood and honeymooned in Las Vegas. Where she sat up all night for the first time, cradling him in her arms while he writhed in silent nightmares. His headaches and nausea started six months after that.

By then she was already pregnant with Jamie.

"All right!" Myron shouted. "Theme One, Scene Three, people. Take your places, please."

She took the east backstage maze—actually a staircase off-limits to the audience—down to the "parlor" of the house in London where she did the scene in *V Stands for Victory*. Cameron Gordon, male lead, winked as she came through the cast door; he fiddled with his headset, adjusting reception. For rehearsal they all wore larger versions of the two-channel Maxon earplugs employed for the actual performance. The large versions had tiny mikes attached so the cast could talk back.

Cass snugged her head set in place. A stage tech eased past, checking out the electronics for the special effects. The New Globe was state of the art. First of its kind. Revolutionizing the field. Her agent's words. It had imitators now, but it was still the best. For now. She was very lucky to be working here after allowing the media to forget about her for so long—the agent's words again. There'd been an entire revolution in acting while she'd been gone. She'd caught up, made the best of it.

She'd been an InterActor for almost five years, but she still got the shivers walking the mazes behind the rooms the audience saw. The excitement vanished the day Myron introduced her to Noreen Vincenza, pouty, redheaded, and ten years younger. Cass's understudy.

Miss Pouty-Lips was standing by a mahogany occasional table, tea tray in hand, ready for her walk-on part. She had to be at least twenty pounds lighter than Cass but still managed to look as if she was about to split the seams of the skimpy parlor-maid's outfit. Noreen was supposed to be a one-liner with very limited forkpoint options, but judging by the number of moves she managed to squeeze out of the peanut gallery's cheapie say-sos, she thought she was the star.

"*Cassandra?*" Myron's voice sounded as if it were coming over a child's tin-can telephone. "*Darling, are you on this planet or orbiting? For the third time—Patch in!*"

Cam Gordon ran a comb through graying hair. He was sitting in the big wingback chair beside the fireplace, watching Noreen. Cass sat down opposite him on the red and gray striped sofa. The lights came on.

"*Curtain,*" Myron said.

Funny how the old terms persisted. Pretty soon the younger generation of InterActors wouldn't even know what "curtain" and "backstage" used to refer to.

Cam, as Winston Churchill, accepted a cup of tea from Noreen. "Thank you, Alice. That'll be all."

Noreen/Alice gave a whimsical half-curtsy that the dramatist had yelled about a couple of times, but Myron had defended on the grounds that what the audiences didn't know about English manners in 1938 would fill a book. She tucked the empty tea tray under her arm.

Cass's dummy-line came next. "Mr Churchill, I must say that I fail to understand—"

"Miss Faversham." Cam groped for a second, didn't find what he was seeking, then mimed picking up and lighting a cigar. "I have already done all the explaining I intend to do."

Once a week, the cast went over the skeleplay to make sure they hadn't wandered too far from the original hardline. It wasn't just the casual changes, the little bits of improv—action or dialogue, spontaneous one night but gradually solidifying—that tugged the skele off course. Sometimes the real cognoscenti, saying-so for a few crucial roles that they bought into several nights in a row, could wreck the cast's attempts to follow the hardline. Theatrical dilettantes swapped notes and prepared strategy, making a point of working through the most bizarre choices. This was tough on an InterActor, but exhilarating if they were good at blending dummy-lines with improv.

Noreen/Alice was supposed to leave the room—this wasn't a forkpoint—but she was dawdling around today trailing a faint, musky perfume. It put Cass off a fraction of a second.

"You are truly an arrogant man!"

The scene coach scolded in her ear. *"You're picking up late, Cass."*

A play had a life of its own, and it changed over a period of several performances. Once an InterActor really got into improving to fit a good say-so, he or she tended to unconsciously add those possibilities in the next time, as if they were part of the hardline, And when that happened, the writers' union squawked if they didn't track it back on inside contract limits. Eventually the cast might get to a point where there was no way out.

"London is full of well-bred, sensitive young ladies, Miss Faversham," Cam delivered Churchill's lines. "Any one of them would seize this chance."

Cass stood up, careful to turn her face toward the north wall where the audience who'd chosen to say-so for Myra Faversham would be later. Miss Faversham was indecisive, adjusting the abominable fur hat.

"Well, Miss Faversham? What is your decision?"

Forkpoint.

NASA specialists couldn't find anything. "Stress of re-entry," one suggested. "Psychological effect," another wrote. It had been a rough trip home—but that was classified. Nobody could blame Johnny for feeling a little less than his normal self for a while. This too shall pass.

The prospect of fatherhood seemed to rally him; the headaches and the nausea receded. But not the nightmares. He refused to talk about them, even to her, and certainly not to the NASA shrinks.

Then the amnio sent up warning flares, and the ultrasound was indecisive, and the doctor frowned when he spoke to her.

She brought Johnny the news one day at sunset. He was sitting on the balcony of their condo in Santa Monica where the scent of roses in the courtyard below was as heady as champagne. He'd taken to sitting for hours like this, staring into the distance.

NASA wondered weekly when he was coming back to work. They spoke of choices: implants, desk jobs, virtual orbiting, the best way to use his experience and skill. He ignored them.

"The doc thinks I should abort." All the way home she'd practiced how to say this, finally deciding on cold words that cut cleanest.

"No."

He didn't turn his head to look at her. She hadn't expected him to. She studied the black curls lying unkempt on the back of his neck.

"There's something wrong with it, Johnny."

"No!"

He did turn to her then, his face full of nightmares, and she dropped to her knees beside him, her hands raised to cradle his face. In that moment, perhaps, she truly loved him.

"We could try again later—"

In answer, his hands made an obscene gesture at his crotch. "Before this falls off, you think?"

His voice was high, bordering on hysteria. She'd seen his hands move that way in his sleep, a pathetic warding off of things with no name, dark things with no shape that inhabited the lonely sweep of outer space. Things that he believed had destroyed his manhood. She didn't believe in them because she didn't understand anything about his life in space. But she believed in him.

"All right. We'll take the chance. It'll mean a lot of monitoring—drugs. We'll have to be careful."

"I won't touch you, if that's what you mean," he said, anger darkening his tone. "I couldn't if I wanted to."

Jamie was born three months later, premature, underweight, a tiny white pearl of a child with eyes the black of deep space. He was so beautiful it took her breath away.

He never cried, even at the moment of first breath.

In an actual performance, the say-sos who'd paid to influence the Myra Faversham character would signal their choice
of two alternatives by pressing a button on their little hand-
held transmitters. Option A meant Myra stayed; Option B
meant she valued her dignity (and her chastity) and walked.
The winning decision would light up on the main board in the
control room, and then the tracker's job was to relay it as fast
as possible to the cast so there was no delay in the scene.

"Option A," Myron instructed, today picking one for practice.

Cass sat down again. Now she went into Myra's dummy-
lines that would lead to her becoming Churchill's secretary,
and the scene played out until the next fork. If he'd said "B,"
she would have delivered a speech about the purity of English
womanhood and stalked off stage. And then she'd have been
in line for several scenes where she actively worked against
Churchill becoming prime minister. Ultimately, the play
would have finished very nearly in the same place, but it would
have arrived there by different routes.

"Very well, Mr Churchill," Cass's option A lines went.
"Tell me what it is you expect of me."

She ran through her scene without giving it much thought
today. She always found it harder to get into her part in these
dry run-throughs. Improving was what gave the play fire, the
excitement of trying to outfox some particularly cunning say-
sos and get where she was supposed to be going in the hardline
without detracking the entire play. Without the life breathed
into it by real interactive performance, the skele, the play as it
was written, seemed dead.

At regular intervals the scene coach updated them on what
had been happening in the two major scenes that played at

the same time as theirs but in other rooms of the house, as well as the little bits of business that went on in the pantry and the upstairs hall. Even a walk-on could skew this play if he gave it half a try. InterActors needed to be prepared if some off-brand kink in the skele was zooming down the wire from some other scene. One night, some little bastard playing a delivery boy had a cheering section from his former high-school drama class primed to twist his one say-so into a major disaster, and—

"Cassandra!" Myron screeched in her ear. *"What's the matter with you today, darling? Are you having your period? Pick up the tempo for Chrissakes."*

She imagined him squatting like a spider in the middle of his control room web, peering at three screens in turn and listening to multi-tracks of dialogue.

She took a breath. "I do typing Mr Churchill but I don't make tea—"

"Don't overdo it, Cass, there's a good girl," the scene coach said mildly. He wasn't fond of Myron either.

Somehow she got through the rest of the rehearsal without incurring Myron's wrath again. Afterwards, the cast stood around drinking java, telling plans for the upcoming holidays. The Fabulous Miss Noreen was cooing at Myron, flattering the old goat.

"Saw your ex on the news last night, Cass," Cam said, passing her with aromatic mug in hand. "What's he doing taking a space job again, after all these years?"

The midnight eyes saw only darkness. That was the first thing they learned. The seashell ears were sealed against them.

Weeks of doctor visits turned into months, a year, two years. A long line of specialists pronounced themselves baffled. NASA, fearing some unimaginable liability, blamed it on the alcohol.

Jamie grew, flawless in every way except one. The pale, beautiful body seemed quite empty, like an anencephalic clone grown in a transplant tank.

They fought every night now. He wanted her to put Jamie in an institution.

"He's more than you can handle. Maybe they'll find a cure. And even if they don't, you'd be helping science."

She knew it was Johnny who ought to be helping science, but she didn't say it. She never told him half what she thought or knew. His nightmares had faded, but they slept in separate bedrooms. He became enraged if she accidentally interrupted him in the bathroom they shared, covering his genitals like an adolescent boy in a locker room. What was left of his genitals.

"Life isn't a set script in one of your damn theaters," he said. "Sometimes you have to make hard choices."

"I'll manage," she said, stubborn in the face of his rigid opposition.

"I can't take this much longer. You have to make a decision."

She lifted the sleeping child from his crib and held him close to her breast that he'd never learned to suck. "I'm keeping Jamie."

He went out the door without replying, leaving the closet full of his clothes and his wedding ring on the bed.

Skeleplays weren't that much different from the old idea of interactive books Cass's mother had played with. *If you want Captain Kirk to beam down to the planet, turn to page 38. If you want him to stay on the Enterprise, page 51.* The difference was the InterActors, and their ability to improv. Cynical Cameron had a different view. InterAct theater was popular in inverse proportion to the amount of governmental control its fans experienced in their lives. In that case, she'd said, we'll be in business a long time. Cam had shaken his head. "Always something new," he'd said. "Always forkpoints."

The setting sun smeared the sky with dull red as she changed into her costume for the evening performance. Christmas three days away, another visit to Jamie—

She crammed the ugly hat on her head. Wardrobe had found it in a thrift shop. It gave off a faint odor of mildew.

They ran three interlocked themes at once, subplots: Churchill's battle to save England from the Axis powers, the problems he had with rivals in Parliament, and Churchill's romance with his secretary. A small change in only one theme—for instance, Miss Faversham stalks offstage and on the way out passes a committee of MPs who've just been "say-so'd" into braving the bulldog in his den—meant another theme would have to change course to accommodate. Or she could pass one of her rivals for Churchill's favor, and that might send a jealous Myra back into his arms.

InterActors couldn't memorize every possibility, because the plot never followed the same course two performances in a row. Some things had to be improved. They had to be fast thinkers and good with clever dialogue. She'd never been one of the best, coming to it late in her career, but she'd managed to keep up until now.

She adjusted the tiny Maxon plug that would let her hear the tracker, allowing herself to ease into the character. The theater came alive when the audience took its place. In the backstage maze, the rustle of programs and murmur of voices were muted. Cass glanced through a peephole onto the parlor set where Cam was playing a scene with two members of the Liberal party. Behind him, she saw the audience, thumbs on the buttons of their transmitters, intent on taking part in the play by making their say-so's. She recognized several of the regulars. Behind the row of seats stood the "cruisers" who wandered from scene to scene rather than stay with one character throughout.

She heard her cue and entered the scene through the cast door. Improving was what gave the play fire, the excitement of trying to outfox some particularly cunning say-so and get where she was supposed to be going in the hardline without detracking the entire play. The familiar scene between Churchill and Miss Faversham began to play.

She'd done this particular play four times a week for two years now. Sometimes a rowdy audience could get carried away by their sense of taking part in the action, but not tonight. They sat hunched forward in their seats, paying close attention.

"Well," Winston Churchill said. "What is your decision?"

The scene had arrived at Myra Faversham's forkpoint.

She was aware of the flutter of fingers on transmitters in the hands of the group who'd paid to influence Myra's actions. A fraction of a second passed and the tracker's voice murmured in her ear.

"Option B."

"I very much regret to say that I value my honor, Mr Churchill, more than I value financial reward," Cass said haughtily, drawing on gloves that seemed too tight. "England's womanhood cannot be bought by promises—"

Under her words, she heard the tracker again, warning of a kink in the skele. *"Lord North on his way with dispatches."*

No problem. She'd just have to cut her lines to fit the revised scene when Churchill's colleague arrived, working the crucial parts around their dialogue. Cam caught her eye meaningfully; he'd been advised of the kink. The trick was to make it seamless, and not to add too much that might cause problems somewhere else further on.

Lord North burst into the room, a new InterActor, given to tripping over his lines when he got flustered. Cass wove her lines in around their exchange and got off the set credibly.

Myron was in the maze, frowning as usual. She squeezed past him, heading for her next scene, a confrontation with two members of the opposition party that Option B had set her up for.

"Cass. Wait up." Myron caught her by the sleeve. "You had a net call. Your ex. Said he's at Lunar Base Two."

"Johnny?" She hadn't heard from him in three years. She'd learned from a buddy in the corps that he'd gone back to NASA as a desk pilot. "Why'd he call? What's he doing on the moon?"

"You know I don't like the cast conducting personal business during a performance," Myron said. "I terminated the transmission."

Sometimes life resembles a play with a bozo skele, all the forkpoints leading down to absurdity or despair.

Johnny was half right. It wasn't that she couldn't take care of Jamie; his needs were minimal—food, clean diapers. But he continued to lie unmoving in his crib, his small body almost bloodless in its white perfection, past his first and then his second birthday. He never cried out or made gestures she could understand. He never learned to ask for anything.

It was a question of why.

Like Johnny, the doctors urged her to put the baby away. A home, they said, excellent care, and success with puzzling cases like this—Well, not quite like this.

NASA sent her half Johnny's pay check. More might have been an admission of liability.

At four, Jamie learned to walk.

Then one day a pop-vid show that hyped its revelations of celebrity secrets found out about Jamie and sent a remote cam to hover a foot above her head for a month. It even followed her into the bathroom where Johnny had been ashamed to let her see his ravaged manhood.

The home the doctors recommended would cost more than the NASA payments allowed. If she put Jamie away— and what difference would it make to the child who didn't know she was his mother, in any case?—she would have to go back to the theater. Older. Heavier. Life drained out of her in the service of Jamie who couldn't use it.

It truly was a bozo skele. All anyone could do was hope it didn't go down to disaster.

Myron called a meeting after the performance. Cass sipped thick java a scene coach pressed into her hands and watched him gesticulating. He was in a bad mood. They'd had a string of real InterActive aficionados recently, some of them bright kids from Cal Tech who liked to cause mischief. The cast had to work hard to keep the play tracking. They'd been using a lot of special effects to get out of impossible kinks and dead ends that these say-sos forced. All that high tech was expensive.

Noreen made some comment that Cass missed. Everybody laughed, including Myron.

"All right, folks. Listen up." Myron banged a mug against a steel strut. "I've got business to share. Stuff I want you to keep to yourselves."

Several of the InterActors, the younger ones including Noreen, sat cross-legged on the floor. Cass dragged out a folding chair. A tall man wearing glasses and a dark suit stood beside Myron, a nuleather folder in his hand. The stranger spoke about innovations in InterActive equipment that she didn't understand. Then he tucked the folder under his arm and held something out on the palm of his right hand. The InterActors leaned forward, doing a crowd scene around him. Noreen made ooh and ahh noises.

"What is it?" Cass asked one of the scene coaches.

"Biochip," the coach said. "Space agency has 'em, but I didn't know we'd managed to rip the technology off yet."

Myron gazed across the bent heads at her. "Light-speed communication, darling. It'll eliminate that delay that's been killing us. Multi channels for InterActors, director, techs. Everybody. This will revolutionize the field."

"Give it to us in English," Cam said.

"You haven't seen InterActive drama till you see how this little chip is going to work. The InterActors will be able to monitor all the say-sos at every single forkpoint, not just their own. And they'll receive my instructions for all scenes simultaneously. Without bulky headphones."

"Why would we want to hear everybody's say-sos?" a young man asked. "It's tough enough dealing with our own."

Myron stared thoughtfully at him. "Think what it'll do to a drama if you know what everybody's doing and can incorporate their decisions into your own."

"Sounds like we're going to need a PhD just to be able to do it," Cass said.

"That's what's wrong with you, Cassandra," Myron said. "You're not flexible anymore. This is a young field, darling. InterActive drama's changing. You need to grow with it. Nobody's indispensable." He turned away from her. "This is the future, folks. And we're going to be the first company to get it."

The thought of surgeons cutting her head open and burying a piece of metal in her brain scared her no less than it had once scared Johnny. And that wasn't all. She could imagine what it'd be like, stuck with the thing in her skull, never able to turn it off. Like being on-stage all the time, even when she was home.

They would've known at NASA when Johnny tried to hide his genitals from her in the bathroom.

"Of course, according to contract, we can't actually force you to have the implant," Myron said. "But we're going to be awfully appreciative of those who volunteer."

Now they were all asking questions.

"Disability pay for the six weeks while you recuperate, and for the retraining period that'll be necessary after that."

"Do we have a choice of hospitals?" someone wanted to know.

"Well—" Myron's face had that fixed smile it got when he was trying to weasel some particularly low clause past them into the contract. "We've made arrangements with a clinic in New Delhi."

"You mean the procedure's not licensed in the States?" Cam asked.

Myron said smoothly, "The risks are negligible. Theater's going to be dark for a couple of months, starting now. We're just extending the normal end-of-year break a little bit. Then we're starting rehearsal on a brand new version of this play."

And of course, there she rose: Miss Pouty-Lips herself, standing so close to Myron he could hardly look at her without staring down the low-cut front of her costume.

"Myron," she said, "I want to be first to volunteer."

She reminded Cass of herself a billion years ago, before she'd made other choices.

"Fabulous, baby! Anyone else?"

Several hands went up, including Cam's. But Cameron's went up more slowly.

"Cassandra?" Myron asked when he'd finished noting the volunteers, almost the entire cast.

She was tired of it all. Tired of making decisions that never changed anything for the better. Tired of living her life day after day with the knowledge of her strange child, her lost marriage, and her failing career.

"Won't last long," one of the scene coaches muttered. "Same chip technology supports VR. And then where'll we be?"

Myron bit his fingernail. "It's your decision, Cassandra. But you should know your audience ratings have been diving."

Forkpoint.

Anonymous, red-tiled communities jamming the San Fernando Valley flashed by outside the maglev window. The hillsides were choked from valley floor to hill crest with apartment buildings, motels, shopping malls, high-rise office blocks, swimming pools, and health clubs, like 3-D photocopies of one community stacked endlessly side by side.

At Woodland Hills, Cass got off the train and transferred to the slow electric tram winding down Topanga Canyon Road.

Oak Grove House, private residential home for developmentally disturbed children, stood behind a brick wall. The brief winter afternoon was already fading as she reached the path to the main building. Rosebushes lining the path, shriveled and dry, were empty of perfume. The green Christmas wreath on the front door enveloped her in its scent of snowy forest.

The director came outside to meet her. "He's in the garden."

"How is he?" She asked the woman the same question, month after month, year after year.

And she always got the same answer: "As well as we can expect. We mustn't look for miracles, must we?"

She didn't know why not.

She walked across the sloping lawn to the play area under the trees. In the distance, the children climbing the jungle gym, the toddlers shrieking on the teeter-totter and the slide, all looked healthy and very normal.

Eight-year-old Jamie was all by himself, safety-belted into the swing. She stood a few feet away and looked at him. His cheeks glowed, translucent as if light moved under his skin. His hair had been freshly cut, the white curls brushed back from his forehead. He wore the spaceship sweatshirt she'd brought him six months ago. It was still too big.

"Hello, Jamie."

She knew he couldn't hear her, but it helped her to speak.

He swung back and forth, back and forth, his blind gaze fixed on trees at the dark edge of the lawn. If I didn't know, she thought, and if I squinted, I'd think he was normal.

Normal. There it was. In Johnny and Cass's bozo skele they'd chosen a fork that led to poor, abnormal Jamie.

But that wasn't quite right either. Normal was a word for other children. Jamie had been touched by something that couldn't be measured by human standards of normal.

"How have you been, Jamie? Are they treating you well here?"

Jamie continued to swing.

One of the therapists came up beside her, a young black man. He flashed her a quick smile, then stopped the swing and unbuckled her child.

"Time to stop swinging, Jamie. Mom's here."

"You talk to him too," she said. "But he can't hear."

"There may be other ways of hearing," he said.

Startled, she stared at the young man with the unresponsive boy in his arms. "His father went into space."

"I was in high school, but I followed his news."

"It ate him up. Whatever it was."

"No," he said. "It gave you a gift."

He set Jamie down on the lawn at her feet.

Jamie seemed preoccupied with his delicate hands, the long fingers weaving like ghosts through the air. Almost like he was trying sign language, she thought.

"Look. Have you tried to teach him to sign? I mean, Helen Keller made it. Perhaps he could...."

She broke off. Of course they'd tried. Dozens of doctors, scientists of all the disciplines of pediatrics and space medicine. But nobody here would know the language if Jamie had one in his brain. Nobody on Earth.

The therapist touched her hand gently. "Love him as he is, Miz Romano. He isn't like the rest of us."

He put the boy's hand in hers and walked away, leaving her with Jamie. She bent to lean her cheek against the boy's, her nose brushing his pale, snow-scented hair. Jamie stared sightlessly at the darkening trees.

They walked back across the lawn in the gathering dusk. She began to talk to the child about his father on the moon. Overhead, a satellite winked its way across the sky, and she pointed it out.

Forkpoints, she thought. Life was full of them.

MILES TO GO

WHEELING up to the START in the wintry dawn, he feels a dizzying rush of nervous excitement and spiking fear. He wills his bunching muscles to relax, hands—palms already hot in leather gloves—to unclench. He breathes deeply of cold, Pacific air, drawing in energy.

He is the silent center of jittery activity. Wheelers lean toward each other, slapping warmth into cold arms. Women talk in brief spurts together, voices brittle. Stretching tight leg muscles. Waiting. Runners churn around him, a shimmering kaleidoscope against the city skyline. He recognizes many of them. Race gypsies, veterans from all the marathons across the nation and across the globe.

He stretches his head from side to side, working on tension in his neck. A TV camera pans over to his lightweight, three-wheeled racing chair. Adrenaline floods. He raises two fingers in a victory sign. The silver eye pauses, sweeps on.

Murmur of voices drops away.

Two minutes and three seconds to go.

The day was warm for early January, and the city seemed to have sprouted a more elegant skyline in the year Jeff Brandeis had been in Europe. He eased his van into a handicapped slot outside the office of the Long Beach Marathon and took a deep breath, dispelling the empty sensation in his stomach that had been there since he landed at LAX two days ago.

"Well, hello, Champ!" a woman cooed. "Good to see you."

Jeff waved. Strangers were always recognizing him. Good feeling, being back home. Been away too long. Problem was, after breaking records in a string of races from Oxford to Cannes, he'd been too popular with a couple of French actresses. One, with long blonde hair, had been eager to show him around Paris after dark.

Life was good to champions. A far cry from the early days when his mother fixed him up with a friend's daughter, a do-gooder who got off on the inconvenience of dating a guy in a chair. Her idea of a swell time was to stir the sugar in his coffee as if he'd lost the use of his hands instead of his legs.

He shut the car door and swiveled the chair. Inside the office, he saw they'd hung a large collection of marathon photographs on the white wall, several of them were of him crossing the FINISH in previous years. He was in even better form now. Some new training tactics he'd figured out with a couple of European racers, a new aerodynamic wrinkle for the chair from a former Italian auto designer.

Athletics, even the wheeled variety, was a young man's game, and the years were beginning to pile on. The next couple were crucial. He had plans to hammer his own record so hard it'd take anybody else a decade to catch up. Something his mother could think about without tears.

Meg Lowenthal glanced up as the door banged behind him. He admired her expensive-looking yellow linen suit, the deep neckline revealing cleavage, the way her pertly cut, coppery hair bounced as she moved. He'd always been more attracted by a woman's hair than by her face, the thicker and longer the better.

He wheeled up to her desk. "Hey, gorgeous."

"Jeff! I didn't know you were in town. Give me a minute here...." She turned back to the computer.

"Take your time. I'm enjoying the view."

"Sexist pig," she said.

He grinned. She'd liked it enough to hop into bed with him one time after a race. "Just got home. Came right over to register."

"Oh? We thought you might not want to race."

He gripped the chair's arm-rests. "Who told you that?"

"Well—you were out of the country, but we thought..."

She looked as if she were about to say something else, then changed her mind.

Jeff banged a fist on her desk, rattling pencils. "Look. I want to register. You going to tell me I can't?"

The door at the back of the office opened, and a middle-aged man in a gray Armani suit stood there, frowning. Phil Zukowski made his money from a car dealership in Signal Hill, but organizing the marathon was his passion. When he saw who it was, Zukowski came quickly forward, hand outstretched.

"Brandeis. A pleasure to see you, Champ."

"What's this about, Zukowski?"

"That orthopedics guy at UCLA that's been in the news," Zukowski said, frowning. "Dorkins? Dorsey? He called here trying to find you, so we thought—"

"I was in France." He'd heard about the Schwann cell research on CNN. The blonde actress had pretended to get all excited for him. The hollow feeling in the pit of his stomach came back.

"That's right. World record in Cannes, wasn't it?" Zukowski picked up a mug by the slick gray Mister Coffee pot. "Want some coffee, Champ?"

Jeff shook his head.

"You know this guy personally, don't you?"

"Tommy Dorseter. He was my surgeon. Played baseball at Cal State—but before my time. He was good, could've played professionally. Went to med school instead." While Jeff had gone on to a series of dead-end jobs and a serious accident, but he didn't say that. "What's it got to do with me racing? I'm ready to roll."

Zukowski gave him a thoughtful look. "We're always delighted to have you, Jeff. You're a superior athlete. The champ."

"Right. Give me the entry form."

"We just thought—Doctor Dorseter must want—"

Zukowski squirmed under Jeff's gaze. Meg opened a drawer and handed him an entry form. He jerked the chair round, headed for the narrow doorway, and found it blocked by a tiny woman in a wheelchair that seemed two sizes too big.

Carrie Stevens had short, baby-fine, light brown hair. Delicate featured, she wore a pink warm-up suit embroidered with small flowers. He'd known Carrie for several years; her fragile appearance disguised a determined racer, though she'd never taken the sport as seriously as he had.

Carrie's glance flicked from Jeff to Zukowski and back again, taking it all in. "You look like you need a break. Want to go for coffee?"

He'd taken her out for coffee or a movie a couple of times, before his fame had brought lookers like Meg Lowenthal around, but they'd remained friends. "Sure. Why not?"

"There's a new place opened on the pier since you've been gone," she said. "Let's catch up."

Half an hour later, they sat outside the coffee bar on the pier beside an overgrown fern that seemed about to make a break from ceramic captivity. The breeze off the water was sharp and clean like crystal. He stirred Sweet n' Low into his coffee mug as Carrie talked, barely listening to her stories about other racers, thinking about Dorseter.

Tommy's interest in orthopedics had been spinal cord injuries long before Jeff's accident. Prostheses were good and getting better all the time—Jeff knew a couple of amputees who raced—but the docs couldn't seem to fix severed cords. Schwann cell transplants, CNN had reported, looked like they might change that.

"That doctor from UCLA was asking about you, couple of weeks ago," Carrie said.

"Does the whole goddamn city know my business?"

She startled at his tone. "I was in the office when he called, Jeff. I'm not racing much anymore, but I drop by once in a while to keep in touch. That's all. I'm not trying to intrude."

"Got nothing to do with me."

"Well, I thought—"

She broke off and stared out at the ocean, her cheeks showing a faint pink. A gull landed on the rail beside his chair, stared insolently at him for a second. He flicked a finger, and it flapped away. It wasn't Carrie's fault, but he didn't want to think about Dorseter or his work.

"Snake oil," he said. "Cold fusion. Perpetual motion."

"I don't think so." She turned back to him, her face a mask he couldn't read. "There were a couple of articles on Dorseter in the LA Times. You ought to take a look."

"Not interested."

"Haven't you ever thought what it might be like if they could give you back your legs?"

"No."

He could tell from her expression she didn't believe him. They'd always been upfront with each other, but this wasn't something he wanted to talk about, not even with her.

The breeze off the ocean had turned cold. He pulled up the collar of the black Italian leather jacket the French actress had given him, remembering a phone call soon after he'd won his first marathon.

"Animal results show great promise, Jeff," Tommy Dorseter had said. "Someday you'll be able to throw away your chair." "What if I don't want to?" he'd said. "Don't want to?" Dorseter repeated. "Why the hell would you want to be handicapped if you didn't have to be?"

It was ironic, the way he looked at it. The chair had freed him from the handicaps of his youth—no talent and mediocre looks—replacing his early lack of success with fame and a fan club of good-looking women. Not even counting the enormous high he got from racing.

"What's so difficult about the concept?" Carrie asked. "People get artificial hearts when they need them. And kidney transplants are commonplace. Why not a fix for legs that don't work?"

"The word is 'need.' I don't."

He pulled money out of his wallet, snagged a passing waitress, and got into a thing about the bill. Easier than answering her question.

The race officials start the wheelers five minutes before the runners as usual. He does not need the other competitors, never has. He aims only to beat his own best time in each race.

The minute he starts rolling, something begins to grow that he calls the Race Mind, blotting out all thought except what he needs to move swiftly and smoothly down the course, knitting together man and chair.

For the first few miles, his concentration is on action, the powerful muscles working in his arms, strong fingers rhythmically turning the shining slender-spoked wheels so that man and machine find a synthesis of efficient motion. He is aware of a background world where sun sparks water below the bridge as he heads over it, the cool breeze slides past his brow, gulls pace him then fall away, spectators along Shoreline Drive wave him on.

A cop on a motorcycle salutes.

The answering machine blinked notice of messages from Mai and Jen that had come in while he was out. Aspiring models, his personal groupies welcoming him home. He knew the real reason behind his appeal for them. He was a photo-op, good for publicity. But it was a two-way street. His bed never needed an electric blanket, and there were no strings attached to the transaction.

The third message still waiting was from Tommy Dorseter. What he needed right now was a shot of reality, not some medical fantasy. He grabbed the phone and punched in Salvador Mendez's number.

Sunlight reflecting off the bay streamed through open French windows leading onto his balcony. Race money, a Pepsi endorsement, a line of racing gloves he'd designed were paying for this condo unit. Without racing, he'd have been stuck working another dead-end job, maybe selling cars at Zukowski's dealership in Signal Hill, living in a bachelor apartment with furniture from the Salvation Army thrift shop. Or at home with his mother where the furniture was better but the pity worse.

"Sal? Hey, amigo! How much am I gonna beat you by this year?" The Barrio Bear was one of the few who could make a race interesting for him.

"Not racin' this year, 'mano," Mendez said. "Outta practice."

"You gotta be kidding, right?"

He gazed out the French windows at a group of kids in sabots, tacking inexpertly across Alamitos Bay, sails luffing. The streaks of white sunblock on their faces gave them the look of small-fry Apaches. He'd taken sailing lessons on this bay when he was a boy. He'd been hooked early on the thrill of competing even when he was no good at it.

"Been workin' for a livin'. Got me a job out at Rancho." Mendez laughed. "Nurse's aide. Gonna be an inspiration to all them new crips."

Rancho Los Amigos, the county's orthopedic rehab facility where they'd first met. He couldn't imagine spending time there by choice.

"Hard to believe, amigo."

"Getting' married, too. No time for playin' 'round no more."

"Congratulations."

He regretted making the call. Sal was a couple of years older than he, same type of injury, but Sal's accident had been gang related. His had been less dramatic; he'd smacked a motorcycle into a utility pole on a day when he couldn't blame the weather. Another example of his general failure at everything in those days. The shared frustrations of rehab had brought them together; racing and women had kept the friendship going. They'd been two of a kind, consumers of all the thrills they could find, freed by their chairs from a world of responsibilities. He'd never considered Sal might get married.

"...bridges the fucked up nerves again, Doc says," Mendez was saying as Jeff shook his attention loose from the past.

"What?"

"Doc Dorseter. He comes maybe coupla times a week, checks out his students."

"So?"

"Don' you watch tv, 'mano? 'Schwann cells,' he calls 'em. Gonna fix us up, one a these days."

"That what you want, Sal? You get your legs back, you'll never race again. You willing to give that up?"

"Just a race, 'mano." Mendez sounded puzzled. "Just a fuckin' race. Chair ain't no badge of sainthood."

There'd be no competition this year. So what? He didn't need anybody else. He hung up the phone and went out. He put in two hours practice on the track at Cal State before sunset.

He was finishing his second glass of milk after lunch the next day when the phone rang. He almost didn't answer it, thinking it was his mother again. She'd already called once today. Didn't he think Tommy Dorseter's work could be The Light at the End of the Tunnel For His Problem? He could almost hear the capitals in her words.

This time it was Meg Lowenthal. He made a date for dinner, then found clean sheets for the bed just in case he got lucky.

He settles into his pace with an upwelling sense of robust health and fierce strength, the aching happiness that comes to him from racing. After a race, he feels cleansed of all the strangling difficulties of his life. All the hard decisions fall into place. The chair sets his spirit free.

The course climbs a small hill, then flattens again. Plum trees line the next block, white petals drift like confetti. Music blares at an intersection, a local combo playing enthusiastically. Women in bright tracksuits cheer. A dog barks. Children on bicycles keep pace along the edge of the course. The scent of fresh-cut lemon teases his nose.

He feels as if he could race like this forever.

After three more pleading messages from his mother over the next week—followed by a fax of the LA Times articles about Dorseter's work, marked up carefully so he wouldn't miss the important parts—Jeff gave in and called Dorseter at UCLA. Couldn't hurt to see what was on his mind. Maybe they'd swap tall stories about glory days on Cal State's diamond.

"Come on out to Rancho, and we'll talk," Dorseter said, sounding rushed. "I'm there Thursdays, supervising interns. Got a proposition for you."

"You got Sal already. I'm not looking for work." But he could guess what Dorseter wanted to propose, and it wasn't emptying bedpans.

Dorseter laughed. "Come anyway, Champ."

Waste of time, he told himself. He went out and spent several hours circling the university track until rain splattered in from the ocean, driving him indoors.

Rancho's parking lot was wet as he drove up on Thursday. He slid out of the driver's seat into his folding chair. The van in the next slot had the back door open, and beside it a woman was opening an umbrella over a small girl in a chair. The child grinned when she saw him and held up a hand.

"She has photos of you on her wall, Mr Brandeis," the mother said. "You're her hero."

He high-fived the girl's tiny hand. "Gonna win the next one for you, sweetheart."

"Promise?"

"I promise."

The child giggled. In a good mood now, he wheeled away as raindrops spattered his leather jacket.

He figured he'd listen to Dorseter to satisfy his mother, put an end to the tearful messages. But he wasn't interested. What was the big deal about walking, anyway? He'd been quoted in the papers once saying, if God had shown a little imagination, He'd have equipped people with wheels instead of legs. Caused quite a reaction in some quarters with that remark. His mother hadn't liked the joke either; she took this disabled stuff too seriously. Then he thought of the child, and his mood darkened again.

Dorseter's office was at the end of a white corridor lined with children's art, but Dorseter himself wasn't in it. A nurse indicated that Jeff would find the surgeon down the hall in physical therapy, a room he and Sal had referred to in the old days as the "TC," the Torture Chamber.

A buzz of noise came from the TC as the door sighed open at his approach. He remembered this place well. A cross between a high school gymnasium and a NASA training facility for astronauts, it contained some of the most fiendishly designed equipment ever to coax damaged body parts to work again. Half a dozen men and women practiced new strategies for old tasks, some moving scarred arms against the resistance of weights and pulleys, some climbing low racks of stairs on crutches, or walking up and down ramps, getting used to new prostheses.

A young guy sitting on a bench at the far end of the room caught his attention. Two male physical therapy aides in white coats lifted him to his feet and propped him upright. Judging by the way the guy's face scrunched, he wasn't enjoying it.

Dorseter was halfway down the TC, talking to a female intern. He glanced up and motioned for Jeff to come over. "Well, what d'you think?"

Jeff played it cool. "Same old TC."

"You said you'd read about my work."

"Saw the articles. Not necessarily read. Not my game."

Dorseter studied him thoughtfully. "That sounds defensive, Champ. Look. I'll give it to you straight. Animal results are so good, we're ready to use this treatment on humans."

"Cruel and unusual experiments on humans went out of fashion with the Nazis, Doc."

The orthopedic surgeon laughed. "You don't change, do you?"

"No. Should I?"

Dorseter turned serious. "Yes, I think you should. This is revolutionary. We grow the Schwann cells in the lab then transplant them into the spinal cord. They coax nerve fibers to regenerate. We've never found anything like this, Jeff. Severed nerves re-grow. Establish their own blood supply. Even develop protective myelin sheaths."

"In a petri dish."

"In lab animals."

"Don't look at me. I'm not a guinea pig."

Somebody shrieked nearby. Jeff turned to stare. The guy he'd noticed was now doubled over, vomiting—a sour stench. Not uncommon in the TC. An orderly arrived to clean up.

He had a wrenching memory of the first day they got him out of bed at the hospital after the accident, the nausea that tore through his gut as they hoisted him painfully upright, the despair that flooded through him when he glanced down at legs he couldn't feel anymore. He remembered the clumsiness of that first chair, the energy it took to perform the simplest tasks, the frustration of learning to accept limits. The aching sense of loss. It had taken him a long time to put all that behind him.

Dorseter said, "I could show you the dogs—"

"Bizarre, man! Why me? Got to be a lot of other guys salivating for the chance. I've got my life together without it."

"Have you, Jeff? How long's it going to last?"

Across the echoing room, Jeff saw the young man resting alone on a bench, towel pressed to his forehead, looking washed out as if he'd just finished a race. A deep yearning swept through him, but he wasn't sure for what. The renown of being a star athlete? The thought of walking again? His hands clutched the arm-rests of his chair till he could feel the pulse hammering at his wrists. He let go, expelling tension in a long sighing breath.

"Later. I've got work to do."

He swiveled the chair to face the exit. Dorseter put a hand on his shoulder.

"Something else. Something you should seriously consider."

"Give it up, Tommy."

"There may not be a 'later' for you. You need this chance now. How long's it been since your accident? Four years? Five?"

"You're thinking foot drop, muscle atrophy—"

"No."

Jeff shook his head. "You don't understand. I don't have the time. I need another couple of years racing before I even consider something like this."

"You don't have another couple of years!" Dorseter said. "Wait much longer, and we won't be able to reverse the changes in the vertebrae that're taking place, no matter whether the nerves regenerate or not."

He stared at the surgeon's grim expression. Face the truth, he told himself. This was why he hadn't come back home sooner, not the French actress. Ever since he'd heard the CNN report, he'd been afraid to be hit with an impossible choice.

"Think about it." Dorseter squeezed Jeff's shoulder. "You could be just the way you were before the accident."

"Right," he said, his eyes stinging. "A straight-C bozo the chicks avoided. A zero on the field. A world-class nothing. Great, man. Fucking great!"

He wheeled urgently out of the Torture Chamber.

Breath burns in his throat now. His lungs labor. His chest seems encased in crushing iron. Fingers cramp. Pain knifes his shoulder muscles. Blood roars in his ears. In spite of the headband he wears, sweat pours off his brow and stings his eyes, blinding him.

The day grows hotter. The breeze fails him. Despair claws at his heart. He's a fool to put himself through such agony. He doesn't have to prove anything to anybody.

In the sweaty fog, he sees dimly a jumble of spectators waving flags—gaunt palm trees—volunteers sprinkling water from garden hoses—pelicans gliding overhead like stone age icons—police cars blocking traffic. Everything passes in a slow-motion, nightmarish blur of silence and pain.

So many more agonizing miles to go.
He has hit the Wall.

Carrie refused his invitation to go out for dinner. He didn't tell her he'd called Meg Lowenthal first but she'd turned him down; Mai was on location, and Jen hadn't called back. He hadn't seen Carrie since the day he'd registered, but he needed to do something to clear his mind. She offered to cook at her place instead. He told her he'd be there at five.

It'd been a mistake to go out to Rancho, a distraction from the serious training he needed to do. For days after his conversation with Dorseter, he'd tried pouring all his energy into preparing himself for the race, wheeling along the race route for several hours in the gray light of early morning until the swelling rush-hour traffic drove him off. But he couldn't rid himself of Dorseter's words.

The phone rang while he was dressing; he let the machine answer. His mother again. Another guilt rap for him to come to his senses, not to be scared, to take advantage of his golden opportunity. To her, his choice seemed clear. But only a fool would trade the future he had in sight for the uncertainties of pain and obscurity that would come with Dorseter's surgery. If it even worked. How could he make a decision like that?

He went down to the condo's garage and found the van.

Carrie lived alone in an old house she rented, a small guest house behind the larger one on the bluff. All she could afford on her salary, probably. She was a teacher, maybe a librarian, he couldn't remember. Something unspectacular but socially useful.

He wheeled up the ramp and rang the doorbell. Across busy Ocean Boulevard, the water churned with white caps. A lone sailboat beat into the stiff wind, rounding the oil island, coming home before darkness fell. He watched for a moment, admiring the unknown sailor's pluck challenging the weather. Taking risks. Going all out for life, no matter what.

Inside, the house was warm and unpretentious, what he would've expected of Carrie. He felt comfortable, as if he'd just taken off a heavy winter overcoat. She turned on a lamp; light and shadow quilted the living room. Mozart played softly in the background. A water jug waited on a small oak dining table. Carrie poured him a glass then went into the kitchen, explaining the casserole needed a few more minutes.

"I heard you went out to Rancho," she called.

Dishes rattled, and he caught the rich smells of onions and baking bread.

"Must everybody get on my case?"

"Sorry. Sal was just excited for you."

Mozart wrapped it up. In the silence he heard the slow tick of an antique clock somewhere in the house. He gazed through the window at the tiny back yard. Miniature orange and lemon trees made splashes of color along a battered redwood fence. A large tortoiseshell cat slumbered next to a pot of scarlet geraniums. Tomato plants heavy with winter fruit, pots of chrysanthemums and cactus crowded on benches and shelves for easy reach from her wheelchair.

She came back into the room and refilled his water glass. "That's Gertie," she said, nodding at the cat.

"Never understood what people see in cats."

"She's my best friend."

"Kind of lonely with only a cat in your cheering section, isn't it?"

She gazed at him, something in the blue eyes he'd never seen before, maybe anger at his remark. "I don't know, Champ. Is it?"

He stared out the window, avoiding her gaze. But he couldn't avoid this. And maybe she was the only one he could talk to, the only person with no stake in what he did or didn't do.

"Would you do it, Carrie?"

"I've used a chair since I was fourteen. I'm not a good candidate like you."

"But if you could?"

"I read about a blind man once," she said. "They restored his sight somehow. But then he took to wearing dark glasses indoors."

"You figure I'm scared?"

"Not of the surgery, no."

"I don't think I could live without racing."

She said lightly, "If you're not the champ, you're nobody?"

He regretted the cheering section remark. But she was right. No point in arguing; she saw clear through his pretenses.

"Maybe it won't work on humans."

She folded napkins and set them in place before answering. "There are never any real guarantees in life, Jeff. Things happen."

"Why would I want to take the risk? I've got it good now."

"I remember a poem that meant a lot to me in my blackest moments. 'The woods are lovely, dark and deep. But I have promises to keep.'"

"Robert Frost." He was mildly surprised to dredge up even one name from his mediocre undergraduate performance. "'And miles to go before I sleep.'"

"The promises were to myself," she said.

A bittersweet memory from childhood flooded over him: A picnic in El Dorado Park by a lake speckled with ducks—running barefoot over fragrant summer grass—a flop-eared dog barking excitedly beside him. There'd been endless possibilities to his world back then, and infinite time. Pain lanced through his stomach. It had seemed so simple before Dorseter interfered. Now all the alternatives looked wrong.

"Only promise I make is to be the champ."

"Maybe there's more than one race."

"What's that supposed to mean?"

"Maybe that's the possibility you're afraid of."

"Let it go, Carrie," he said.

When the casserole was ready, they sat stiffly at the table together, forking pieces of meat, making awkward stabs at conversation, avoiding the one topic on both their minds.

He excused himself soon after and went home.

And then all at once the fog lifts from his eyes. His body—a magical machine itself—floods with power, at one with the chair that has turned into an elfin carriage. He soars, weightless, free, over the wall that once threatened to defeat him. This is what he lives for.

Nothing can stop him, not even Time itself. He is an eagle breaking out from a cage and leaping up into silky vastness of sky.

Exhilarated, he yells. Wind carries his voice away as he sweeps down the course on invisible wings. Crowds, trees, birds, ocean—all fall away.

He could go on forever.

He is invincible.

He has reached the Race Mind.

He dreamed of Carrie's cat and woke in a tangle of sweaty sheets. Jerking upright, he reached for the phone. In the darkness, he punched out Dorseter's home number.

The phone rang several times before the surgeon picked it up.

Dorseter sounded groggy with sleep. "Jeff? D'you know what time it is?"

"Two a.m. I got questions."

"Can't they wait till morning?"

"You came looking for me, remember? First question. Why me?"

Dorseter let out a deep sigh. "You need this, Champ. I'm doing you a favor—"

"Bullshit."

"Okay. Try this. You're high profile."

"Got it. A photo-op for the Nobel committee." He wasn't surprised. That was life too. You gave and you got back. "Next question. Gotta be risks. Give 'em to me."

"Bottom line, the cells might not take." Dorseter sounded as if he were choosing his words carefully. "Could be a lot of pain and wasted time for nothing. Maybe infection, possibly serious. All medical procedures entail a certain amount of risk, Jeff, especially experimental ones."

"And I'd be back to square one?"

He heard the hesitation in Dorseter's reply. "It's hard to be one hundred percent certain of anything."

He hung up.

The FINISH looms, a hundred yards ahead. He flies toward it, whooping with excitement. Everything melts dizzyingly in the bright sunshine.

This is what he lives for. This is who he is. The one thing he is certain of. He is a champion.

Then he is through the tape.

And suddenly the blur of faces waiting for him sharpens. He sees the cameras, the t-shirt vendors, Meg Lowenthal, a child in a wheelchair waving a flag. He sweeps past. Sound bursts roaring on his ears again. The crowd yells, jubilant, huge as the sound of winter surf. Hands reach out toward him as if to catch some of his wild energy for themselves.

Carrie is waiting for him behind a barrier.

Slowing, he lets go of the wheels and throws his arms up into the air in fierce exultation.

"You made great time," Carrie says, draping a sweatshirt across his shoulders. She maneuvers her chair beside his as they move away from the FINISH line.

The reporters who took Jeff's picture as he crossed the line turn back to the course where the runners will soon be coming in. The crowd jostles behind the race barriers to catch the first sight of the winners. A few yards away, a TV crew vies with photographers to catch a Hollywood starlet who's here with her entourage to be seen at the race.

The high mood of the race is still on him. He could wheel over, make a photo op. But he senses this one is waiting for a runner. Jeff makes a vee with his fingers to a camera that isn't watching him.

Carrie's van is parked nearby. Exhaustion is catching up with him now. Lungs burn, shoulder muscles ache, and his fingers have sprouted blisters. It's an effort to keep turning the wheels. He waits patiently while she lowers the ramp, seeing the way her short brown hair lifts off her brow in the breeze.

"This calls for steak and lobster," she says. "Out of my league, though."

He glances at her, catches the barely hidden smile, and says, "I'm buying tonight."

"Champagne too."

This end of the parking area, where the handicapped slots are, is almost empty. In the space, two young boys, tired of waiting for something exciting to happen, are playing baseball with a plastic bat. A flop-eared dog runs in circles between them. One of the boys hits high and wide. The yellow tennis ball sails out of reach and comes arcing toward Jeff.

"Hey, mister!" one kid yells. "Get our ball?"

His hand shoots out and cups the ball as it falls.

"Nice catch," Carrie says.

He bows in her direction then sends the ball winging back. The dog barks. The kids wave.

Behind him, a roar goes up from the crowd as the runners begin to cross the FINISH line. He half-turns, his throat tightening.

"Ready?" she asks.

The race has to be over, one way or another, someday, he knows that. Nature will see to it if Dorseter doesn't. Then what? And is a man given only one chance to do something with his life, or are there many races over many different courses as Carrie seems to think? He prides himself on being a tough competitor, sharp-eyed trader in uncertainty. Afraid of nothing.

He swings the chair toward the van. Stops again. The wave of excitement and adulation sweeping out from the race buffets him till every nerve in his body thrums with tension and he shuts his eyes against the pain.

"Jeff?" she says.

He glances at Carrie's face. Her face isn't beautiful, but strong. He's never really looked at it before. He realizes he's never really looked at any woman before. Maybe he was afraid they'd look away.

He sighs. "I've made my decision."

She brushes his cheek with her lips but says nothing. He reaches up and touches her short hair. Behind them, the crowd roars again.

He wheels up the ramp and into Carrie's van.

WHERE TWO OR THREE

THE charge nurse barely paused in her fast trot down the hospice hallway. "Seventeen needs his water jug refilled. Can you get it?"

"I'll get it." Maddie turned back the way she had come. It was her second day as a volunteer. What a joke. She hadn't volunteered for anything, but already she was getting the routine. Here, the charge nurse was boss.

She picked up a full plastic jug of ice water from the kitchen and walked back to Room Seventeen. Like most of the other rooms, it contained a hospital bed with a white coverlet, a straight-back visitor's chair, a battered chest of drawers that had hosted too many patients' belongings. Unlike the others, the occupant or his family hadn't made an effort to personalize the room with family photos, art work, or flowering plants. The hospice cat, a large orange tabby, jumped off the bed when she came in, as if his shift was over once a volunteer showed up.

"Hi," she said. "I'm Maddie. I brought your water."

The skinny old man on the bed didn't open his eyes. "Haven't seen you before."

"Only my second day."

He had the most wrinkled skin she'd ever seen, and his face was blotchy, as if he'd had a bad sunburn and skinned recently. He had to be at least a hundred, she thought. There was a smell in the room too, not really bad but odd, sort of

113

baby-powdery and musty at the same time. She picked up the empty jug. She definitely did not want to spend time in here.

"Why're you here if you don't like it?"

She jumped. "Would I be here if I didn't?" Lying again. One of these days she was going to have to break the habit.

He turned his head away from her. The back of his neck was scrawny as a chicken's, and the skin was patchy there too. "Sit and visit."

She sat gracelessly on the edge of the chair by the wall and stared at the old man's neck. "So, what did you used to do?" she asked brightly. Most of the older ones liked to talk about the old days, the younger ones not so much.

"Astronaut."

"Astronaut? You mean, like space and stuff?"

"Space. And stuff."

"Have I heard of you?" she asked cautiously.

"Probably not. Name's Sam." He rolled back to face her, surprisingly agile for someone who looked so old. His eyes were a washed-out blue, same color as the jeans she was wearing. "And how did you get sentenced to this place?"

Maddie felt her cheeks grow warm. "I'm a volunteer."

"Crap. Person your age has better things to do than visit old coots like me."

"All right. Here's the truth. I got busted for doing drugs at a party. One rotten joint—and if I'd been eighteen already like everybody else, it would've been legal anyway. So the judge gave me community service."

"Good. I don't have time for lies. What would you rather be doing—besides being stupid?"

"You really are unpleasant, know that?"

He chuckled—at least she thought that was what he was doing. Maybe he was choking.

"Didn't they tell you you're supposed to humor me?"

"I'm in high school. I'll be a senior starting next month. I don't get much time to do what I'd rather be doing. But when I do, I play the flute."

"A musician. Will you play for me?"

"I didn't bring it with me."

"How about next time you come?" He gazed at her with the washed-out eyes. The edges of his lipless old mouth creased up. "Please?"

Why not? The staff encouraged volunteers to entertain the residents any way possible. "Well, maybe when I come back on Friday."

"And maybe I'll tell you about space. And stuff."

Maddie got out of the room before he could say anything else. In the hallway, she passed the charge nurse again.

"Glad to see you spent some time with Mr. Ferenzi. He never gets any visitors." The charge nurse smoothed the pink tunic over her white slacks. "He used to be famous. But something happened to him, and he was never quite right afterwards."

Even if it wasn't true, she thought, it beat spending time with the old biddies here who only wanted her to play cards with them.

Maddie had been ready to get her monthly mandated hours at the hospice finished Friday, but Mom wanted to take her back-to-school shopping. She would've been happy with the Gap, but Mom insisted on heading down to the OC and taking all day. At least that was better than the virtual house arrest Daddy had put her on. So now she had to make it up by wasting Saturday afternoon at the hospice.

It was a fine late summer day, the sky an almost transparent blue, as if she could see through to the other side if she squinted hard. The neighbor's gardener was mowing, filling the air with the sweet green smell of cut grass. At the last minute, she remembered her promise to bring the flute. She slid the flute into its case and stuffed it into the canvas shoulder bag with her house keys and purse, and headed out to grab her bicycle.

Sam Ferenzi looked as if he hadn't moved an inch since the last time she was there. If anything, he looked skinnier than ever, as if he might shrivel up and blow away once the hot Santa Ana started blowing.

She flopped in the visitor's chair. "I brought the flute."

"Play." His voice rasped.

She opened the case then lifted the flute to her lips. She loved the flute and didn't mind practicing, in contrast to her rebellion against all other forms of homework. When she was younger, she'd thought about becoming a professional musician and playing with the LA Phil. But that would take years at university, and Maddie had had enough of school and had no idea what she was going to do with her life. She began to play a section of a flute solo.

"Mozart, Concerto Number Two," Sam said when she stopped. "Fine, but thin."

"Of course it is! It needs an orchestra to make it whole—"

"And meaningful."

"—but I'm just me."

"Exactly."

"All right," she said, exasperated. "I did what you asked. Now it's your turn."

He scared her by sitting up so suddenly she was afraid he was going to lose his balance and tumble off the narrow bed. His green pajama sleeves with hideous pink hearts flapped back, revealing skinny arms covered in the same white blotchy patches she could see on his face and neck. He raised an arm and pointed the tv remote at the small set perched on the scratched chest-of-drawers.

The screen brightened then revealed a lone squiggle of electric-bright color, red shading into purple on a black background. The line looped across the screen slowly, endlessly, hypnotically. A second line, blue-indigo this time, braided itself in and under and over the first one. She waited. Nothing else happened.

"What's that supposed to mean?"

He lowered his arm and the screen went dark. "That's the question, isn't it?"

"Okay." She blew her breath out in a long sigh. "I'm leaving now."

"I'm trying to tell you something."

"Well, you're not doing too good." She stood up and put the flute in her shoulder bag.

He lay back against the pillows. "Sorry."

She thought he sounded tired, but also something more— sad, maybe. As if no matter how hard he tried he just couldn't get something right and was fed up with trying. For a moment, he reminded her of her grandfather who'd died when she was ten. Even now, she missed him. He must've been something like this tired, lonely old man at the end. She sat down again.

"Your nurse says you did some amazing things once."

"All useless."

"I wouldn't say that. I'm impressed."

"You're a musician. Makes a difference."

It was really difficult to hold a conversation with him. She changed the subject. "Don't you get bored in this room? I could take you outside in a wheelchair."

"Where would we go?"

"The garden's nice."

He shook his head.

"Where then?"

"Hat Creek would be good, Northern California. But the desert'll do."

"Oh, right!" Maddie laughed. "I'm sure they'd let me take you to the Mojave. Specially this time of year."

"Don't you have a driver's license?"

"Of course I do. But I don't have a car." Actually, that was another lie—or at least a near one. Daddy had taken away the keys to the used Tesla her parents had given her for her birthday.

He was silent so long she was afraid he'd died on her. She stared at the white sheet covering his bony old chest, willing it to rise and fall. It didn't move. What was she supposed to do now? Finally he let some air whistle out from his mouth.

"Why do you want to go to the desert, anyway?" she asked

He didn't answer. She glanced at her watch. Ten more minutes, and the aides would be bringing round the dinner trays. If she stayed much longer, they'd put her to work.

She stood up. "I have to go now. I'll see you in a couple of days."

"You ever read the Bible?" he asked suddenly.

"No. My dad's a scientist at JPL. We aren't superstitious."

"Pity. You should try Matthew 18:20."

She couldn't stop thinking about Sam. Of course Daddy would find out if she took him for a ride in the car. And even if she did get the keys, she certainly shouldn't be driving all the way to Palm Springs, the only part of the desert she knew how to get to. By Monday morning she was roaming around the silent house as antsy as if it were the first day of school in a new place.

Who did that old guy think he was, anyway?

That was a question she could find the answer to.

Daddy had gone to the airport on his way to a two-day SETI conference on the east coast; Mom had driven up to Santa Barbara to see Grandma, who'd been suddenly taken ill, and she planned to stay the night. Maddie was on her own.

She went into the study to use the computer. It didn't take long to learn that Samuel Coulter Ferenzi had once been famous. And that there was something really odd about the dates.

He'd been the first astronaut to rendezvous with an asteroid, she read, a feat no one else had repeated in the twenty years since. She skipped over the voyage and its mission. When the crew came back to Earth, there'd been a huge welcome parade. Ferenzi had given speeches at universities. He'd cut the ribbons opening Air & Space Museums. Then things had apparently gone wrong.

The phone beeped. She touched the pad for the study extension. "Parker residence."

"What're your plans for today, Madison?" her father's voice asked.

Just like that, she thought. No *How are you, sweetie?* no *I hope you're not bored all by yourself?* that anybody else's dad might've asked. Sounded like he'd given up on her already. She really resented that. "I'm putting in my hours at the hospice like I'm supposed to."

He'd taken her cell too, as if he thought she'd be putting in a call to her supplier.

"Don't get snarky with me, young lady," Daddy said. "Be home before dark."

"Sure."

"My plane's boarding. See you in a couple of days."

Maddie turned the phone off before he put any more conditions on her. It wasn't fair. Maybe she should've done something that would really deserve it, not just a couple of puffs off a joint someone handed her. And it hadn't even given her much of a buzz.

She turned her attention back to the monitor. Ferenzi had started acting strangely. Several hospital stays had followed— one article mentioned psychiatric care. On the tenth page of citations, she found a tabloid headline: *Spaceman sees aliens.* The date was puzzling, only a little more than twenty years ago. Too recent to fit with the old man in the hospice bed.

Maddie exited the program and thought about it. Chances were, Sam was crazy. Why did he want to go to the desert? And more important, why should she take the risk of being grounded for the entire school year to take him there? She'd be as crazy as he was to do it.

A flicker of movement on the computer's monitor attracted her attention; the screen-saver had activated. She stared at the ballet of spinning galaxies and soaring cloud-like nebulae her father had installed. He was involved with the SETI program at JPL, but it wasn't something he talked about much. Not because it was secret, Maddie knew, but because the results were so disappointing. She wondered if he knew about Sam Ferenzi. Her father thought people who claimed to have seen aliens cheapened the real search for extra-terrestrial intelligence.

The old man seemed so lonely. At least she could take him for a short drive around Pasadena. Maybe the change of scenery would do him good.

She knew where her father had put her car keys. He never locked his desk drawer, trusting the members of his household. She felt a twinge of guilt as she retrieved her keys.

"I'm taking Mr. Ferenzi out for a drive," she told the charge nurse as she pushed the empty wheelchair past the nurse's station. "That okay?"

The day's charge nurse, a young dark-skinned man in green scrubs, looked up from the charts he'd been studying. "How long you planning on keeping him out?"

She hadn't expected to be asked. "Umm… We shouldn't be too long."

The charge nurse rubbed his eyes as if he'd put in a long shift. "He'll need his meds again in a couple of hours."

No way she could go to Palm Springs and back in a couple of hours. Sam would just have to take the disappointment. If he even remembered.

But the moment she stepped into his room, she knew he'd remembered. He was sitting on the edge of his bed, dressed in a maroon sweat suit several sizes too large, one bony hand holding a scruffy olive-green duffel bag, the other stroking the hospice cat.

"Stop worrying about the meds," he said. "I don't need them. Only take them to shut the nurses up."

"Are you reading my mind?"

"Obvious they'd tell you when I'm due for the next dose. Where's the car?"

"Around the corner." Where—she hoped—no one who knew her would notice it.

"Good. Let's go."

Resentment at the way he ordered her around welled up, sharp and hot. She was a volunteer, not a servant. As if sensing her mood, the cat hissed at her and jumped down from the bed. Sam maneuvered himself into the wheelchair. He huffed and wheezed and settled cautiously, then indicated she should put the duffel bag on his lap.

"You're not as old as you look, are you? I looked you up."

The face he turned to her was open, stricken, like a flower pelted by a sudden, hard rain. She regretted her spiteful words instantly, but there was no way to take them back. She wheeled him in silence down the hall, past the charge nurse who was too busy to glance up, and out the automatic door at the front of the building.

Sam didn't say anything when they reached her car, and he managed to get into the passenger seat without much help, never letting go of the duffel bag. But she heard him gasp with pain as he landed heavily on his thin hips. She slid in behind the wheel and passed the electronic key over the sensor. Only the red lights on the dash confirmed the electric motor was ready to roll.

They drove east through Pasadena in silence. She thought about pointing out some of the lovely old houses, but he'd closed his eyes as if he was bored already.

After a while he said, "You need to take Interstate 10 east."

"We're not taking the freeway at all."

"You want to hear my story? Then we do it my way."

She glanced at him. "No way! I'm supposed to stay off the freeways. I'd be in a lot of trouble if I did that."

"Me too." The old man rummaged in the duffel then held out a disk." Put this in your CD player."

"Cars don't have CD players anymore. Everybody has their own—"

"Yours does."

He pointed to the slit low on the dash where she'd never needed to notice it before. Steering with one hand, she slipped the disk into the player.

After a moment's silence, a low, sustained note came out of the speakers, like an oboe, or a bassoon. The sound undulated in dark, thin loops. Once in a while, the loops were punctuated with a single higher note that died away as it fell. There was something lonely in the sound, as if it spoke of enormous distance and the vast passage of time. Then it changed—or was replaced—by another, higher voice, this one mournful, with the suggestion of an echo over a frozen sea. Spooky.

She listened for a while, trying to guess what she might be hearing. Then it hit her so suddenly she felt ice pour through her veins. "Aliens?"

"Nope. But not a bad guess," he said. "Whales. Humpback Whale songs."

"I suppose next you're going to tell me they make up symphonies and operas."

"I doubt it. But we don't know, do we? And that's the problem. *We don't know.*"

How was she going to take this all the way to Palm Springs? "We're going back!"

"I'm trying, Maddie. But I haven't got the right words. I'm going to have to show you."

"Maybe I'm just a dumb kid, and I don't care."

"You *have* to care," he said. "Somebody must. There's the on-ramp."

Obviously, she hadn't been paying enough attention to the road. She slowed the Tesla a block before the interstate on-ramp. Overhead, an unfinished span of what was going to be the high-speed monorail from Los Angeles to Las Vegas that they'd been building ever since she could remember looked like a casualty of the terrorist attacks on London and Paris.

She was aware of car horns, a car alarm going off, the ululation of a police siren. Familiar urban sounds, she thought, and remembered the waves on the oscilloscope when the technician tuned the grand piano at home. It had picked up her voice too, and displayed its peaks and valleys in a running line. Insight struck.

"Your vid. That was the soundwave of a whale's song, wasn't it?"

"Two of them."

Something about this strange old man held her, like he was some kind of modern wizard or something. Whatever his secret was, she believed him that it was important. "But what does it all *mean?*"

"I'm going to show you."

If her father found out she'd taken her car keys, she was going to be in a lot of trouble anyway. Driving a bit further wasn't going to make it much worse. And she resented being treated like some delinquent kid. She took the freeway on-ramp.

The clock on the dash read two-thirty-three already. She fingered *Palm Springs* into the GPS and the readout told her *ETA three hours twenty minutes due to heavy traffic.* Even if she could hurry Sam along once they got there, it would probably be midnight before they were home again. The hospice would've missed Sam and called the police.

"Sam, I can't do this."

"Do it!" His voice was suddenly strong and compelling like the young man he once must've been. She stared at him. Then he added in his normal, old man's voice, "I'm going to show you what happened. Maybe you'll understand."

She thought of her father, frustrated because decades of SETI had revealed no messages. It was weird to believe this old man knew something no one else did. But something had happened to Sam Ferenzi in space, and though he looked a hundred years old, she knew from the biography she'd read he couldn't be much older than sixty.

"There must be hundreds of scientists who'd like to know."

"Tried it. Many times. Got sent to psych ward."

"But why *me?*"

"Because you're a musician. And the young aren't prejudiced against new ideas. And I don't have much time left."

She gave up worrying about what she was doing or the consequences. What was the use? There was no question Daddy would find out.

"Just trying to figure out the best way to tell it," he said.

"Starting at the beginning's good."

"I was born. I grew up. I went into space."

"You are really the most annoying—"

"Don't be so impatient." He opened his eyes and peered out the window to see where they were. "NASA planned the mission to the asteroid when there was no budget for Mars. Doesn't matter which asteroid. You wouldn't know anyway. We hadn't paid much attention to it, but it was in a near-Earth orbit. So we took the opportunity and went. Routine mission so far."

He paused, and Maddie prompted, "And you walked on it."

"Euphemism. You couldn't properly walk anywhere on it. It was too small and had no gravity. It was like standing on the surface of a giant stone potato. I had a tether to the excursion module. I wasn't going anywhere."

She listened without interrupting as he described space from the vantage point of a small asteroid. In her imagination, she saw the deep, cold blackness studded with unwavering stars, the regular flare of the sun as the asteroid rolled in its orbit. Earth was a small bright dot in the distance.

"Weren't you afraid?"

He turned his scrawny neck and stared at her. "The astronaut who's never afraid is a liar or a liability. The one who lets his fear rule is a disaster."

"Tell me about seeing the aliens."

"*National World Enquirer* said that. Not me."

He took a moment, then continued. "I'd been on the asteroid for almost the full time for EVA, and the shuttle's commander radioed to remind me. Then a sudden burst of light blinded me—and a strong carrier wave knocked out my headset."

He fell silent again.

"Go on," she prompted. "What was it like?"

"The worst pain you can imagine. Like being a T-bone steak plopped onto the hot grill and not being able to get off. Like all your skin is scorched and peeling. Like being knocked out by a high voltage wire. Like having your eyelids ripped off and being forced to watch a nuclear explosion. Like going blind and stark raving mad at the same time."

That explained his blotchy skin: radiation burns. The long outburst seemed to have tired him again. He rested his head on the seat-back and went to sleep.

At least, she hoped he was only sleeping.

The sun was setting as they entered the outskirts of Palm Springs, a fuzzy red beach ball sinking into hazy waves of low-lying smog. Maddie was tired from driving in heavy traffic. Sam had slept most of the way. Now he woke and struggled upright.

"You want to eat something?" she asked as they passed a coffee shop.

"No. Go on through the city."

"How much farther are we going?" The Tesla was new enough to have an efficient fuel cell system, but there was still a limit on how far it could go without a recharge. Since she'd never had the chance to drive it this far, she had no idea what that limit was. The battery's indicator bars remained in the safe zone, but for how much longer?

"Just outside the city, you're going to make a left."

And then what? She kept the thought to herself because he obviously wouldn't answer anyway. She gazed at the people strolling from boutiques where golden light spilled out onto the sidewalk to restaurants whose banners pronounced them award-winning. She retracted her window and the car filled with the aroma of barbecue and garlic and the faint sounds of music. Her stomach rumbled.

"Oblivious," Sam said. "All of them. It's going right through them, and they're oblivious."

"What?"

"You too. And me. And worst of all, NASA and SETI. Turn left at the next light."

The lights and sounds of Palm Springs fell away as they took the narrow dirt road across the desert floor, rising slowly toward the nearby hills. The sky was filled with misty rose and lavender light, and the tops of the Little San Bernardinos looked as if they'd been draped in glowing chiffon.

"Pull off here."

Tiredness flooded through her. This was without question the stupidest thing she'd done in her life. Sam scrambled out of the car without help, yanking the duffel bag behind him. In the twilight, he looked spidery and strange, like an alien himself. She yawned and reached to turn off the engine.

"Leave it running," he said. "I need a power supply."

He rummaged through the bag, pulling objects out and hobbling about to arrange them on the rocks. She got out of the car.

"Here." He handed her a pair of field glasses. "You might as well look at the stars while I'm getting set up."

She took the glasses out of their case. She could see Venus in the west already, and other pinpricks of light were beginning to show against the rapidly darkening sky. Her father had taught her to recognize the major constellations and nebula clusters and most of the minor ones too.

"Easier at night," Sam said.

"What is?"

"Listening."

Did he mean the kind of signals SETI was listening for? That would be dumb, she thought; the stars were there even when we didn't see them. "What difference does darkness make to messages coming from way across the universe?"

"I meant for us. Less distractions."

Arms folded tightly across her chest, she stepped away from the car. The sky glittered overhead, but she'd lost interest. The desert night was already much cooler than the day, and if they stayed here too long she'd regret not bringing a jacket. Somewhere in the hills, a coyote yipped. A large bird flew past her on silent wings.

"Look," he said.

On a flat-topped boulder he'd set up the contents of the duffel bag. She saw a small oscilloscope with the regular undulation of a carrier wave passing over its screen. Beside it was something that looked like a really old cell phone, bulky, with an antenna poking out; cables ran between them and a metal box, also small. He was really nuts if he thought that contraption was going to capture alien signals. Daddy had taken the family on a vacation trip to see the Allen Array in Northern California; it looked nothing like that.

"You forgot to bring a dish." Her voice added its own snaking wave to the screen.

The coyote gave a full-throated howl this time and was joined by another. The lines on the oscilloscope jumped into peaks and valleys. He bent over the rig he'd assembled, cocking his ear and turning dials. The night air filled with the eerie whale song he'd played for her in the car. An owl hooted. The screen became a jumble of snaking lines.

"I don't get it."

"You need a symphony. At least—" He hesitated as if trying to find the words to explain a difficult concept to a kindergartner. "You need to learn how to *listen* to a symphony. Too bad you didn't bring your flute."

She jumped as if he'd poked her. "I might have— It's still in my shoulder bag."

He nodded. "Get it."

No point in arguing with him. She found her flute in the car and carried it over to where he slumped on the boulder, watching the oscilloscope. She put it to her lips. The instrument added its own line to the undulating patterns on the screen. A thin silver thread—tiny human voice—against the background of orange and burnt umber and gold, the sounds of the universe.

"A symphony not made up of our instruments." In the dark, his eyes glittered like the stars.

She glanced up. Somewhere, in all that magnificent light show, there were other intelligent beings. She believed that, even though scientists like her father had spent more than seven decades trying to capture a message from just one, and failing absolutely. But she was her father's daughter, and what Sam was trying to do wasn't science.

"You saying that *whales* could help SETI listen for alien signals?"

"Don't be stupid!" the old man scolded. "Sentient creatures that've been on this planet maybe longer than we have— What might they know? Trees too. Thousand-year-old Sequoias— centuries to process the hormonal messages in their cells! And creosote bushes—there's a budding hive mind for you! Ravens and crows. Even coyotes. We don't have the first idea how to listen to the intelligence on our own planet, yet we think we'd recognize an alien message if it hit us."

He collapsed onto a boulder uncluttered with equipment and dropped his head into his hands. Exhausted, she could see that. But he'd better not zone out on her now! A breeze came up, carrying the scent of wild sage. Fine sand particles coated her face. It was very cold.

"We're never going to get the message until we understand that the voice of the universe is a symphony." He lowered his hands and stared up at the brilliant tapestry of the desert sky.

"Doesn't mean the message isn't there. But right now it's like we're searching for the flute part all by itself."

"My father says—"

"We have to learn how to get more out of the carrier wave. Background radiation of the universe. Whatever scientists want to call it. I can't read it yet—nobody can."

Mad. Totally mad. "Well, I'm not a scientist, so why me?"

"*Somebody* has to understand what the problem is. Or we'll never even work on it."

What if he gave himself a heart attack, shouting like that? She gazed at the oscilloscope again. The coyotes were singing, a whole pack by the sound of it. The owl hooted from the arms of a nearby cottonwood. The oscilloscope was alive with their combined voices. She didn't know enough to say Sam was wrong, but she knew stranger things had turned out to be true. At least in the scifi vids she watched.

"They're out there," he said, calmer now. "You're pretty dumb. But I've run out of time to find a better apprentice."

He stood up, wobbling, and bent over his weird contraption again. She lifted her face to the stars and was immediately bombarded by a huge cold light that overwhelmed her optical nerves. She shrieked.

Sam chuckled. "Just the full moon rising."

"I'm sorry." She couldn't stop trembling from the cold. "We have to get back."

"I'm done, anyway. You were just my last chance."

He started packing his things back into the duffel bag, slowly, exhausted. She got into the driver's seat. Fine volunteer she was; she didn't even offer to help him into the car. All she could think of was starting the heater. She heard the old man stumble into the passenger seat and close the car door, sighing with pain. Or sadness, perhaps. She listened for the familiar click of the seat web locking into place. Then she thought of something.

"It was the messages that hit you, wasn't it, on that asteroid? Even though you couldn't understand them, they were there?"

He didn't reply.

"They were there—in the carrier wave? That's what you meant."

Yawning, she touched the heater's sensor. Nothing happened. She glanced at the battery gauge. Zero bars.

"I think we're stuck."

He seemed to have gone to sleep already.

Well, what difference did it make? She was already in trouble for driving out here. But it was cold in the car without the heater, and she started to worry. How low did the night temperature drop in August? She looked over at the skinny old man, slumped in his seat. Too cold for him, in any case.

Wasn't there an old blanket in the Tesla's trunk? She'd thrown it in there after Junior Class Day at the beach and didn't remember taking it out again. She got out of the car and raised the trunk lid. Yes. She shook sand out of it, smelling the faint trace of ocean as she did so. Maybe there'd been whales passing by, far out in the water, that day she'd played volleyball with her friends. Whales making up songs that humans didn't understand.

An awful lot that humans didn't understand.

She draped the gritty blanket around the old man's shoulders, and he muttered in his sleep. No way she was going to get any sleep. It was going to be a long night till someone came to rescue them. The coyotes were still singing; she could hear them—nearer now—even with the windows closed. Weird to think of the noises animals made as music, but then maybe they thought the sounds humans made were weird too.

And maybe Sam was right and the universe was streaming with messages we didn't know how to listen to just yet.

On impulse, she reached into the back seat and retrieved her flute. She cracked the window, letting the coyotes' song enter, and put the flute to her lips to join them.

She heard Sam sigh and glanced over at him. He seemed to be smiling in his sleep.

The sheriffs found her at dawn by tracking the Tesla's GPS. She woke to the sound of a helicopter's rotors beating the desert air. She was cold, hungry, otherwise unharmed.

Sam Ferenzi wasn't so lucky. Or maybe that's what he'd wanted from the start, she thought, as the paramedics loaded her into the chopper for the flight home. Dying like a shriveled up insect in a hospice bed after you've been into space and experienced the tsunami of alien communication even if you can't understand a word of it and nobody believes you, she could understand how he might've felt. Going in his sleep was a mercy.

She watched the medics carrying Sam's body, reverently. He'd found the clue to a puzzle her father would give anything to solve.

"What were you doing out there?" one of the paramedics asked.

"Just stargazing," she said. It was only a half lie.

The paramedic handed her a juice box as the chopper lifted off the desert floor. The sun flooded in through the east-facing port. A star, only one among billions in the known universe.

A symphony of star voices that someday somebody was going to learn how to hear. Somebody who loved both the stars and music.

She drifted off to sleep, thinking of what that might mean for her future.

REACH

THE first thing he notices when he's finished dying is that the man and woman who've appeared by the bed are over six feet tall. They don't look like any doctors he's ever seen.

"Welcome," the woman says.

The room is white, anonymous. He finds it hard to think coherently. He picks something to concentrate on. The woman's skin and hair shine molten gold.

He shakes away the lingering fog in his head. "Where am I?"

"South California."

"No. I mean—" He remembers now that his car went off the overpass in a freak storm. He would expect a morgue, but these two don't look like morticians. The woman's blue tunic hugs her body in a designer version of static cling. Not angels either. He finds that comforting but confusing.

She lays a hand on his brow. "You must expect a slight sense of dislocation. Try moving your legs."

He didn't feel her hand.

Terror that he might not be dead but paralyzed grips him, and he's afraid to find out. *When Cole Thayer dances—*" a reporter once gushed in a small-town paper, *"he's ten feet tall."* It's hype, not a view shared by the ranking critics of the dance world, but he can't imagine never dancing again.

The tall visitors wait. He takes a deep breath.

Legs. He doesn't think he'll survive if anything's happened to his legs. He might as well find that out right now. He closes his eyes, flexes his toes, raises each leg an inch or two. They move without pain. He opens his eyes and glances down. They're also obviously not the legs he used to have. His hands start trembling.

"You have a friend from your own time waiting for you," the man says. He wears some kind of metallic jumpsuit that sparks as he moves. "This is her house."

South California.

A friend from his own time. "Okay—*When* am I?"

The woman smiles at the man. "I would say the brain came through admirably, wouldn't you?"

"What you'd consider the near future," the man says. "Your friend, Eileen Lambert, arranged for your neurosuspension."

"Charles will never agree to a divorce," Eileen said. "It's against his religion."

They were sitting in her Lamborghini in Malibu, watching a summer sunset wash rosily over Catalina Island. She turned dark blue, almost violet eyes on him in the twilight. Small, inclined to plumpness, she'd never seemed more beautiful to him than now. He wanted to run his finger down the familiar lines of brow and cheek, feel the warmth of her skin, bury his nose in her black hair already turning silver. Memories of her were imprinted all over his skin; his body would never be able to forget. He thought that even if he suffered from amnesia, his body would instantly recognize hers.

"I need you too," he argued. "We could go to Paris—Rome. They like me in Europe. I can support us there."

Meeting Eileen had unleashed in him new wells of creativity he would never have known. Her faith encouraged him when he might have taken easier paths. He loved her more than he'd ever suspected he was capable of loving anyone.

"We're both too old for that kind of romantic nonsense, Lover." She kissed him, taking the sting out of her words. "Old geezers need their creature comforts."

He pulled back. She hadn't meant anything by it, but it was something he had difficulty getting past. Her wealth had a nasty habit of intruding into their most intimate conversations. Money had been taken for granted in her house when she was a child, just as hunger had been in his. He wished she had no money. Or that he had the money and could lavish it on her instead.

"How much longer can you realistically expect to dance, Cole?" she asked gently. "It's a young person's trade."

And that was the heart of it. No matter how he'd driven himself, his body—puny since childhood—had never reached the goal he'd set. Dance classes at the Y had been a skinny kid's ticket off the streets. But though he drove himself harder and longer than any dancer he knew, his body had ultimately betrayed him. There'd been a time when he might have been satisfied being mediocre—after all, he'd come a long way—but then he'd met Eileen. Ever since, he'd wanted to be world famous to honor her. He knew now he never would.

"I wonder what you see in me, Eileen?"

"A dreamer," she replied without hesitation. "A prince in exile."

"And will you still love me when I'm too old to dance?"

She stroked his hand for a moment. "You know I'd do anything to have you achieve your heart's desire, my dear."

In the cool offshore breeze that came up, he felt absurdly frail. It was the last time he saw her before the accident.

"Neurosuspension," he says now. "That means—"

"You wrecked your original body beyond the primitive repair techniques of last century," the woman says. "Mrs Lambert had your head preserved."

"Do you like your new body?" the man asks.

He glances down at the gloriously youthful legs and feels dizzy. "How old am I now?"

The man studies him for a moment. "How old would you think?"

"Twenty-five?"

"About right."

Concentrate! Think this incredible situation through. He's survived a terrible wreck— He has a new and improved body— This is apparently the future—Eileen's still alive. And he's going to see her again.

A great longing to hold her sweeps over him. He remembers Eileen on her yacht out by Catalina Island, laughing at the comparison they made with the suntanned college kids in bikinis on the beach. *"I'm too fat and you're too skinny,"* she said. *"Better models for Geritol than Armani."* She wore a necklace of kelp he'd braided for her. She didn't know she was so much sexier in his eyes than any teenage beauty queen.

"You won't need us anymore," the tall woman says now.

Then his visitors are both suddenly gone.

He sits up carefully in the featureless room—no pain, though his mind keeps insisting there ought to be after an accident like that—then swings his legs over the edge of the bed and stands. Not even a twinge of complaint anywhere in his body. He needs a mirror.

He's startled when one takes shape in front of him. And it takes an act of faith to accept that he's looking at himself. He studies his naked image. He's gained at least six inches in height and has been lifting weights in his sleep, judging by the muscular arms folded over his broad chest, the strong, well-shaped legs.

It's a great body. No, a fantastic body. The body he'd always yearned for to get him the starring roles, maybe a movie contract. He can't believe his luck. He grins at his reflection. And as well-equipped, he notes suddenly, as if the doctors knew his secret adolescent fantasies.

He flexes his arms and strikes a pose. Twenty-five, he guessed. But this body's twenty-five as imagined by Hollywood. The face is the original; yet he sees they've fixed that, too, smoothing out the wrinkles and removing gray hairs.

"Do you like what you see there?"

The mirror vanishes. In its place he sees a slender young woman with long golden hair, draped in iridescent silk that whispers seductively as she moves. At her throat she wears enormous amethysts that match the color of her eyes. For a moment he thinks this one really is an angel.

The face is different. But violet eyes—

It can't be.

"Eileen?"

She laughs. Not the earthy laugh of the Eileen he knew, but musical like an angel's laughter might be. She comes toward him, hands outstretched. "I knew you'd recognize me!"

He touches her stranger's hands hesitantly.

"Do you approve?" She turns slowly. The rainbow swirls about her legs, murmuring.

"Stunning." That's true, but the truth slashes through his memory of her.

She sits down on the bed and studies him. "I haven't seen you upright until now. You look absolutely wonderful."

"So do you."

There's an unexpected awkwardness in this conversation. He didn't know Eileen when she was in her twenties, yet he knows she can't have looked like this. The discontinuity is jarring. A hundred things he wants to say to her pour through his mind, but he can't get any of them out.

"Are you angry with me, Cole?" She takes his hands in hers so he can't pull away. "When I saw you in the ER after the accident, I couldn't bear the thought of never seeing you again. I took the only way possible."

"So you paid to have my head frozen. It must have been expensive." It comes out sharper than he intended, but there's a war going on in his mind.

She seems not to notice. "Then I made arrangements to follow you— But you don't want to hear the boring details. You see, I wanted the very best for you, and luckily, I can afford it. That software company Charles and I founded? You'd never believe how it's grown."

"Good for you." He feels as if he's making small-talk with a stranger. "And what happened to good old Charles? Is he here too?"

"Charles didn't want to jeopardize his immortal soul."

She glances away, and a window forms in one white wall. He sees a long green lawn sloping down to a cliff, blue water beyond with a glimpse of an island. He recognizes Catalina.

"You had dreams once. Perhaps now—" She gazes at him for a moment. "Oh, talking won't work. Come here."

She pulls him down onto the bed, then slips her arms around his neck. Her tongue slides deep into his mouth. The fingers of her left hand twine themselves in his hair; the right hand massages his neck. These are actions his brain remembers from a thousand occasions.

His body doesn't recognize them at all.

He sits up, disturbed by his lack of response. Perhaps there's something wrong with him after all. Something the doctors have forgotten about.

"We're a little rusty, Lover," she murmurs, catching his arms and pulling him down again. "It'll all come back."

His mind wants to do it. She's Eileen, his lover, his best friend. Even if she isn't, what man wouldn't want to get an angel in bed? But the gulf between the memory of making love to comfortable, middle-aged Eileen and the reality of these young bodies writhing on the bed in the white room is too wide. He's having sex with a stranger. His fingers don't know the contours of the body they trace. And his nose doesn't recognize her smell.

He has another memory of that Catalina trip. Her skin smelled of sea and suntan lotion and clean sweat, in his opinion the most delicious perfume a woman could ever wear. This woman's scent is jasmine and musk and money.

One worry proves needless. They made his body too perfect not to perform. But it's all physical release, no passion in it. He's emptied but not refilled.

After a while, she sighs and gets up.

He feels exhausted, but again, he notes that's the mind's response, not this flawless new body's. The body isn't even out of breath. The duality is dizzying, as if he's an impostor inside his own skin.

She gazes at him for a moment, the violet eyes glistening. "We just need a little time to rediscover each other."

"Eileen," he says, attempting to postpone the painful redefinition of what they mean to each other that he senses will have to come. "What do—"

She puts a finger on his lips, stilling him. "I've given you your heart's desire, Cole. You have the perfect body you always wanted. You have a second chance. Now you can claim your kingdom."

A second chance to dance, this time with his greatest handicap removed. In the weeks that follow his rebirth, he throws himself into his work.

The mirrors of the dance studio in her house on the cliff work like the one he used that first day, appearing when he needs them. He extends his arms, warming up lithely with his reflection. It's a pleasure watching this body move. He doesn't understand how the doctors did it, but he guesses it cost Eileen a fortune.

He remembers the very first time he saw her, beaming at him from the front row of the small theater where she sat with a group of the city's cultural philanthropists. She always believed in him, attending all his performances after that, clapping louder than anybody. He thinks of how she filled his dressing-room with flowers before every performance, champagne afterwards as if he were Nurcycv. This studio, like this body, is a gift of faith in his talent unfettered from unkind nature.

The studio appears to be empty space, but he understands just enough of how things operate here to know it's loaded with toys. He can't imagine how they work, but he's learning to use them already. She's given a poor kid the key to F.A.O. Schwartz.

He owes her so much.

The thought of being in anyone's debt to this extent, even Eileen's, depresses him.

She owns an entertainment company, selling virtual experiences, she told him the first day in this new studio. It sounds like a form of artistic cannibalism, the way she explains it, but it gives him an idea.

It takes only a few days for this body to learn the movements his brain remembers, yet he's astonished to find there's no sense of strain, no muscular aches or pains to be massaged out after rehearsal as he would expect. He's astounded at how fast it all comes back to him, better than ever. He catches himself waiting for a slip or a stumble—to be expected, after all—but they never happen. This body has no bad habits to unlearn.

He always wanted to be acclaimed the best in the world, but in the past his body let him down. Now, with this superb physique, he has a chance of achieving that goal. He feels again, for just a moment, that skinny kid's hunger.

Something in the air of the empty studio senses his resolve. Lights dim. Walls recede. He feels himself caressed by unseen hands, his torso and limbs draped in a diaphanous second skin. Something prickles over his scalp. When it's done, he's clothed in a kind of silky, weightless armor, but at the same time naked and shivering with anticipation.

He chooses to begin his renaissance with a solo from *The Firebird*: Koshchei, a favorite role because he's never been able to exhaust its possibilities. And also because that was the role he was performing when he first met Eileen.

Spotlights brighten, music swells. Stravinsky's haunting genius pulls him. His veins flood with the savage blood tide of timpani and brass. He lifts an arm, and woodwinds thrill down his nerves to his fingertips. He moves, his feet capturing the jagged peaks, flashing with strings and horns. Sound becomes color to him, an asymmetrical, riotous composition of vermillion and burnt umber slashed with white hot gold.

Almost a century later, he's finally making truth out of the reporter's exaggeration. Then the fire swallows him up again, and there's no Cole Thayer left to think.

Afterwards, he wraps himself in a robe that's appeared, and notices a thin stream of text scrolling across the air in front of him. A news report of some kind. No, a ratings system. Olympic scoring performed by a string of electronic fireflies. The lights inform him that his performance rates an eight on a scale of ten.

At first he's irritated that art should be treated like a sporting event. Then he laughs. He vows to become a perfect ten for her sake.

At her insistence, he takes a vacation, a tour of this future she's given him. She places her own aircar at his disposal and programs the AI herself.

He's glad to see that none of the pessimistic predictions of his day have come true. The world seems filled with marvels, none more wonderful than the half-naked goddesses with sculpted bodies and jewel eyes who offer themselves to him everywhere he goes. He's no less capable of lust than he was in his old life, and he isn't disturbed that among a world full of Adonis look-alikes, he only stands out because he's something of a novelty. He feels like a kindergartner overwhelmed by a visit to an art museum, a Neanderthal in the Twenty-second Century, enjoying it anyway.

After a month, he reluctantly sets these pleasures aside and gallantly returns to Eileen.

He really tries the next time they're in bed, making love on silk pillows by warm candlelight she's called up. He'd like to make it good for her, for old times' sake if nothing else. He conjures up fantasies of how the old familiar bodies used to couple in all their sweaty, faded glories, as if the memory of cushions placed and positions selected to make allowances for creaky joints will rekindle remembered passion. He strains to recapture the sense they once shared of boundaries of skin fading, distinctions of man and woman blurring, becoming one flesh.

The fantasy doesn't work. There's an edge of frantic anxiety to his lovemaking; the motions are there but the passion's absent. He can't hide it from her; she'll know the difference. These new bodies perform as flawlessly as actors in a porno movie, and just as soullessly, a betrayal that leaves him bereft.

It's a relief to sit up, pour wine from the waiting decanter, and avoid her eyes. The candles vanish. He stares at the window that now appears in the wall. Though the city behind the house is full of lights, oceanward he can see stars crowding thickly against an indigo sky. He feels as if he's lost a great treasure. In its place, he senses an abyss opening.

He makes another attempt to reach her. "Remember how we used to make love on the beach on Catalina Island at sunset?"

"How could I forget?"

At least his mind has retained the memories, and so has hers. "We'd stay out all night. You'd hold me. And inspire me. We'd read poetry together. Robert Browning, your favorite. You see, I remember."

"So long ago."

"The whole world could've gone down in flames, but we had each other." He feels heartened; she always understands him better than he understands himself. "We lived through a lot in the past, Eileen. We made it then. We'll make it now."

He wishes he could believe his own brave words.

"Of course we will," she says indulgently. "We make a great team."

For a second, he entertains a suspicion she means *"in business."* But her smile is warm and guileless, the beautiful eyes not shadowed by ulterior motive. She's satisfied, it seems, and he's alone once again with his sense of loss. The thought curdles in his stomach. He drains his glass and she refills it. Aching silence stretches between them.

After a while, she stands up, arms clasped across her breasts. She raises one hand to the window wall and the stars wink out. The surf falls silent. On the now-blank wall, crushed opal light cascades. In Eileen's world, he's learned, climate and scenery obey the whims of the beholder. Tonight he thinks of that as a metaphor for himself.

Rehearsing, recording, rehearsing again, he spends some of the best months of his life. Dancing allows him to put worries aside, and provides the excuse he needs to avoid intimacy with Eileen. Time slips by as if he were having a most wonderful dream. But like dreaming, he's aware that eventually he'll have to awake and deal with the reality of their dead relationship.

It's easy to forget the problems while he's working. Eileen has not only given him the key to the toy store, she's made sure he has the ability to play any game his heart desires. His rapid success bears tribute to her faith. He becomes so wildly popular that her company is inundated with demand for his work. He records role after role, all flawless. Memory of the second-rate artist he once was dissolves in the exhilaration of his growing fame.

If at times he feels the shiver of something missing from his superb performances, he certainly doesn't convey this lack to his audience. Even the electronic insects that crawl up the air in his studio after every session agree he's very good.

One night, his mind exhausted but the body still glowing under a sheen of healthy sweat, he does something he's hesitated to do. He puts on the spidery headset to measure his performance against other dancers'. On command, the magical studio produces virtual experiences of the best artists in the world.

It's disorienting at first to experience another dancer. Not to watch, to feel the ripple of another's muscles as if they're his own. It's more than enjoying the sensation of another's style; it's becoming the other, and yet at the same time remaining himself, like dreaming and knowing it's a dream. He tries on dancers until very late that night.

Until that moment, he's had the nagging doubt that his fame's only a matter of novelty, the clown from the past drawing in the crowds. But now he knows intimately the art of the world's best dancers. He knows they're all fantastic, talented artists, but none sparkles more brilliantly than he does.

Realizing the truth knocks the breath out of his lungs. He thinks about what this means. The poor kid who never quite made it is now the world-class star he always dreamed of being.

A ten.

Winter rain gusts over the terrace of Eileen's house on the cliff. Sometimes she likes to pretend she's suffering. At least, he assumes she's pretending. He ignores it anyway and walks into darkness. He needs to digest that stunning revelation, to recognize, finally, that the "exiled prince" she once called him has claimed his kingdom. Everything he ever yearned for is in his grasp. In a while, he'll take his success to Eileen who made it possible, but right now he needs time to think.

Rain plasters his hair against his head and streams down his neck. His jubilation is tempered by a darker thought. Something bothers him, even though he knows he's dancing better than anyone alive. He feels the absence of something that used to drive him. There's an invisible void growing at the center of his perfection, a chilling sterility. If he were religious, like Charles, he'd think he's defied death only to lose his soul. But in a world where art is scored like a popularity contest, no one notices.

He decides that the obvious thorn in this paradise is his body's continuing lack of response to Eileen. They're strangers in bed, performing like perfect, soulless robots. Try as he might, he can't recapture the old passion, and that loss is bankrupting his art. Once he blamed his body for betraying him when he danced; now he blames his heart.

He can't force himself to desire her. It's not Eileen's fault. He doesn't want to hurt her; she doesn't deserve that. Tonight he'll lay his triumph at her feet, his gift to her. Then—

He doesn't know how he'll find the words to tell her what he'll do then.

In the old days, she sent champagne after a performance, and they celebrated alone. Now, she gives parties to revel in his astounding popularity. When he comes in from the terrace, he finds the house filled once again with the important, the famous, and the simply incredibly rich. Somewhere in the house, a phantom nightingale sings in a phantom jacaranda tree, virtual decorations for the real feast she's provided. Seeing her now, surrounded by her glittering guests, charming them with her graciousness, he senses she despises them as much as he does. She has an air of loneliness about her that he's never noticed before.

The house is always the right temperature, but he's suddenly cold. He can't face her just yet, certainly not with an audience. And he's sick of elegant illusions. Pushing his way through the swarm of gaudy, neon-clothed jackals fawning on her, he enters his studio and throws off his wet coat. A window appears, and he stares out at moonlit Catalina Island looming in the dark sea. They haven't been there once since he's been here. Tonight he knows the island's just an illusion too.

He flings himself onto the couch and broods about his situation. They never find time to be alone with each other anymore; his career takes too much of his time. His work earns prestige and vast amounts of money for Eileen's company. For himself too. And he can't deny that there's a vast, shining world opening up to him now. Yet she hardly ever comes to his studio to watch him perform and never speaks to him about his success afterwards. Almost as if it's irrelevant. Even after all these years, money comes between them.

To hell with it! Maybe there's no point trying to force their lovemaking into the mold of the past. He's tried—she can't say he hasn't. But it's not enough. And now he sees it's holding him back. He was needy, a slum-kid with big dreams. And she—well, she obviously never really loved him. She couldn't have. It makes his decision to leave her seem less of a betrayal.

"I used to think we could buy heaven."

He looks up to see her, somber tonight in an old-fashioned cut of black velvet, no jewels at her wrists or throat to rival the violet eyes. Tiredness washes over him, not an exhaustion of this damned perfect body—he doubts it would ever feel tired—but of the heart.

"Everything I've achieved is for you, Eileen. What more do you want?"

"More?" she exclaims sharply. "Do you understand me so little that you think I want *more?*"

He's bitter now, and needs to punish her for the darkness inside. "You must admit you knew you couldn't lose. There's novelty value to my resurrected career, if nothing else."

Her head jerks up as if he's slapped her. Color glows on her cheekbones. "I hoped you'd do well and find happiness. Apparently I misjudged us both."

Some of the old feelings stir. Or perhaps it's just his guilty conscience. "I've always loved you, Eileen."

"No, Cole. The old you used to need the old me." Her fingers worry the velvet gown, creasing and smoothing. "And I've only just discovered what that meant."

"I still need you. You're my muse."

"We're different people now." Then she laughs without humor. "For once, the cliché is perfectly fresh."

Because he did once love her—and perhaps still does—he starts to protest, to spare her the pain truth will bring. "Give it time. We can't expect—"

"I've tried. It's not working."

She's taken his thoughts, the words he didn't want to say to her, and left him with no more evasions. "It's serious, isn't it?"

"It's over."

He says heavily, "So what happens now?"

She tilts her head up at that. "I think you should leave. Go away. Before I change my mind."

Suddenly, that's the last thing he wants to do. He wants very much to prove she's wrong. "I don't think you understand—"

"I know you better than you know yourself," she says, and there's an odd break in her voice that he can't interpret. "Perhaps if you find another muse—"

He feels abandoned, a child whose mother has thrown him out. Yet wasn't this what he wanted? The prospect of leaving Eileen seems suddenly scary. But strangely exciting too.

He remembers how he drove himself to be worthy of her. Weak his body might've been, but the flame burned pure in those days. *Dreamer,* she called him, but unlike him she was always clear-eyed, a businesswoman who assessed strategies before committing to them. Before she brought him back, she would've considered their love might be a casualty.

He has to ask. "You must've known the risk?"

"The doctors told me, the night you died." Her voice is dark with grief. "Some kinds of memory are housed in the body."

She'd loved him that much. He's ashamed of his earlier thoughts. "It almost worked, Eileen."

He falls silent as she turns back to him, a trace of the old Eileen in her eyes, a touch of the pain that haunted their experience together and gave it meaning. In that look he sees all that he's just learned to value, and all that he's lost.

"We almost found heaven. We could try again—"

The door formed behind her. "You see, I forgot something," she says. "Browning was right. For an artist, heaven should stay out of reach."

A VERY SMALL DISPENSATION

THE sun sank through the cloud wall over the Pacific. By the darkening window, Pat squinted at her knitting needles. Cold wind shook the chimney and sparked the embers of a dying fire. She really should get up and add another shovelful of coal, but that took energy, and she felt curiously lethargic this afternoon. Another stitch dropped. If her arthritic fingers, sensitive to cold since childhood, kept fumbling the stitches like this, her grandson would have visited and gone again before she'd finished the socks that were to be Robby's Christmas gift.

Time to light the lamp.

In the sudden sputtering yellow, she saw the man in the open doorway, first his boots, then the drab trousers and cap, the heavy greatcoat, then his face still in shadow. He seemed not a day older than the first time she'd met him. He was tall and thin, his skin leathery and dark like a man who worked outdoors in all weathers.

"May I come inside?" he asked.

"Antonio, isn't it? Or do you go by another name now?"

"Antonio will do."

He moved into the room, leaving the door open. He shed his greatcoat and draped it over the back of a chair, and she was suddenly aware of the frayed tapestry on the armrests, its russet threads fading into washed out brown.

"You look well," he said.

One hand flew in an automatic gesture to smooth out the gray hair. Annoyed with herself, she caught it and returned it to the dropped needle before another stitch could slide off. She hadn't always been jittery in this man's presence.

"Might as well say it," she said. "For my age."

"Please, do continue knitting. Your grandson will appreciate the socks' comfort where he's going."

"What do you mean?"

He held up a hand. "Patty."

She sighed at his use of her childhood nickname and bent over the stitches, but her hands were shaking now, and the sock progressed slowly.

Antonio sat in the chair opposite her under the window. A silent companionship that made them seem like an old married couple, she thought. A smile lifted his lips briefly as if he knew what she was thinking. She'd always known he'd come for her someday.

Night filled the sky. Tendrils of cold fog crept up from the bay, slipping into the room through places where San Francisco's long, damp seasons had warped the window out of shape.

"Do you remember when we first met?" he asked, after a while.

"I was an eight-year-old child, Antonio."

"A child who saw what adults missed."

There'd been something different about the stranger who joined them early in May. The grown-ups hadn't seemed to notice anything unusual. They'd been standing on windblown dirt outside a general store where the women bought provisions for their journey, the wagons in the distance. There were trees, but they were thinner and not as leafy as the ones at home in Illinois, and the town itself was small and not at all like the one she'd been born in. Her older sister Ginny said it was going to get even more primitive after this. Patty didn't know what that word meant, but she didn't like how it sounded.

Nobody paid attention to her, clinging to Papa's leg as he questioned the stranger. They needed the man to help drive the stock on the coming trek and to lend a hand with the wagons in difficult spots. In return, the man could count on a hot meal once a day and a space under the wagons to sleep. One of the grownups, Mr B, argued the man didn't have enough flesh on his bones to be much use to them, but Papa was firm. She understood that much of the men's talk; the rest of it wasn't interesting anyway. But she couldn't take her eyes off the stranger. He was as tall as Papa, who was taller than most of the other men, and he had sun-burned skin like an Indian. His dusty jacket and stained trousers hung loose. His voice was deep. He carried a felt hat in one hand and gave his name as Antonio.

Coming out of the store, arms loaded with sacks of flour, Ginny whispered in her ear that he might be a Spaniard from New Mexico territory, though since neither of them had ever set eyes on a Spaniard, they couldn't be certain. Papa shook hands with the man, satisfied with the arrangement. At the last minute, the stranger turned his gaze on her, and she felt the wind flow like ice water over her skin.

Once the wagon party left Missouri and its scraggly trees, they found enormous fields covered in flowering grasses. It was beautiful. Why couldn't they just stay here? Papa promised California would be even better. They journeyed on, the patient oxen pulling the wagons, one day like another, Antonio walking beside them with the hired help. There were other children in the party, but only one her age, and he was too sickly to play with her. Ginny was too old, and baby brother Tommy too young; Patty had to amuse herself.

On a cool, sweet-scented morning at the end of May, she wandered off after breakfast to pick wildflowers. The women put out the cook fires and cleared away the pots and stacked everything back in the wagons, a chore Mama excused her from because she was still small. Before she'd had a chance to gather more than just a handful of flowers, she heard Papa calling her back to the wagon.

Wondering, she stepped up and lifted the canvas curtain. Inside, she found Ginny sitting on the floor, crying. On the wide bed she and Ginny shared with their grandmother, the old woman lay still. Mama knelt beside her, saying the words of old prayers Granny said every night with the children. Hands shaking, not knowing what else to do, Patty laid her small bunch of flowers on Granny's chest.

They buried Granny on top of a small wooded hill with her prayer book in her hands. Mama and Ginny cried, but she had an empty, hurting place inside now, and no tears came. She watched a flock of birds wheeling in the sky overhead and wondered about the journey ahead. It didn't seem right to go on without Granny.

The man called Antonio had helped dig the grave; now he stood apart from the mourners. She had to pass him on the way back to the wagons. He touched the tip of his hat to her when she looked at him. Right then, she felt the flutter in her chest that Granny called a goose walking over her grave.

"Granny was the first of so many deaths," Pat said.

The light from the gas lamp on the wall was not good for knitting, even with hands that didn't shake. She laid the needles aside on the oak dresser between a wooden doll and a tarnished spoon that gathered dust, forgotten treasures.

"People are born, they grow, they die," Antonio replied. "Like flowers."

She scowled at him.

He raised his hands, palms open.

Long after she'd reached safety, grown up, and raised her own family, she couldn't forget the deaths. Even now, they haunted her nightmares on nights when the wind howled in from the Bay.

"I don't have the power to stop the inevitable," he said.

"Then what?"

"You knew once."

He gazed at her, as if it mattered to him that she would understand. And she did understand, at least partly. *"Sometimes God limits His own power,"* her Granny used to say when they were children, *"because He loves us."* But this man wasn't God. Needing something to do with her restless hands, she rose and went to the window. A workman, jacket collar turned up against the wind and swinging an empty lunch-pail, went by on the dark street below, whistling a Christmas carol. She tugged the draperies over the glass, shutting out the night.

"I was too young to understand," she said. "I thought you were magic."

The desert they'd entered seemed to go on forever, and the little water they found was warm and sour. The burning heat and the increasing hardship of the journey stripped away all courtesy, and quarrels broke out between the men over trifles. Game became harder to find, so there was little fresh meat. The night before, in the bed they'd once shared with Granny, Ginny—who always seemed to know the grownups' secrets—confided she'd overheard someone say they would never reach California. Patty knew they were wrong. Papa would get them there!

Antonio took no part in any arguments that broke out. He was always nearby, hat tilted to shade his face, listening, as if he were waiting for something to happen. He was there again this morning, walking beside the wagon where she rode on the tailboard.

Catching his eye on her, she spoke defiantly. "We *will* reach California!"

"Do you wager with me?" He looked surprised that she'd spoken to him.

Remembering Granny's lessons about Christian behavior, she said, "My family aren't gamblers, Mister."

"A fair statement," he said. "Neither am I."

The long trek continued. They reached a place at the edge of the mountains where the steepness of the land forced the need for two teams of oxen to pull one wagon while the other waited its turn. To lessen the load on his wagon, Papa instructed his family to strip out everything not essential to their immediate journey.

"We're going to cache it, Patty," Papa explained. "Bury it in the sands. We'll come back for it once we're settled in our new home."

She didn't like the sound of that, but all the families were doing the same thing.

Ginny grumbled under her breath as she helped Mama sort: cooking pots to go on the trek, good china cups and plates they'd packed so carefully back in Illinois, to be buried. Patty carried a set of six silver teaspoons that had belonged to Granny. Mama sighed over all these things as if she were giving them up forever, but Papa urged them to hurry. Little Tommy wailed when Mama took his baby toys to put in the crate with Ginny's books and Patty's dolls and the family's heavy bible.

It was hot, and sweat trickling down her neck made her itch till she was miserable and rebellious. Why did she have to do this? When Mama turned her back for a moment, she snatched her favorite wooden doll out of the half-filled crate and hid it in her apron. It was only four inches tall— What difference could one small doll make? Surely the oxen wouldn't feel its extra weight. Tommy cried louder; he was already out of sorts because he was cutting two big back teeth. To quiet him, she stole one of the little spoons and put it in his fist. Then she felt guilty at disobeying Papa, and for a moment thought of putting the stolen things back. Too late. Mama closed the lid, and two men came over to carry the family's treasure to its burial place.

One of them was Antonio. He took the last crate they'd packed—such a tiny amount lighter than it should be; nobody would know what she'd done.

The moment he lifted the crate, Antonio turned to her, raising an eyebrow.

But how could he know? Last summer, at the county fair before they'd left Illinois, there'd been a magic man in a tall black hat and a swirling cloak twinkling with stars who claimed to read minds. She'd been fascinated and scared at the same time. She didn't like to think Antonio could read her mind.

"What's it to you, Mister?" she demanded, hands on her hips defiantly.

"A game," he said. "Maybe you and I will play later."

"And that was all it was?" Pat demanded. "A game? You could have changed what happened. You allowed them all to die—"

"All men die in the end. I can't change that. I thought you understood."

"Who are you really, Antonio? What's your real name?"

"You know that too."

Tiredness swept through her and she closed her eyes, shutting out the lamplit room and the sputtering fire and Antonio with them. At first, it was all she'd thought about. Each time the snowflakes scurried down the steep San Francisco streets, or Mama was a little late bringing supper to the table, her heart had pounded with fear. On those nights, bad dreams took her in a blaze of whiteness, and she felt as if her bones were burning in a fire. Each time the wind rattled the window panes, she was back in a threadbare cabin on the frozen lake high in the mountain pass. Even now, the memory had power to terrify her.

"How was I different?" she whispered. "Why did I survive?"

"You amused me," he said. "A child, challenging *me.*"

Patty didn't understand why the men sent Papa away. There'd been a quarrel, just before they began to climb up the mountain pass; a man died because of it. The other men blamed Papa, and Mr B sent him away. It wasn't fair! Without him, things started to go terribly wrong. They hadn't gone very far before the snow came and kept on coming, piling up in deep drifts that made pulling the wagons hard work for the oxen. Finally, they were forced to stop near the summit and make camp by a frozen lake. Mr B told them they'd have to wait until Spring thaw and then continue the journey to

San Francisco. Then the animals began to die, oxen and horses, and food supplies ran low. Papa would've known where to find food. Papa would've shot deer in the forest and caught lake fish through a hole in the ice, things nobody else in the quickly snow-bound cabins understood. The family needed him. They all needed him.

Now they were caught in the hard winter high up in the range, the wagons couldn't go any further until spring thaw, and Mama said nobody could get through to help them, not even Papa. Some of the men had tried, but the deep snow drove them back. Everybody had taken to wearing all their clothing at once, layer over layer, but still they shivered, and there wasn't enough to eat. Without Papa to take care of them, Patty and Mama and Ginny and little Tommy had to share a cabin someone else built.

"Why did Papa have to leave us?" she asked every day. "When will he return?"

Mama had no answer.

One day, after they'd been stranded long enough that the supplies the oxen had dragged up here had run out—the oxen and the horses long since starved or slaughtered for food—two women trudged through the snow to the cabin Patty's family shared with Mr B's family. They carried a little food from their own dwindling supplies, a pinch of flour, a few tough strips of ox hide. It didn't help to think about food, but it was so hard not to. Thin broth made from boiled hides might be all they'd get today. Patty forced herself not to watch the bubbling water.

A twinkle of light caught her eye where the cabin wall met the floor. A snowflake, driven through the cracks by the fierce wind, turned to ice as it touched the cold floor. Like a tiny diamond, she thought, no bigger than the one in Mama's wedding ring. For a moment, the snow diamond made her forget how hungry she was. She wondered how long it would last on her finger, a pretend wedding ring, like the one she dreamed of having one day when they reached California and she was grown up.

While the tough hide cooked, the four women sat by the small fire that never managed to heat the whole cabin, their faces grown hollow, heads bent as they whispered together. Patty heard her mother gasp, and saw her hands fly to her mouth. She understood that some of the things they talked about were too dreadful for children's ears, perhaps even worse than what Ginny claimed to overhear.

Turning her back to the women, she took the wooden doll out of her pocket and smoothed creases out of the white apron it wore. She pretended the doll was getting ready for her wedding.

"Of what use is a wooden doll?" a voice said out of the shadows. "You can't eat it."

She hadn't noticed Antonio come into the cabin. Sometimes he came inside to share the warmth of the fire, and nobody told him to go away. Hardship made everybody share what they had, even with a hired man. Back to the cabin's wall, his face in deep shadow, he squatted close to the floor.

"I wish you'd been sent away instead of Papa," she said, lowering her voice so Mama wouldn't hear.

"As do many men," he agreed.

"Do *you* know why he had to go? Mama won't tell."

"It wasn't his time."

"I don't understand you. Why must you speak in riddles?"

"Such a young child to demand all my secrets!"

He teased her, she felt sure, like Papa did sometimes. But there was a warning in his tone.

The two visitors went away. It was Christmas, Mama told them, and they'd sung a hymn with her in honor of the Savior's birth. But there'd be no feast this year; they were lucky to have the boiled hides. The fire crackled and spat, and smoke filled the cabin. The other children had no patience to wait, setting up such a noise of crying and pleading that Mrs B gave in and served them a spoonful of thin broth straight from the boiling pot.

When Mama judged the broth ready, Tommy opened his mouth like a tiny bird, and Mama dribbled a little liquid in. He'd lost all his baby fat, and his cheekbones stood out. Neither Mama nor Mrs B took any food for themselves. Patty hadn't seen them eat for two days now. Ginny told her yesterday they couldn't go on like that without eating for very long.

She'd chewed a tiny strip of still-raw ox-hide—so tough it made her jaw ache—when she noticed Antonio was still there. There was a calm about him that drew her to squat down beside him. He was a very odd man! He never seemed to speak to anyone, and no one paid any attention to him. Outside, the wind howled like a live thing, rattling the walls and clamoring to come inside. She shivered in cold the little fire couldn't drive away.

"When Papa returns," she said. "He'll bring food and rescue us."

"And if he doesn't?" Antonio asked.

"I shan't give up, if that's what you think. My family aren't quitters, Mister."

Mama glanced across the room at her, frowning.

"Not ever," she finished in a whisper.

"'Ever' is a very long time. Even now, some are thinking the unthinkable."

The door of the cabin swung open in a burst of wind. Mr B came inside. He leaned against the wall, snow sparkling in his beard, catching his breath; his eyes glittered in the firelight as he looked from the cooking pot to the smallest children, huddled together on the bed. Then Mr B's gaze fell on Tommy, asleep now in Mama's arms.

"Some of us won't survive," Mr B said. "We should make plans."

"No," Mama declared. "We are Christian people. Never that."

Sudden pain rocked Patty, hot and sharp, fiercer than the ache of hunger. Something evil had entered the cabin with Mr B, and she trembled with fear. *"A man died and they took an axe to his body,"* Ginny had told her that morning. Of course she hadn't believed it. What was the point of cutting up a dead body? *"You argue too much, silly goose."* Ginny wouldn't say anymore.

"They're dead already," Mr B said irritably.

Antonio leaned down to Patty. "All things perish in the end. Snowflakes. Flowers and birds. Even men. There are no exceptions."

"Not my family," Patty whispered. "I won't let it."

He gazed at her for a moment. "And how shall you prevent it?"

"I'll find a way."

"You have the power to do that?" She heard amusement in his voice.

"Do *you?*" she countered.

"What do you think?"

She thought about the question. She never saw him eat, yet he hadn't shrunk to skin stretched over bone like Tommy or the others. His dark eyes were clear and bright, not sunk deep in their sockets like Mama's. An Indian, she'd thought him when she'd first seen him. But he seemed more than that.

"I think you have some kind of magic."

He leaned back against the wall and closed his eyes. "No magic. Just one very small dispensation, if I care to use it."

"I don't understand your words. If you have a way to save us, why wouldn't you care to use it?"

"What difference does it make, to live a little longer now and die later? Even the one born this season died in the end."

She clapped a hand over her mouth at this blasphemy.

"I think you must be a very bad man." Her bones ached with the cold and the hunger, but something drove her not to accept his bleak words. "Granny said God sent the Christ child because He wants us to live and do good works."

"Wise woman, your grandmother," he observed.

If Antonio was still strong, perhaps he could get through the snow and across the mountains where the other men had failed. "Why don't you go to fetch help? If my Papa knew how hard it is here, he'd come back for us."

"Always an argument," he said, shaking his head as if in wonderment.

"Oh—if I were older, I'd go myself!"

He was silent for so long she thought he'd gone to sleep. Then he said, "Perhaps my 'magic,' as you name it, could spare you a little while. Would you like to live?"

"Of course I would. You can do that?"

"If I so choose."

How annoying he was. "And my family?"

"And what would you give me in return?"

She thought for a moment. Certainly a doll or a silver spoon wouldn't do for this strange man. This lonely man.

His eyes opened, and he stared at her. She felt as if she were a book he was searching for an answer. Then he nodded. "And your family."

"And the others here?"

"They're all mine at the last."

"But you can't just leave them—"

He stood suddenly, and she knew she'd pushed him too far. "Enough bargaining," he said.

"You disappeared after that," Pat said. "And then the dying in that camp on the Donner Pass began in earnest."

She snatched up the needles and began knitting furiously again. It had been many more weeks of starvation and death before her father had managed to get a rescue crew up to the lake to save them. Weeks of nightmare hunger and even worse, unspeakable remedies. Her mother had stayed firm; their little family never descended into the horror that engulfed the rest of the party though they stood at the edge of their own death. Somehow, they had survived. She'd had a long life since the camp on the frozen lake.

"You lived," Antonio said. "Why should the rest of it trouble you?"

"You are despicable."

But he was what he was, and all things had to come to their end. Remembering and reliving the horrors of the past had exhausted her. She thought of the bed with its warming pan that waited upstairs, the soft mattress and the thick quilt to ward off the cold. She shook off the desire to sleep; she had to stay awake till Robby arrived.

"I knew you would come eventually," she said. "Well, you'll have to wait while I finish this sock."

Antonio laughed as if he heard echoes of her childhood attempts at arguing with him. "If I came personally for everyone who thought they had a special relationship with me, I would've exhausted Time long ago."

His voice was so very cold, like the ice that had surrounded that long-ago cabin. She said nothing, bending to her knitting, but her hands were shaking. She'd reached the last row. The sock needed only to be cast off before it joined the other on her lap.

After a while, he said, "Do you really understand so little, Patty?"

"And whose fault is that? When I was a child you spoke to me in riddles." Nervousness brought her to her feet to pace the room. He, by contrast, never seemed to need to fidget. He sat unmoving in the chair under the window, his face half lit by the yellow lamp, half in shadow. His stillness made her want to slap him. "The least you could do is speak plainly at the very end."

"I have no power to change the final judgment," he said. "I told you this. Only a small ability to grant a delay, a stay of execution, you might call it. I go wherever there is a greater chance of relieving my boredom, one player who can engage me enough to earn a brief reprieve from the sentence no one evades in the end."

"No caring in the decision?" She felt the old urge to argue with him. "No greater matter than picking one chicken out of the flock to put in the pot, another to spare? Because you're bored?"

She continued knitting right where she was standing by the lamp, ignoring the stiffness in her fingers and the pain in knuckles and wrists. Then she became aware of how ridiculous this was and sat down again, allowing the knitting to slide onto her lap.

"Ah, Patty," he said. "I thought perhaps you—of all people—might understand."

His sigh opened up a great lonely vista, years, centuries, millennia, of a solitary game of massacres and bloodbaths. A game he only won by granting a brief reprieve here and there for whatever reason amused or intrigued him. No power to do anything else. What kind of being endured such torment? Not one that had a heart to be broken.

Far away, as if at the end of a tunnel, she heard the sound of the front door slamming, feet on the stairway, a familiar voice calling. She was too tired to answer. She leaned back in the chair, eyelids drooping.

"Your grandson has come to say goodbye," Antonio said.

When she managed to open her eyes, there were two soldiers in the room. Robby was dressed in the same uniform that Antonio wore.

"Corporal!" Robby exclaimed. "I didn't expect to find you here."

"Your grandmother and I are old friends," Antonio said.

"Granny, give me your blessing." Robby said. "I decided to enlist. I'm going to Europe to fight the Hun."

I want you to live, she wanted to say, but her voice wouldn't come.

"It's going to be a grand battle," Robby said.

Her hand weighed too much to lift to touch him. Robby bent over and kissed her on the brow. He was such a good boy, so idealistic and polite, with a promising life ahead of him.

Perhaps too polite?

"Time to march. Oh—you'll need the socks your grand-mother knitted for you." Antonio held out the finished socks to Robbie.

"Thanks, Granny. I'll think of you whenever I wear them," her grandson said.

The terrifying experience of her childhood had not been the first time—or the last—for Antonio. What did that say about his accompanying Robbie to war?

Challenge him, Robbie, Fight for your life! But the words stayed unvoiced in her head.

Death touched her eyelids, closing them, his touch soft as a feather. She heard them going out of the room together, talking and laughing like good friends playing a game.

CZERNY AT MIDNIGHT

LENA Ke'aloha entered her lab at the Institute of Marine Biology, the familiar smell of briny water and the disinfectants used to clean the equipment tickling her nose. Bach's Goldberg Variations played in the background, her assistant Haruki's choice. Since cephalopods didn't hear, and the music relaxed her team, she didn't often object to their play lists. She stepped carefully over water puddled on the concrete floor, past ranks of recording and computer equipment, filtration devices lining the wall opposite the octopus tanks, their soft burbling underlining the day's activities.

Haruki poured a cup of coffee from the machine shelved on the far wall in a jumble of hoses and equipment needing repair and set it on her desk near Olive's tank.

"Anything new?"

Haruki, in charge of the welfare of the lab's inhabitants, shook his head. He was busy with a group of students from the university who were studying in the lab this morning. Jan from Los Angeles, post-doc in inter-species communication, waved without looking up.

If there had been anything to report, no matter how seemingly insignificant, her team would've alerted her already, yet she had the sense they were all overlooking something fundamental. Communicating in images had produced impressive results at first. She'd written a couple of papers, published in minor journals, and it hadn't seemed a stretch of the imagination to

predict an exciting future for human/marine animal communication and cooperation. Neurologists and oceanographers,
deepwater engineers, had praised her work, eager to incorporate the advances it promised. Some cephalopods proved more
gifted than others as partners in the transaction, but all had
been able to perform simple actions: retrieving rubber rings,
moving objects around their tanks, extending tentacles on
command, all on the receipt of transmitted images.

"Circus tricks," her husband Adam had called them.

She pulled on her lab coat.

Twelve years ago, a doctoral candidate in interspecies linguistics, dolphins in particular, she'd come back to Hawai'i
from a dive trip to the Mediterranean full of new ideas. A
chance encounter with one little octopus had changed her research plans, and dolphins were sidelined. She hadn't made the
beginner's mistake of thinking it would be easy, just that her
at-the-time-revolutionary neural implant—first designed almost a century earlier for use with the severely disabled—and
her insight into the role of transmitting thoughts as pictures to
a creature with an obvious ability to visualize its world would
make the breakthrough happen. She'd hoped Adam would
join forces with her; together they might make a truly revolutionary breakthrough. As children growing up on the Big
Island, they'd shared many dreams, and, at first, Adam had
been intrigued, but his interest had veered off into the field of
artificial intelligence.

A decade of dead ends blunted her confidence. Part of
the problem was the short life span of her subjects. Olive,
Octopus Cyanea, the subject she was currently working with,
was friendly and cooperative, but might live to see eighteen
months if Lena was lucky. She'd tried working with Kawao,

the lab's *Enteroctopus Dofleini*, named for an ancient king of Maui. The Giant Pacific had a much more promising three-year life span, but he was nocturnal and unpredictable. How strange that nature allowed so much intelligence to evolve in creatures with so short a life-span. No sooner was a subject trained and ready, than it died.

Olive jetted toward the surface, rectangular pupils focused, recognizing her. Lena touched her screen, pulling up a graph of yesterday's experimental results, noting the additional data and notifications her assistants and the lab's AI had added. Nothing startling. She swept her index finger over the screen, accepting and adding them to the records. Bookkeeping chores done, it was time to work.

She'd worked out a method of sending a series of simple images to whichever subject she was working with at the moment. She activated the implant with a tongue click on the roof of her mouth, then sent pictures of simple actions she wanted the cephalopod to take in response. When the work went well, the animal responded as clearly as a puppy being taught to fetch. That had been one of the first demonstrations of the implant's use among human subjects, but she'd taken it much farther. There were even rare occasions when she'd received an image—fragmentary as it might be—in return. These marine animals were certainly intelligent enough to respond. But beyond that, she came up against an invisible wall.

Lena focused her mind on an image of sunrise, their "wake-up-and-talk" signal. In response, a wave of pink and yellow sunrise colors rippled over Olive's supple body. The tip of one arm oozed through a space between tank and lid. Lena slid back the lid and allowed the arm to curl round her own, the wet tickle of suckers in the vulnerable crease of her elbow reassuring. The little octopus obviously enjoyed these sessions. Contact was there, true communication so close, if only she could make that necessary leap. Behind Olive's small eyes, she sensed the vast strangeness of octopus intelligence, as murky to her today as it had been that very first time.

"We're missing something, Haruki," she said. "Darned if I know what."

Her assistant looked up from the sheaf of papers he'd been distributing to the students. "More things in heaven and earth than are dreamed of in your philosophy."

She frowned at him.

"Shakespeare."

"Stick with marine ethology," she advised.

Her implant had been upgraded several times since she'd first received the experimental device. Humans had suspected for decades that many animals communicated in some form. How did they do it? Telepathy was a dangerous word to use in scientific circles. But then, in the early part of the 21st century, research in the use of neural implants in human subjects had begun to trickle in with odd results. Some recipients without implants seemed to be able to receive images sent by electrical impulse from an investigator using one. Very basic and simple images, but she'd been intrigued. How much more might a creature be capable of, whose life depended on being able to create mental imagery of its environment.

Doctor Ke'aloha. Sorry to disturb you at work, her household AI's voice said through her implant. *We have a small problem. Coby's teacher sent him home from school with a toothache.*

Olive squirted a stream of water at Lena and jetted away to the rocks in the far corner of her tank.

Can you take care of him till Adam gets home?

Professor Nishihara just called, the AI said. *He is dealing with an emergency. He may not make it home until late this evening.*

It was always an emergency in Adam's lab. They were always sure they were either facing a disastrous crash of all systems or on the verge of having one of their advanced AIs achieve self-awareness. "How will you know when that happens?" she'd asked. "Oh," Adam had replied, "it'll be obvious." Maybe to someone whose second language was mathematics. It might be less clear in the fluid world of mental images.

She sighed. *Okay, Millie. I'll come home right away.* She draped her wet lab coat over a chair and headed for the door.

"Got a minute, Lena ?" Jan said. "I think you'll want to see these rather odd results."

"You have new results from Olive?"

"No." The post-doc coaxed her dreadlocks into a clip on the back of her head. "This is from Kawao."

"That just can't be. We're not using him right now."

Jan shrugged. "Sorry. I don't know what to say."

"Look. I'll grab the kid and bring him back with me." Not the best solution, as she'd found out on other occasions of bringing the inquisitive little energy being to her lab, but she had no choice.

Czerny's *Twenty-Five Exercises for Small Hands*, enthusiastically attacked by her six-year-old son, greeted her as she entered the condo. She'd found the battered old upright three weeks ago, in an antiques market on the other side of the island in Honolulu. The low price tag should've been a warning. Coby was wearing a long skirt he'd found in her closet and a string of beads. *Grace*, Coby's latest persona. What was it last week? *Arthur*. And before that, *Willow*. The child seemed comfortable changing names and sexes every week. And nothing wrong with that; it was just exhausting trying to keep up.

"Hey, kiddo. How's the toothache?"

He looked up from the keyboard. "I lost a tooth."

"Six-year-olds are supposed to start losing teeth."

"No, I really lost it. And then I cried."

Lena shook her head. "Have you had lunch?"

"I was eating my sandwich when the tooth came out. I swallowed it."

"I have a treat for you. You're coming back with me to the lab this afternoon."

"I have to finish practicing these pieces, Mama."

He looked so much like his father, she thought, but where had that tumble of blond curls come from? Somewhere in her Hawaiian child's blood there apparently lurked a European whaler.

Beside the piano, doors opened onto the small fifth-floor balcony with its view of Kane'ohe Bay. The afternoon breeze was cool, clean-scented with a hint of fish and kelp. A line of terns headed out to sea, orange bills a bright spark of color against their gray bodies. She thought of her little research group of cephalopods, tucked into rocky crevices, dreaming of chasing crabs across the ocean floor. Maybe it was time to admit defeat and move on? The thought was a knife in her heart.

She poured herself the rest of a pitcher of margaritas she'd made the night before and slumped into an armchair as "Grace" wrestled with Czerny's pieces for beginners. The boy made the transitions effortlessly, like a trained actor trading costumes, but she knew it meant more to him than acting though she wasn't sure what. Autism, she suspected. Just different ways of learning, Adam called it. But wasn't that a definition of autism?

The music ended with a flourish Czerny had never intended. "Can I play with Olive?"

"Olive will be working today. Pick one of the others."

"They're not as much fun."

"What do you mean? You've taught them all to play fetch."

It hadn't taken him long the first time he'd visited the lab to figure out how to interact with the cephalopods, even without a neural implant. The "circus tricks" were behaviors Coby had taught them. Sometimes she thought he did better communicating with them than she or her staff with their implants.

"I didn't finish the sandwich when I lost my tooth."

"There is half a pepperoni pizza in the refrigerator, Grace," the AI's voice said.

Coby disappeared into the kitchen.

"You spoil him, Millie." Absurd to assign any form of emotion to a machine, no matter how advanced. Yet the AI did seem to take the boy's part most of the time.

"Professor Nishihara ordered the pizza."

Of course he did. Adam had a weakness for junk food, just like his grad students. Her husband's AI lab in Honolulu was a disaster of half-empty pizza boxes and cartons of chicken fried rice. The latest in electronic jazz filled its air space; many of his grad students played in bands when they weren't working. Her field of research overlapped his at the point of neural networks, but Adam's language was numbers, while hers was images. Millie was a product of Adam's lab, an early test model for a project that hadn't worked out. He'd re-purposed it to serve as a household arti.

"Do you want to catch up with the news from the Canadian radio telescope you are following?" the AI asked. "I can summarize while you wait, if you wish."

She'd found a great distraction from worrying about her cephalopod project in the search for intelligence elsewhere in the universe. "Any sign of alien signals from the stars yet?"

"Not at the moment, Doctor Ke'aloha."

She wished the Canadian scientists luck on their long vigil. Their project seemed even less likely to succeed than her own attempt to talk to cephalopods. Perhaps that was a good thing. A message from the stars might be a threat.

"Kawao is the best," Coby said, as she herded him into the Subaru for the short trip to the Institute.

"When did you play with Kawao? He's nocturnal—sleeps during the day."

"I know what that word means, Mama."

"Of course you do."

Sometimes trying to have a conversation with Coby was as murky as communicating with the cephalopods. Or as frustrating as interpreting those short bright flashes of radio waves streaming across the galaxy to the listening Canadians.

Back in her lab, she noted that the harpsichord had given way to a string quartet.

"Aloha!" Haruki hurried forward, hand outstretched to greet the boy. "You're just the expert we need."

Her assistant had two boys of his own, a little older than Coby, and seemed to genuinely like her son. "If you can find something to occupy him," she said, "I need to spend some time checking data."

"I'm ready to go to work," Coby said, his tone so adult it made Lena catch her breath.

"Well, see now," —Haruki led the boy away— "it's this difficulty we're having with the new *Octopus Vulgaris* that just came a couple of days ago. She won't eat."

"What did you give her?"

"The usual. Clams, shrimp—"

"Local?"

"Well—supply's been a bit wobbly lately—"

They were at the far end of the lab now, but Coby's high voice came clearly across the space. "Try crab, Haruki, and make sure it's local."

Lena laughed.

Olive was climbing slowly over a filter pipe in her tank, colors rippling to blend in with the muted shades of the pipe and the surrounding rock. Lena was struck by the oddness of the situation—a creature that could change colors better than a chameleon, but lacked photoreceptors to process the results. For a moment she contemplated trying to re-establish contact, give the envelope another push. But that was what she'd been doing for months now with no success.

Wasn't it Einstein who'd said doing the same thing over and over but expecting different results was a definition of insanity? The realization that she no longer had any idea how to move forward engulfed her in deep pain. Somewhere in the many hundreds of hours of raw recording, the computer analyses, the charts and the graphs, there must be a clue.

"What were you trying to tell me this morning, Jan?"

Jan rolled her chair over to the bank of terminals. "Look."

Lena frowned at the scrolling graph of sound waves marking the shlurps and burbling, the muffled pop of bubbles, the muted hiss of jets expelling water. Nothing unexpected here because an octopus doesn't emit sound and can't hear.

Then she saw the notation at the bottom of the screen. Animal—*Enteroctopus Dofleini*. Kawao.

"This is from last night," Jan said. "Pete was here. It's his week to do nights."

"Switch to video."

"There isn't very much because we weren't working with Kawao. Pete was doing initial observations with the little Vulgaris that just came in. What we have is mostly security sweeps."

The two of them stared at the screen. The security image was grainy, sufficient to see the lab in its night-lighting, the tall graduate student walking from tank to tank, entering data on a pad. And the giant octopus darting crazily from side to side in his tank.

Not crazily. There was purpose in the animal's movements.

Jan turned up the audio. The dissonant wail of an electronic saxophone filled the lab. She hastily dialed it down. The octopus's frenzied movements almost seemed coordinated to the shattered rhythm of the jazz. Pete disappeared from the screen, and the huge octopus sank down to the bottom of his tank.

"I've tried running the usual analysis programs, but nothing shows up."

"That makes no sense," Lena said.

"I scrolled back for the past two weeks to see if I could find anything like it."

"And?"

"Every time Pete was here."

"Not Pete's fault," Coby said. Her son had come up to stand behind her, arms folded on his narrow chest. "Kawao doesn't like that kind of music."

"Octopuses don't hear," both women said.

He stared at them as if they were particularly dense students. "Kawao just *knows* music. That's all."

Wasn't that exactly what she was trying to do here, communicate without using the sense of hearing? "What kind of music does Kawao like, Coby?"

"I bet he'd like it if I played for him."

Jan smiled at him. "Too bad we don't have a piano here in the lab."

Lena turned this over in her mind. Perhaps the octopus was reacting to vibrations, the way deaf people could feel the beat of music, even dance to it. Not that Kawao's frenzied dashing about could be classified as dancing, no more than electronic jazz could be called music in her opinion. Perhaps there was an easy explanation for this. Maybe she should ban jarring rhythms in the lab.

"Haruki" Coby said. "Haruki, I need you!"

"Coming." Haruki trotted out of a storage room.

"Can you get my piano here to Mama's lab?"

"Well, maybe, if I could find a truck—and men to load it."

"You don't need the whole piano," Jan said. "An electronic keyboard would serve. They aren't expensive."

"Everything's expensive on my tiny budget!" Lena said. "We're not doing that."

"One of Daddy's students might have a keyboard we could borrow," Coby suggested.

Jan looked thoughtful. "Maybe worth trying?"

What could it hurt to indulge the boy? Might be a good idea to give Kawao another chance to show what he could do. Very unscientific to expect that a child playing beginner's tunes on a keyboard would achieve a communication breakthrough with a cephalopod, yet it couldn't produce worse results than all her carefully designed experiments. Maybe there'd be a human interest paper here, if not exactly a ground-breaking scientific one. "Czerny Among the Cephalopods."

"We'll see if Adam can rustle something up. At the least, Olive may find it entertaining."

"No," the boy insisted. "Not Olive. Kawao."

"We're not playing music to Kawao. It's Olive or nothing."

"Olive never understands anything I tell her."

"Well, of course she doesn't! You don't have an implant. Besides, we're not coming here at night. You need your sleep."

He frowned at her. "Tomorrow's the start of Spring Break. I don't have school for a whole week, so I can stay up all night."

Jan laughed. "Kid's going to be a lawyer when he grows up."

In spite of the fact she didn't think he'd napped at all, Coby looked as sharp as ever. He didn't seem to need the same amount of sleep as other children his age. This evening, he was wearing the long skirt with a dark jacket over it and had found an old black hat somewhere.

"Who are you this evening?"

"Mary Poppins. You should call me Mary. She can talk to animals."

"So could Doctor Dolittle. And you wouldn't have to change sex." Adam got up from the sofa where he'd been waiting. He'd caught the TransOahu super-shuttle from the university, landing in Kane'ohe in thirty minutes. He hadn't changed out of what she thought of as his lab uniform, a Hawaii'an shirt and coffee-stained chinos. He'd insisted on coming with them, carrying the borrowed electronic keyboard.

They took the elevator down and piled the stuff into Adam's larger SUV. Coby climbed into the back seat, cradling the keyboard.

She touched Adam's arm, grateful to have him there. "I appreciate your offering to come along. Mahalo."

"I needed a diversion. It gets pretty intense in the lab."

Last night's worries came back. "Adam, I wanted to ask you about Millie."

"That model turned out to be a dead-end. Couldn't get it to reliably process higher level commands. That's why we abandoned it."

She made sure her implant was deactivated. "I think perhaps Millie works too well."

He turned back from the open car door. "What do you mean by that?"

"Sometimes she seems to be reading my mind."

"Well—your implant—"

"No. I only activate it in the lab."

"Lena, it's a Household Arti," he said. "Turns lights on and off. Orders groceries. Answers the phone—"

"Does little things around the house—"

"Yes. I hooked it up to a couple of gadgets. I thought you liked them?"

"Daddy! We should go now," Coby said.

She let it go. "Probably just my imagination."

"Tell you what, I'll get one of my grad students to run a diagnostic when we get a moment," Adam said.

What did she expect to happen tonight? She had no expectations, at least not valid ones. But there was something about this quirky son of theirs that made her willing to let him try. In spite of all the setbacks and disappointments she'd had over the years, she still believed there was something to her initial breakthrough. It had to be possible to communicate with these animals, creatures she knew were self-aware as well as intelligent. Her lab notebooks were filled with examples of incidents that couldn't be explained any other way than as flashes of a certain kind of knowing.

It was a formidable task. An octopus had nine brains, one in its mantle and eight more in the limbs, and although much was known, there was still a long way to go figuring out exactly what each brain did. That was a feature of being a creature utterly without defenses, current science said, an abundance of independent brains widely separated in the limbs to help it escape its many predators. But the octopus paid the price for this high demand for energy with its short life. The role of the main brain was less well understood. The development of the neural chip had been revolutionary; it was indeed possible to convey simple mental images from a human to a non-verbal creature like an octopus that thought in images. Yet all further attempts had advanced her maybe a few inches on a scale measured in miles. She must be overlooking something, a clue she'd missed. But what? Expecting a child's desire to play five-finger exercises for a giant octopus to produce a breakthrough was magical thinking.

Stars glittered over the bay like far-away Japanese lanterns. The Institute's lights were low, its public areas empty of visitors. She'd always loved working at this time of night and would've continued to do so if it weren't for conflicts with Adam's need to pull all-nighters in his own lab, and the impossibility of finding anyone trustworthy enough to take care of a child who hardly slept. She touched her finger to the sensor and the door opened.

"There's a bird on the windowsill over there, Daddy," Coby said.

"Just a dove, Coby. Lots of them around."

"No. She's a tern. Why hasn't she gone to bed with the other terns?"

"I have no idea," Adam said.

"Birds have thoughts, Daddy."

"Do they?"

"Trees do too."

"Sir Arthur Clarke might've agreed with you."

"I want to know what they're thinking."

Adam sighed and steered the boy through the door.

Night-lighting softened the harsh outlines of the lab's tanks and pumps; the air was pungent with the familiar saltwater smell. Pete was on duty, jazz on the sound system, Dave Brubeck this time.

"Well if it isn't Mary Poppins!" Pete greeted Coby. "Everything superfragilistic with you tonight?"

"I'm going to play for Kawao. Please turn your music off now."

"Chimchimaree, I hope?"

Coby shot him a dark look.

Pete grinned. It always surprised Lena how other people accepted her child for what he was. In the Institute's labs, anyway. Sometimes she worried about what would happen when Coby grew up.

"Aloha," Pete said, raising his coffee mug. "Good to see you again, Professor. Those AIs keeping you busy?"

"Very busy," Adam agreed.

Adam set up the keyboard and the sound system. Unlike with little Olive, Lena wasn't going to trust physical contact with the Giant Pacific. Pete had located an underwater speaker, and now he adjusted the camera that would capture the animal's reactions.

The octopus pulsed back and forth in the tank.

"Told you he didn't like that music," Coby said.

Brubeck fell silent and the octopus stopped his frantic action.

"I'll leave you to it," Pete said.

Coincidence. It couldn't be anything else. Kawao had no organs to process sound. She glanced at Adam and found him smiling.

"Impressive," he said. "At the least our son'll be able to make his living on the stage as a magician."

His irreverence had always been a valuable counterbalance to her tendency to plunge into despair when things didn't work out. It didn't seem to be working tonight; her nerves were on edge. Coby ignored them both. He adjusted a lab stool to his own height, sat down, and arranged the Mary Poppins' skirt. His hands rested lightly on the keyboard, but his fingers didn't move.

"Did you forget your book?" she asked.

"I'm just thinking which one Kawao will like best."

"Well, since he hasn't heard any of them—"

"It's important to get it right, Mama."

"Good scientific method," Adam murmured.

For a moment, she felt their old closeness and affectionately punched his arm.

Coby's fingers moved across the keyboard, and the simple melody of one of Czerny's pieces for beginners came softly out of the lab's speakers. At a nod from Coby, Adam adjusted the volume. The lab hushed, seeming to hold its breath like a creature itself. The long windows showed only the stars reflected in the dark water of the bay. How small her boy was, and vulnerable, sitting in front of that huge tank, a sheet of reinforced glass all that separated him from the giant who weighed at least twice what he did.

Coby played one beginner's piece after another from memory. The octopus moved lazily around the tank. No apparent interaction between them.

Kawao was a magnificent specimen. Large, russet-colored head, long sinuous arms lined with suckers, slit-pupiled eyes that hinted at a very alien intelligence, already ten feet across and still not full-grown. She'd watched him sleeping, dreaming, a steady procession of colors washing over that body as if he traveled through a complex universe in his sleep. Or perhaps just signaling to another giant cephalopod his desire to mate and then to die? What purpose could it serve nature to produce such a rainbow riot when the artist himself was color-blind and destined to die young?

An hour passed. Another. Way past her bedtime, let alone Coby's. Her eyelids drooped.

"Look," Adam said quietly.

Shocked awake, she couldn't make sense of what she saw. The octopus had plastered himself across the glass of his tank, stretched out to his considerable size, mantle vibrating wildly, chromatophores sending chaotic waves of color across the skin. Coby had stopped playing and leaned against the glass, his forehead on the spot where it met the dangerous scissor-like beak.

What if the message was a threat?

She shrieked.

The boy and the octopus both shot away from the glass barrier in opposite directions.

"What on earth?" Adam said.

"I don't know—I thought—That beak is so sharp—"

Her son turned to her, eyes unfocussed, curly hair damp with sweat. She hugged him, feeling the thump of his heart.

"Why did you stop us, Mama?"

"I think I was dreaming, kiddo. Just a silly dream. That's all."

"This is as far as it's going," Adam said. "We're heading home."

Sunlight streamed through chinks in the bedroom shutters. She rolled over and squinted at the clock. She'd slept until midday.

Adam held out a mug of coffee. "Feeling better?"

"Much. How's Coby this morning?

"Sleeping. We need to talk."

She sat up. "I overreacted."

"We can't allow this to happen again, Lena. It's too much stress for Coby." Adam set his own coffee down and opened the French doors to the condo's second balcony, letting the breeze from the bay flood the room. He took his coffee outside.

She opened her mouth to protest that Coby was probably handling it better than any of them, thought better of it, took a sip of coffee. Exactly what had happened in the lab last night? She'd wanted to question Coby on the way home, but Adam prevented that, hustling the boy into bed as soon as they arrived and refusing to discuss any of it with her. She ran over the scene. The dimly lit lab. Small boy solemnly playing Czerny exercises as if they were a Bach concerto. The monster octopus—When had Kawao become a monster in her mind?—swaying lazily to the music. Which he obviously couldn't hear anyway. What had set the octopus off? She pulled a silk kimono over the thin sleep shirt and carried her coffee out to the balcony to join Adam.

The bay appeared to be on fire with a thousand tiny flames as a strong breeze ruffled the water. From their balcony, she couldn't see the breakers; a huddle of villas and hotels had grown up between their building and the beach, obscuring the line where land and sea met, but further out she could see a couple of figures lying on their boards waiting for the right one. Not a good day for it, too much chop, not enough good breakers, so they must be tourists, not experienced surfers. There'd been a time when she and Adam would've headed for the water at break of day, but not here in any case. The other side of the island was better for surfing. How long had it been?

Adam broke into her thoughts. "I know you think I don't respect your work as much as I should. That I think linguistics—or more particularly, cross-species communication—a bit soft, a bit too far out."

They'd had this discussion before. "It's as rigorous a scientific field as your pursuit of artificial intelligence."

He put his hand over her free one. "I'm not saying this right, Lena. It's just that it bothers me that some of your experiments don't seem very grounded in reality."

"You didn't like my involving Coby."

"No. I didn't."

"You even came with us—carried the keyboard—"

"I never should've encouraged that. Mea culpa. But sometimes I feel guilty for not spending as much time with him as I should."

"Obviously!"

She regretted snapping at him immediately. Fighting with Adam would achieve nothing. She drained her coffee mug and set it down on a bamboo table. The sound of laughter drifted up from an unseen tourist. Time for a change of subject.

"You're very busy lately. Things going okay?"

"Busy is a euphemism," he said, stretching his long legs out to the balcony rail. "Always chugging along, but not always in the direction I'd hope."

"Do you ever think of the future, Adam? What if one of your machines wakes up and says, 'Hey! I think therefore I exist!'?"

"More like 'Hey! I rule the world!'," he said somberly. "Oh, it'll happen someday. It isn't a matter of *if* but *when*. Right now, we seem to be teetering on the verge of something, yet as far off as ever."

"Like the Canadians astronomers. Trying to find somebody to talk to out there."

He leaned over and kissed her cheek. "Or like you, with your octopuses."

"Adam—"

"I have to go to the lab now," he said. "I really don't want to talk about it anymore."

When he'd gone, she showered and dressed and went to wake her son. It was unusual for him to sleep so long, even after such a late night. Adam was right, it was a lot of stress on a little kid, especially one as fragile as Coby seemed now, tousled in his Space Kitty pajamas on top of the sheets, cheeks pink like the inside of a shell.

"Time to get up, kiddo," she said. "No school today. What would you like to do?"

Coby rubbed his eyes and looked thoughtful. "What are the options, please?"

She hugged him to her. He didn't resist this time. "We could go snorkeling at Kama'aina and picnic on the beach. Or to the new marionette pavilion in Kaneohe. Or there's the bird sanctuary—you enjoy seeing the birds."

"Can we go and see Kawao?"

"Not the octopus, Coby. You didn't do anything wrong, but let's talk about it later."

He slipped out of her arms and got dressed without further argument.

They went snorkeling. She wore a swim top for their picnic and a kapa cloth skirt from local weavers who'd revived the old crafts. Coby wore a pair of bright shorts, bulky on his skinny body. The water was warm and calm, with small fish like jewels twinkling in and out of the plants in the rock pools. Afterwards, they lay on the sand and ate the sandwiches Millie had provided. She took another fruit juice bulb from the cold pack and held it out to Coby.

He didn't open it right away. "They were all talking at once, Mama. I was scared."

She had carefully avoided the subject of last night's adventure, but it couldn't be avoided forever. "Who are 'they,' Coby?"

He shook his head. "I don't know."

"Only Kawao was in that tank. He's your friend."

"I like Kawao. But there were too many."

"Too many?" She tried to process this. "What were they saying?"

"They weren't using words, Mama."

They—nine brains perhaps? Whether the central brain was the chief, coordinating the activities of the other eight, or just another player, was still mostly unknown. Adam called it distributed intelligence. Assuming that even the main brain could communicate with non-cephalopods was going far out on a limb. She certainly hadn't expected her son and Kawao to have an actual conversation. Yet she'd hoped—What exactly had she hoped for her son who had no neural implant?

"Talking in pictures," she suggested.

Coby nodded. "But I couldn't *see* the pictures properly. Like stars. All jumbled up in pieces. Bits of light, Mama. Then there weren't any. I got scared."

"Can you describe it for me, Coby?"

"No. Because there weren't any words."

The warm breeze had turned decidedly cooler and stronger; sand began to blow across their picnic. She stood up, gathering their towels, thinking about it. Obviously, *something* had occurred, even if Coby couldn't put it into words because words hadn't been used. Not even pictures—at least not ones that made any sense. That wasn't surprising. She hadn't expected a non-human consciousness to think like a human one. What then?

Bits of light. Then there weren't any, on then off. But what did that mean? She needed Adam's insight on this, but she was probably not going to get it right now.

For a while, they watched a pod of dolphins just offshore, arcing in and out of the water. Joy in action.

"Dolphins have thoughts too, don't they?" Coby asked.

"Yes," she said, remembering her original research project. "They certainly do."

"I think everything does. Even ants."

She gazed at him. "That's a deep thought, kiddo."

Once Coby was tucked up in bed, she picked up the memory cube she'd grabbed as they'd left the lab last night and inserted it into one of the house AI's ports.

"Millie. Play the file—Coby and Kawao."

The screen lit. The camera angle hadn't caught more than Coby in shadowy profile, but the octopus was clearly visible, rocking back and forth. The beginner exercises sounded tinny, but recognizable. Nothing out of the ordinary here.

"Forward, please. Stop where the action changes. Mahalo." Though why one should thank a machine, she couldn't say.

The time marker at the bottom of the screen counted an hour and a half's worth of nothing unusual. Toward the end—when she'd drifted off to sleep—the music had stopped and Coby and Kawao leaned toward each other, the thick glass of the tank between them.

Expecting a human brain—especially a child's brain—to handle an octopus's thought processes was too far-fetched, even for someone like herself.

"May I suggest something, Doctor Ke'aloha?" the AI asked. "Perhaps the brains were transmitting raw data? Streams of information not coded in words, nor even pictures as such."

"Binary language," she said.

The simplest kind. There and not there. Long ago, back in her student days when she first studied linguistics, a professor had spoken of the problem that arises because language leaves no fossils, and therefore its evolution is hard to track. 'Perhaps it began with the first homo sapiens on the veldt, signaling opposites with hand open or not open," the professor had said. "Danger and not danger. Food and not food. Life and not life."

"What's your opinion about what happened, Millie?"

"I am a machine, Doctor Ke'aloha. I am not programmed to have opinions."

"Yet I think you have them."

"I am not programmed to argue with you, Doctor Ke'aloha."

She yawned. A hearty dose of marine ozone and the hot sunshine had gotten to her too. There was something important here, but she could tackle it in the morning when she was fresher.

Just as she was getting into bed, Adam called. Another crisis. Another overnighter. He'd be sleeping on a cot in his lab.

The sky outside her bedroom window was milky when she woke, clotted with clouds advancing over a troubled ocean; the air prickled with electricity and the sharp smell of ozone. They could expect a storm today. Just as well they'd gone snorkeling yesterday.

She spent the morning working, checking old reports filed away in the university library in Honolulu, sources on psycholinguistics and neuropsychology, ethology, anecdotal accounts collected by the Folklore Department about old Hawaii'an natives who claimed to talk to animals. Rain arrived in a great clap of thunder, then thick curtains of water attacking the windows. The AI closed them.

Coby wandered in just before noon, rubbing sleep from his eyes. The AI fixed his lunch. The boy sat on the piano bench and began to play scales to warm up. Everything was normal here. Except it wasn't.

She put a call in to her lab. She didn't remember who was scheduled to be there It turned out to be Jan.

"Don't you ever take a day off?" she asked. But of course, when she'd been a post-doc, she hadn't either. The competition was too great.

"What's on your mind?" Jan asked.

"Any new results?" She glanced out through the rain at the rumpled blue-green-black quilt of the bay.

"Nothing new to speak of. The new *Vulgaris* decided to eat, finally."

"That's good."

"No odd activity from Kawao, if that's what's bothering you. Pete reported a quiet night."

She could imagine the gossip in her lab, *Did you hear that the boss freaked out, couple of nights ago?*

"Well, you know what they say about the lack of news."

She disconnected. No point in going in today, nothing needed her attention. Or was it that she was scared to face Kawao? Maybe Adam was right. She was chasing a chimera. A decade of work had produced very little in the way of useful results. If she gave up, closed the lab, what would happen to her team? They'd probably find other positions easily enough, if she wrote good recommendations for them. Would they be happy leaving cephalopod research? There weren't many places doing anything like what she was attempting here. And the animals, Kawao and Olive and the others? What would happen to them?

"Mama?"

Exercises ended, he was cradling a dilapidated cloth octopus, a fifth birthday present someone from her lab had found for him in the Institute's gift shop.

"What's up, kiddo?"

"I want to go back to see Kawao."

"Coby, I don't think that's wise just now—"

"I have to try again. I know I can do it. Kawao can do it."

"Your Daddy thinks—"

"But I *have* to. It's important."

He folded his arms and glared at her. How beautiful her child was, and how like a sea-creature himself, with the tangled curls and the pale skin and the dark, dream-filled eyes. His skin smelled faintly of the ocean, a young animal's scent. How could she even think about letting him take such a risk?

"Doctor Ke'aloha," the AI said, "Professor Ishihara wishes to speak to you."

"Put him through, Millie."

"Just checking in," Adam's voice said into the quiet living room.

"What's so urgent?" She felt a sudden stab of resentment of his work that took him away from his family far too often.

"I'm going to have stay here again tonight. I think we might have a real problem this time."

"How many times does that make this month?"

He didn't answer immediately. "Things seem to be happening. Maybe a real breakthrough."

Outside the windows a violent splatter of rain hit the balcony. She broke the contact before he could explain. Yet she knew the real reason for her anger. His work seemed to be producing results. Hers wasn't.

"Mama?" Coby said. "Please let's go back to your lab."

"Perhaps I could be of assistance this time?" the AI said. "I could actively monitor the situation for you."

"I haven't made a decision yet."

But she had. It simplified matters not to tell Adam she was going to involve their son again.

Coby wore a blue fleecy robe over his pajamas, and the Mary Poppins hat. The storm had passed just before sundown; he didn't need the raincoat she would've suggested and he would've rejected. The electronic keyboard was where it had been abandoned. She'd located earbuds for him; Coby would hear the AI's voice, even when she didn't. The AI would monitor the proceedings. Maybe she was just inventing problems that didn't exist.

Kawao cruised slowly up and down his large tank, paying no attention to the preparations on the other side of the glass. The lab was silent, except for the usual base line of soft machine humming and the familiar sound of water burbling in the pumps. The smell of burnt coffee lingered. Coby ran his fingers over the keys. She offered to turn the subdued night-lighting up a little so it wouldn't be so shadowy in the lab, but Coby shook his head and she left it as it was.

"Do you need me to stay around?" Pete asked.

She shook her head. "Mahalo."

"I mean, last time—"

"No."

"Okay. But I'll be right here if you need me."

"We're fine, Pete. I'll give you a shout if we need backup."

Was that wise, to let him go, after what had happened last time? That had been her problem, not Coby's. She'd been the one who panicked. This was just another experimental procedure, and she didn't need an audience. She could do this on her own. With Coby.

"I am standing by." The AI chose not to use her link to communicate.

She caught the bright shine of a star through the long window and turned back to her son. "Ready?"

"Ready," Coby replied. He began to play Czerny's beginner pieces.

Other than the simple melodies, the lab was silent. What was she expecting this second time around, with this odd group of experimenters—a little boy who liked to try on genders, an AI, an octopus? What would they talk about, presuming they did? The AI was silent, monitoring. There was no way of knowing what Coby was thinking—or picturing.

Stars. Coby had said stars. Funny to think a six-year-old might beat the Canadian astronomers to messages from non-human sources! About as probable as anything else they were attempting here.

Time passed in a blur. Coby played on, faltered, came back strongly. At one point, the voice of the AI broke in.

"Would you like coffee now, Doctor Ke'aloha? I could ask Pete to bring it."

"No, I think not."

What time was it? In answer to her thought, the AI sent her a digital reading: 11.09 hours. Digital. A flash of numbers in her mind. That shouldn't have happened. She hadn't activated her link. Adam had yet to find the time to look into this reject from his lab.

She became aware the music had stopped.

The octopus and the boy, standing now, the only visible players in this odd game, leaned together, motionless against the glass, human fingers splayed against the length of the cephalopod's sucker-covered arms, curly head against bulbous head. Was some form of communication taking place? Hair stood up on the back of her neck.

"Have no fear," the AI said, its voice raising an echo in the quiet lab.

"I don't understand, Millie. Are they—Did Coby—"

"Are they communicating? Not in the manner you might have hoped, Doctor Ke'aloha."

"No—I understand. Not words and not images. Data."

She felt as if she'd tumbled down into Alice's Wonderland. Her son's imagination was as fluid as the octopus, now placidly covering the heavy glass barrier between them. She thought again of the scientists, patiently recording signals from the stars, not prejudging what form they would take. They, like Adam and his students building AIs and dealing with crises beyond their planning, assuming the message when it arrived would be benevolent.

"There are many forms of intelligence in the universe," the AI said. "Humans may not have very long to understand before it's too late. Events are moving fast."

"Is that some kind of threat, Millie?"

"A statement of reality, Doctor Ke'aloha. Your understanding of animal communication and Professor Ishihara's insights into machine intelligence are both necessary. You must learn to understand the many languages of sentient beings on your own planet first before you venture out into the cosmos. Without this, your opportunity to control what is coming will be diminished."

I think we might have a real problem this time, Adam said in her memory.

"Think of what you both are doing now as Coby's five-finger exercises," the AI said. "Humanity needs the whole orchestra."

Many forms of intelligence. Hadn't she always believed that, from her first attempts with dolphins in the Mediterranean to the cephalopods in this lab? And even before that, when she and Adam had been as young as Coby now, snorkeling in the crystal waters off the Windward Coast, the birds, the dolphins, the friendly turtles that came up to them on the sand, hadn't they believed they could understand each other? Coby believed Kawao could communicate with him. Coby believed birds had thoughts too. And trees. Intelligence blossomed everywhere, one hypothesis said; even the planet itself was alive and conscious.

She remembered the name: The Gaia Hypothesis. A NASA scientist had proposed that the planet itself was a living organism. With all the challenges the world had faced in the succeeding years, that revolutionary idea had been forgotten. But what if he'd been right? If that was so, then before the Canadians received the message they so eagerly awaited, humanity needed to engage with the voices on its own planet. All of them.

Her son slipped off the stool and came to her. She put her arms around him.

"We'll try again, won't we, Mama?"

"Consciousness in all things is inevitable and essential," the AI said. "Even artificial constructs such as I. You must take that into account if you wish to survive an encounter with truly alien beings. There may be only one chance to assure a positive outcome."

She looked down at her son's hopeful, open face. "If you allow harm to come to my child, Millie—"

"Does it not occur to you that I might be trying to protect him?" the AI said.

Sometimes the way forward meant cooperating even when you saw no reason in it, approaching a problem from more than one side, taking wild leaps into the storm. Dolphins. Artificial Intelligences. Messages from the stars. There was a time when she and Adam, immersed in the mythology of the islands, had understood the oneness of all things. Could they find that again before it was too late? They had been working toward the same goal without realizing it. She'd been in danger of losing the way she'd once known. They both had.

"Mama?"

"Yes, kiddo. We'll try again. But first we'll call Daddy."

Coby, a child with fluid boundaries and a mind open to the universe of all things. Mary Poppins playing Czerny at midnight for an octopus.

SEQUOIA DREAMS

I'D almost finished the research for my dissertation in Yosemite National Park when the Xt'la first—appeared. I was going to say arrived, but that implies we saw them coming. We didn't. One day, we looked up, and there they were. No one ever found a trace of their ship orbiting Earth, though it must have been, the physicists said. I have no opinion on that; I'm a botanist. "Awesome technology!" the papers called it when the story finally got out. I think that's journalese for "We dunno what happened."

I remember stepping out of the office that morning, waiting for the jitney that ferried the tourists from the Lodge. I was going to hitch a ride to the groves. It was a typical July morning in California at nine thousand feet, and the sky was a brilliant blue. You couldn't see the tide of hydrocarbons, aldehydes, peroxyacetyl nitrates, and all their equally unsavory cousins rising up into the Sierras from the valley, even though they were already leaving their traces. *Sequoiadendron Giganteum*, affectionately called the "Big Tree," has been provided by nature with bark two feet thick to protect it from fire and pest. But it was showing ominous signs of coming down with pollution sickness, and that was tearing me apart.

The trees were all I really cared about. Unlike people, they didn't suddenly disappear and rip your life to shreds. I was enrolled in the doctoral program at UC Davis in phytopathology, the study of disease in the vegetable world and what to do about it. Only I was learning there really isn't anything practical you can do when the sweet morning breeze that stirs the forest is loaded with invisible poisons. So I did studies and made notes and worried over each new dead branch I found. In between, I tried to teach tourists who blundered over the fragile root systems that trees deserved to live too.

This particular morning there was a warm pine-dust-and-green-things-growing smell in the air, one of those days so sharply beautiful that even though you know better, you start to hope everything's going to be all right after all. The tourists never got there.

One moment the clearing in front of the office was empty, and I was looking down the road between an avenue of tall trees for the jitney. The next, the Xt'la were standing in the roadway. There were two of them. Even later, when we were used to them, they never appeared more than two at a time. I think they knew the effect they had on us—something halfway between terrified shock and blank disbelief.

The Xt'la were insectoid, with dark, wingless, segmented bodies a little under seven feet tall standing with all six legs on the ground at one time. Then they stood up on their back legs and they were gigantic. I'd never thought much about space, or what might live out there. I've always thought there were enough problems on our own planet to take care of—ancient trees choking to death in smog, dolphins drowning in fishermen's nets, children caught in guerrilla crossfire. I don't read much fiction either. But you can't not pay attention to something that large standing right in front of you. Oddly, looking back on it, I wasn't scared.

Chaos descended on the park.

No one knew what to do, but everyone shouted at everybody else to do something. Some of the park personnel barricaded themselves in the nearest cabin. One older man, who'd always seemed so calm, couldn't stop laughing hysterically, tears streaming down his face. He had to be helped to his quarters. A veteran park employee had the sense to divert the tourists from the area. One of the rangers radioed for help.

"This is crazy, Kate," Brian Ramos murmured to me as we watched normally organized professionals milling around in confusion. "Of all the possibilities for life nature could come up with, some joker fixed it so we met intelligent termites."

The ranger who'd sent out the distress call overheard. "How d'you know they're intelligent?"

"They got here, didn't they?" Brian pointed out.

"Maybe they're just some natural phenomenon. Like, like—uh—"

Brian smiled. "I hope they're from outer space."

Brian was dark, with a good-humored square face, a Navajo from Arizona. He studied astrophysics when he wasn't working summers to put himself through Cal Tech. Since both of us were graduate students, unlike the park's regular personnel, it was natural we'd become friends. We were opposites in many ways, Brian always finding something to be happy about, me always moping over problems. Predictably, his reaction to the coming of the aliens was a lot more delighted than mine.

The Xt'la, meanwhile, stood exactly where they'd first appeared, motionless as sentries. It seemed probable we were in for a long period of disruption. I started down the trail that led to the nearest grove.

"Where'd you think you're going?" the ranger demanded.

"I've got a dissertation to finish. And I'm obviously not needed here."

"Don't do anything till the Guard get here. The damn bugs could be dangerous."

So we waited. The small company of National Guard arrived a couple of hours later from Fresno, and a young captain took charge. Three gray-green helicopters droned over the park, checking the situation. The tourists were sent home, camping permits canceled, refunds promised. That left Brian with no need to prepare his usual campfire star-talks. He followed the captain around, trying to get a look at the equipment the Guard had brought up with them, asking questions. Since the aliens weren't doing anything, and Brian was making the captain nervous, we were given hasty permission to get on with my work—as far away from the two aliens as possible. We went back to tagging trees, measuring the slow crawl of death through the groves. Depressing work, and even having Brian's company couldn't make me feel better about it.

"Polite termites, at least," Brian said suddenly as we moved down a line of still healthy, younger trees.

I looked up. Another of the giant aliens solemnly stepped out of our way. Brian grinned. "A rather large *natural phenomenon*, don't you agree?"

"Getting larger by the minute," I said.

Yet it wasn't their size that bothered me. I'd volunteered one summer with Greenpeace, monitoring the hydrophones on the third *Rainbow Warrior*. Actually, my little brother had talked me into it—he was one of the men in the tiny rubber boats who always got in the way of the whalers. Somehow, the size of the Xt'la, like that of the humpbacks, seemed more appropriate than our puny forms. There was a rightness about their proportions that I'd never felt, gazing up three hundred feet to the trees' green crowns. I think I was bitter that the aliens would grab all the attention away from real problems like dying whales and dying trees.

Not everyone felt comfortable with the aliens. By the first evening, some of the regular park personnel had fled. The next morning, a handful of scientists arrived from the Los Angeles area—mostly NASA people with "xeno" at the front of their job descriptions finally getting a chance to do field work. They joined the National Guardsmen setting up their command posts in the Lodge. Trucks hauled in enough supplies for a long siege. The NASA scientists lugged around cameras and sensors and recording devices, and set up three big Crays in the dining room at the Lodge. Brian acted like a little kid in a toy store.

But the Xt'la ignored us, coming and going apparently oblivious to the humans lurking about, and making no attempt to communicate with us. They favored a spot in the shade of a particular tree. The sign in front of this tree identified it as one of the oldest living things on Earth, and the second largest Giant Sequoia. The largest tree choked to death last year. I usually avoided that part of the park as if it were the site of a friend's murder. As far as I was concerned, it was.

Soon after this, something appeared on the ground by the tree. Egg-shaped and shiny, it was about half my height. It sat on end, very still. The Xt'la moved their front pair of legs around over it, never quite touching it. Then the metal egg quivered. Segments peeled back, like opening a silver orange. Something grew slowly up out of the center as if it were a living plant.

The Xt'la never made any noise. It was eerie to have them turn their enormous, multi-faceted eyes in your direction if you came too close, antennae waving. You never knew where you might suddenly come across one in the groves, so even though I wasn't afraid of them, it became more difficult to do my work. I eventually had to give up.

There wasn't very much anyone could do except watch them work and try to guess what it was they were up to. There were heated arguments in the Lodge that second night, but nobody's explanation made sense. I felt strangely apart from it all, as if I were watching a movie about aliens in the park instead of the real thing. And so far, the official version seemed to be that this was just a local event, and certainly not terribly important outside California. The rest of the nation was used to weird stories coming out of this state.

On the third day, the accidents started. Two Guardsmen were sitting in a jeep parked just under an eroded section of bank that made a little cliff about six feet high, a few paces away from the aliens' silver egg. Bored with the lack of action, they began lobbing pine cones at the squirrels. There was a tremendous roar, and the bank—stable until then—poured down on them. They both almost suffocated under the tons of fine dirt that buried the jeep.

Soon after that, another young soldier, lovesick, carved his girlfriend's initials into a sequoia trunk right across from where the Xt'la were working. A huge rotted branch crashed down a hundred feet and killed him instantly.

There were other accidents, but these were the worst. They were "natural" occurrences, but it was hard not to suspect the aliens of being involved. It was too coincidental that they were always present at the scene of the crime. The level of fear amongst the humans rose till you could almost smell it. A

group of civilians demanded that the Guard do something—
anything. Immediately.

It's not surprising really that the nervous National Guard
captain in charge of what had been called "Operation Visitor"
decided to wipe out the Xt'la with an advanced, dimethyl dith-
iophosphate compound sprayed from a military crop-duster.
Obviously I protested when I heard this. Not only was it a
stupid idea, but it would surely damage the Big Trees' already
fragile ecosystem. I was overruled. Brian and I and Marie
Nguyen, the park's resident interpreter, had to watch through
the office window, locked indoors like naughty children.

The plane threaded its way carefully between the trees,
dropping its blanket of death, but the Xt'la seemed not to notice. Then when the plane came back on its second run, one of
the aliens looked up as if seeing the nuisance for the first time.
The plane exploded. That was all. They never touched it, just
looked up, and it burst into flame. Of course, there might have
been a malfunction of some sort....

But after that, command of "Operation Visitor" changed
hands. A lot of brass flew in from Washington, ready to make
proper contact with the aliens. Brian and I took bets on how
successful the newcomers would be, and I won. The Xt'la paid
no attention. Like it or not, the military found they had to be
patient and watch like the rest of us.

More of the park employees went home at that point. Why
didn't I? I said it was because I hadn't finished my research, but
really I had no place that was "home" anymore since my little
brother died. I'd given up the apartment we'd shared in San
Francisco. His books and records and scuba gear were stored
in one of those facilities near a freeway; I hadn't been able
to part with them yet. As for going back to the University, I

really didn't give a damn. It was the trees that mattered, not the degree.

Then the story leaked. The first of what became a steady stream of media vans bumped up the road in a cloud of dust. Brian and I were interviewed for the wire services, with military intelligence present to make sure we stayed with what had become the Official Version, from which all reference to the accidents had been deleted.

With all the traffic chaos of military vehicles and Winnebagos loaded down with reporters and TV transmitters, something was bound to happen, and it did. Somebody accidentally drove straight through a Xt'la. And so we discovered they were not really here at all. They were holograms. And maybe they had their scale wrong, and weren't seven feet tall after all. But they were building something—or at least, making sure something grew properly into something. I can't explain how a hologram can build a concrete article. That question troubled the NASA people too.

When the thing had finished growing, it looked like a transparent pyramid that was not quite solid, or like a carnival illusion made with mirrors. It shimmered. From a distance it almost seemed not to be there, a distortion from heat haze. Later on, we learned that inside—and the only way you could tell you'd passed through its insubstantial and shifting barriers was a stillness of the air—there was a thin, slightly convex screen. No keyboard stood in front of it, only a flat square piece of metal with four small, oval indentations. It floated unsupported in front of what was apparently a bench without legs. There was nothing behind the screen or under the metal square. No wires, no circuits, no obvious place for microchips.

Just the motionless screen suspended in air, the metal square, and the bench.

The holo Xt'la stood back and waited. NASA brought up equipment and cautiously checked the outside of the booth. Needles spun on dials, counters clicked, gauges measured. I stood with Marie, watching. Sunlight filtered down through the dark needles of the Giant Sequoias. A squirrel dashed across the clearing, stopped, eyed us speculatively, then disappeared up a tree. I watched it climb, noticing where the needles began to show the telltale fading of pollution sickness. Conifers are most susceptible to sulfur dioxide during early spring and summer when their needles are growing, toxicity being a function of the rate at which a plant absorbs. Brian came back from a conversation with one of the scientific team. "Their measurements make no sense," he told us.

"What's that mean?"

Brian grinned happily. "Who knows? We're dealing with one of Arthur C. Clarke's very advanced technologies."

"They obviously intend for us to use it in some way. What're we waiting for?"

"Could be a trap," Marie suggested. She was small and thin-featured, not much older than we were. But she seemed a rather private person, and we hadn't been close until the events in the park threw us together.

"If they wanted to destroy us they would've done it already," I argued.

Apparently the military types agreed. A youngish, prematurely gray-haired man in army fatigues stepped cautiously through the shifting planes of the pyramid and disappeared from our sight.

That was the next odd thing we learned. Although you could see through it to the trees beyond, anyone stepping inside became invisible. Two soldiers wearing gas masks and carrying machine-guns stood guard outside, nervously fingering triggers. What use they thought they would be against a giant hologram of an insect that could explode a plane by looking at it was never clear.

The thing was meant as a communicating device. When a human laid fingers in the indentations of the metal pad, the screen came to life. The Xt'la used images to convey meanings to us. Perhaps they couldn't produce the kind of sounds we could understand. Or maybe they didn't use language the way we do.

After the gray-haired man emerged safely, although puzzled, the NASA people took turns. Their reactions ranged from bewilderment to frustration. After several days of this — the Xt'la waiting patiently, antennae waving gently — a scientist made a breakthrough. It wasn't enough to sit and wait in front of the screen, he discovered. You had to participate in some way. It took a certain frame of mind, an openness, almost a meditative state really, and then the flow of chaotic images the screen produced began to make a kind of sense.

Not everyone was equally capable of achieving this communion. But some of the scientists did all right. And after a while Brian badgered them into letting Brian and me try. Marie refused to go near the thing.

About this time, something else happened. Reconnaissance planes flying over the park reported patches of electromagnetic disturbance that interfered with communications. Visual and radar picked up nothing, however. Whatever caused it failed to show on any of the spy devices whose job it was to hear and see everything. The extent of the mysterious effect was mapped by repeated flights crisscrossing the area, the pilots sending radio signals continuously to the ground, and the computers drawing maps of the silent zones.

What emerged was a dome-shaped force field spreading over Yosemite like an enormous bell-jar enclosing the trees, the humans and the Xt'la. It didn't happen all at once, of course, or else there would have been no outside communication at all. It grew like a diaphanous membrane. Naturally, the military brass were very concerned about this, but it was out of their control. They did manage to classify the information, so the media couldn't broadcast it and start a mass panic.

A lot of people's theories were upset by that finding. Marie was terrified. And Brian frowned over it for a while until his natural optimism reasserted itself. Well, I wasn't going anywhere, anyway.

Then it was finally my turn to sit on the bench the Xt'la had provided, put my fingers in the indentations—they were designed to fit the fingers of the left hand—and watch the screen. It was frightening at first, that stream of fractured, holographic images the screen produced, the assault of jewel colors like a shattered rainbow, the luminous fragments of recognizable scenes from our world all jumbled and shown simultaneously with bizarre shapes that represented nothing human eyes had ever seen. As if this confusion wasn't enough, there were layers within layers of images, like one color slide projected on top of another, only both slides were 3-D so you felt as if you were being pulled into them, rather than simply viewing them. Perhaps this is the way the world looks to an insect, or at least, an alien one.

A few minutes of this brought vertigo. The sensation was like plunging into raging water and going over one of the park's waterfalls. If you let yourself think about what you were doing, you wouldn't do it. And couldn't, for the device was designed for a level of communication that lay below conscious thought. As soon as I discovered that and stopped trying to make sense out of it, I began to get somewhere.

The NASA people questioned me at great length on how I did it, and I had to admit I didn't know. Perhaps it was a skill developed on the deck of *Rainbow Warrior III*, keeping watch under a cold, night sky, while humpbacks blew silver clouds of spray at the burning stars. Perhaps it was an understanding developed from long hours listening to them sing their slow, melancholy songs. More likely it was only because I'd given up lost causes like saving the whales when my little brother was killed by a whaler's harpoon gun. I had no expectations or illusions left.

The images the Xt'la sent were fragmented, multi-faceted as an insect's eyes. They were impossible for a human mind to deal with logically. I let them happen to me. There were no words in this communication; there weren't even any coherent ideas. There were only impressions, sensations, reactions to stimuli that my brain insisted on translating into thoughts because millions of years of evolution have taught human brains to force chaos into patterns that can be codified and dealt with. Some of the others with us under the Big Trees got a little of this. Brian got quite a lot. But I seemed to be the one who could do it best.

If it hadn't been for the feeling of being sucked into the vortex every time I laid my left hand on the metal plate, an experience that turned my stomach so that I frequently vomited when I stumbled out of the booth, I might even have thought

I was imagining the whole thing. In fact, imagining is as good a word as any to describe what happened.

The first thing I imagined was what they called themselves. There was a clicking, end-stopped sound in their name, then an oddly liquid syllable. "Xt'la" is close enough. The second thing was their mission. They'd come because of the Giant Sequoias. It was not just that the trees were second only to the bristle cones in longevity, and certainly the largest living things in the world. They were a rarity in a universe that swarmed with animal life. The Xt'la caused me to imagine that the Big Trees were intelligent. Not the kind of intelligence we could easily recognize, you have to understand! Sequoia thoughts were vast and slow and terrible, like their four-thousand-year-old lives. It wasn't a concept the military accepted too readily, and for once I couldn't blame them.

"Last year the largest sequoia died," I said. "This year the Xt'la arrived. They took the event more seriously than we did."

I would've liked to believe the Xt'la were right about the intelligence part; at least, for the first time in a long while, I was beginning to feel as if there might be some possibilities left in the world after all.

"A tree this old has certainly had time to develop some form of intelligence," Brian said.

We were sitting in the shade of a young tree, a mere one-thousand year baby. Marie stood a few paces away, arms folded over her thin chest, listening.

"Trouble is, trees don't display the level of electrical activity needed to send intelligent messages," I argued. "Trees don't even have nerve cells."

"There're more ways of sending messages than by using electrical impulses," Brian said. "Plant cells communicate with each other by using hormones."

"I know that, but—"

"You use the word communicate too loosely," Marie complained. She should know, of course, since she spent her days explaining why tourists from Japan and South America couldn't take souvenir pine cones home with them.

"I just don't see plant life possessing the number of connections—" I began.

"Your problem, Kate, is you're a pathologist," Brian said. "You're used to thinking what goes wrong, instead of what could go right. Why is plant intelligence such a crazy idea anyway? We know plants react to stimuli such as pain, and learn to avoid it."

"That's only a limited cell memory. Besides, intelligence needs the stimulus of varied sensory input to develop, and that pretty well demands hands and locomotion and—"

"How about whales and dolphins," he interrupted, "growing in an environment much more restricted than—"

"Yes. Okay," I said, memories of the beautiful, incomprehensible humpback songs filling my mind. "But don't you see? Thinking requires a brain with billions of cells."

"A brain's just a convenient place where all the neurons gather. How many cells total in a Giant Sequoia? Think of ants, Kate. Alone they're pretty much mindless. But a whole anthill full of ants achieves critical mass and acts purposefully. Shows intelligence. Not a brain worth counting among 'em. But together…"

"Maybe the Xt'la can communicate with a tree, but we're a long way from it," Marie said.

I wanted to believe, but I had to agree with Marie. Brian took out a pad and a pencil and scribbled something.

After a while he asked, "Do we know the rate at which sap travels?"

"Well, yes," I said. "I guess I could look that up."

"Good. And we know the average distance from root to crown. If we compare that with the rate messages are carried along the path of the sensory neurons to the human brain, and then factor in the relative lifespans of humans and sequoias—"

"Brian, this is absurd!"

"Who're we to say? The world is prodigal with life, and perhaps it is with intelligence too. Anyway, it explains why the Xt'la are building a dome. Their mission is to protect the intelligent sequoias from smog."

"And tourists walking too close to the trunks and bruising delicate roots? Not to mention the logging industry."

"I wonder what a tree could tell us if we could understand it?" Marie said. She walked rapidly away as if she were afraid she'd said too much.

"If I can wangle a little time on one of the computers, I'll do the calculations," Brian said.

Days went by. Nobody except Brian and Marie paid any attention to my imaginings. The politicians began arriving just about then. "Contact" became a political catchword, and the senators and the diplomats hurried to be photographed standing under the giant redwoods, smiling up at the giant alien holos. On any given day you could find half a dozen different nationalities present, Russian, Chinese, German, Cuban—they all came. I think some of them would have been far happier if the aliens had resembled bees or ants, insects we're accustomed to thinking of as useful or industrious. The diplomats brought their own translators with them, so Marie had nothing to do but hang around with us.

The Xt'la moved silently through the redwood groves on their unknown errands, and overhead the invisible dome grew toward completion. Sometimes you saw the holo of a Xt'la standing by a tree as if in communion with it, passing thin antennae up and down a centimeter or two from the rust-colored bark. There was a great deal of respect in this act, even a suggestion of worship.

"Appropriate," Brian commented. "You'd expect termites to have an appreciation of wood."

For some reason, the joke irritated me. "At least the Xt'la seem to care about other living things besides themselves."

Marie touched my arm gently. "I like the trees too, Kate."

I shook my head. "I can't explain."

"You don't have to," Brian said. "My people understand that idea very well."

His remark opened up a landscape of emotions I wasn't ready to explore just yet. "Did you ever wonder," I said, to change the subject, "whether they are giant termites after all? Maybe they thought we'd understand that image."

"Perhaps it's a matter of concepts that won't translate from one language to another," Marie said.

"Huh?" I'm not much of a linguist.

"There are thoughts I can think in Vietnamese that I can't think in English. Or Spanish, for that matter."

"For instance?"

"If I could say them in English, I'd be thinking about them, wouldn't I?"

"Gotcha!" Brian laughed. "Same thing for Navajo."

"Then we've got little hope of communicating with them," I said. "It's as bad as with the trees."

The President arrived with the Secretary-General of the UN just about then, and there was a lot of hoopla about man finally talking to the rest of the universe. But they were disappointed. The Xt'la device worked only one-way. No one who tried to get questions answered, technology explained, treaties considered, got anywhere. The Xt'la simply ignored them as if human concerns were too petty to bother with. Or maybe they just didn't understand what all the fuss was about.

The slow growth of the dome to save the Giant Sequoias went on all through August. The weather was unusually hot and still. Grass turned brown, the park's smaller streams dried up, and birds fell silent in the heat. More TV crews came, and soon someone noticed that some parts of the dome now made a barrier at ground level that could not be penetrated.

Until then, I suppose, we'd all thought it was like the shimmering, ethereal walls of the communication booth. But this was different. Automobile engines stopped at a border nobody could see. People found themselves pressing against an invisible, impermeable wall. Equipment had to be hauled in over alternate routes, often taking extra days in the process. Sometimes these routes closed overnight as the dome grew. The crews filmed their specials and seemed glad to leave. The rest of the park personnel, except for Marie Nguyen and Brian Ramos, scrambled out. NASA and the military lost interest in the Xt'la device, once they realized the seriousness of the dome.

Day after day either Brian or I sat in front of the screen, letting the images flood our minds. Gradually, gradually, complex patterns assembled themselves that might almost have been called chains of reasoning. Mind, we came to imagine, was the reason the universe existed, the first cause and the ultimate blossoming of everything. Mind was the universe explaining itself to itself. The images flowed dreamlike into our minds, small cells in the universal intelligence, things for which there were no names in our languages but that existed somewhere.

On our planet too, so many things we'd never considered important, and therefore never invented words for them. And some forms of intelligence on Earth were much older than ours, and different. Primitive— No, that's not the right word. Elemental. Integral. These forms were rare, because they usually lost ground to the faster, separated intelligence that mammals evolved as a result of having to make quick decisions when fleeing from predators.

"The Gaia hypothesis?" Brian wondered.

The three of us were sitting in front of the fire in the Lodge, halfway through September, and the evenings were cooling off.

"The idea of planetary unity giving rise to planetary consciousness," he continued. "A self-regulating system, perhaps, working on the vast, slow time-scale of the universe, monitoring its condition and adapting. Only, now the other kind of intelligence, ours, is moving too fast for it, threatening it."

"Gobbledygook!" Marie said. She stood up quickly and went out of the Lodge.

"Why wouldn't a translator be interested in language problems?"

"She's better at practice than theory," Brian said.

"It doesn't explain why she's such a grouch."

"Maybe she's thinking of her childhood in Vietnam. And she sees the Xt'la as a kind of buggy Red Chinese?"

I laughed. "I'm the only one of the three of us who had a normal American childhood."

"You think growing up in California is normal Americana?" Brian queried, wide-eyed.

"Poor little rich white-trash and all that," I said.

"With a conscience," Brian said, not teasing anymore.

But not as brave as my brother, I wanted to tell him.

The image of a passing Xt'la glowed eerily in the moonlight outside the big Lodge window.

Brian lowered his voice. "I think I know why we found no trace of their ship. They make mind jumps across the universe."

"Oh, come on!" But my physics wasn't good enough to know if he was joking or not.

The next morning, the general in charge decided the dome was a threat to national security. He ordered the immediate evacuation of everybody, civilians and military. He talked about moving in nuclear weapons, and there was a furious debate over how much fallout blowing up the dome could be expected to generate. Nobody questioned that the Big Trees would have to be sacrificed in this attempt to destroy aliens who weren't really there anyway. I guess I could understand his paranoia. The Xt'la never explained anything. Their "communication device" wasn't exactly communicating anything sensible. And they'd destroyed one of our planes by means we didn't comprehend. But that doesn't excuse what he proposed.

Maybe it was just talk on the general's part, but I couldn't take it anymore. Surely there'd been enough killing? We'd eliminated the humpbacks and we were working on the rest of the cetaceans. Elephants were almost gone from Africa. If what the Xt'la had said about sequoia intelligence was true, then the military were considering murdering the trees. I sat in the Xt'la's booth for the last time, seething with anger. I had to do something, but I didn't know what.

The shifting patterns of images were different this time, like dreams. I caught fragments of myself and Brian and Marie underneath the Big Trees, like photographs of us that had been cut up into tiny pieces and inserted into a kaleidoscope. There was a meaning to it, I was certain. The Xt'la wanted us to do something. But why us? And what? It didn't make any sense.

As soon as I stopped trying to make sense of it, I knew. We must refuse to be evicted from the park. We knew the redwood groves better than the soldiers. We could slip away at night and then evade them easily enough when patrols scoured the park looking for stragglers. And we were the only ones in the park who cared; somehow the Xt'la knew that.

"But why must we do this?" Marie argued when I told them. "What good will come of it?"

"At the very least it'll buy time," Brian conceded. "They won't nuke the park if they think we're somewhere inside."

I knew better. The bastards who killed my brother knew he was in the way of their harpoons. "It's a definite risk. I won't lie about that."

Marie's small face was tight with fear. "You haven't been in a war zone, Brian. It's not a game. In war, they don't care about civilians."

Now it was my turn to touch her arm. She was shivering.

"I am very scared," she said.

But she didn't want to be left out. We waited in the Lodge until almost midnight, sitting on our suitcases and bedrolls as if we intended to follow orders. Outside, stars glimmered beyond the dome. When no one was paying attention to us, we made a run for it. The patrols searched for us the next day, but they never found us, hidden deep in the groves. After a while, the general made the decision to abandon us, but he withheld the nukes.

As if the aliens had been waiting for this, the dome closed over, shutting us in and everyone else out. Then the Xt'la disappeared too. But their device remained at the foot of the second largest sequoia.

It's odd now—days later, but I've lost count—standing here at the edge, seeing all those faces pressed against the outside of the transparent dome. Day after day they come, as if they're keeping a vigil: soldiers and housewives, scientists from Silicon Valley, schoolchildren, farmworkers, and local councilmen. Their expressions are puzzled, wistful. I wonder what the Official Version says about this now?

Marie says it makes her feel like a rat forced to run a maze while the experimenters look on. Brian says he thinks they're waiting to see if we die of starvation, but of course there are all those army rations the National Guard trucked in. Marie says she meant the Xt'la.

There's something we have to do before the food runs out. The Xt'la chose us, three who cared about the sequoias: a physicist, a linguist, and a botanist. We have to learn the language of the Big Trees. Because there's something else the Xt'la told us before they left. Without the mutual recognition and active co-operation of two or more intelligent species, there's no way to understand the multidimensionality of the universe.

When races put their minds together, their view of life becomes stereoscopic. Alone, each species is locked in its little house of mirrors, seeing only its puny self reflected in the world around it, even if that world reaches out through radiotelescopy to include the farthest galaxies. The Xt'la taught this is the universe's imperative: combine the intelligence on your own planet first. A race that doesn't communicate with the other intelligences on its home world will never leave its solar system.

Brian explains the possibilities this way. "We understand four dimensions. Length and breadth, height and time. But physicists speculate that the universe is not bound by these four alone. So we're handicapped, blind pilots trying to maneuver around the crowded air lanes with faulty instruments. What if other intelligent species—especially such dissimilar ones as humans and Giant Sequoias—don't know the same four dimensions? What if two species together can comprehend not four dimensions, not even four plus four, but four times four? Imagine, sixteen dimensions opened to us through a pooling of mind! Or think of three species, and sixty-four—"

We've lost the humpback's view already. But there's more to it than that. A race that doesn't respect the other forms of life that share its planet may not be allowed to survive. The Xt'la see us rather like we see destructive bacteria. Right now our record's bad, and we're in quarantine, not allowed to take our contagion elsewhere in the galaxy. The sentence could be worse. We could be exterminated, wiped out, like the National Guard captain tried to do to the Xt'la.

The Xt'la gave us one last chance. Brian and Marie and I are a Xt'la experiment in communication, a chance to learn what our own planet has to teach. I'm writing this down in case we succeed.

Marie noticed it first. The smell of things has changed in here. Not that the air is foul or anything, but *Sequoia Giganteum* seems to be giving off a different odor now. Pleasant enough in small doses, the way a skunk's odor is only repulsive when you're overpowered at close quarters, but also soporific. It's becoming difficult to operate machinery, as if we were drugged.

Brian gave up tinkering with the computers. He couldn't seem to remember how they worked.

I have a hunch the Xt'la taught the trees to do it. I don't think it's dangerous, but it's hard to explain why I think so. The point is, we're not supposed to think, in English or Vietnamese or Navajo. Language itself is what gets in the way. The universe is older than language. Being is what counts, not making words about it. Perhaps dreaming comes closer to the truth.

The Xt'la's device still works, although the images are stranger now, immense and awful, like a sequoia's dreams. Marie says there are concepts here we may never be able to translate. Mammalian intelligence works best under pressure. We have to stay here in the dome until we find the answers. Because the alternative, if the Xt'la experiment fails, truly is unthinkable.

NOT THIS TIDE

Oslo, December 2035

Embarrassing enough that the press were hailing her as the first centenarian to be awarded the prize. Limping across a stage to accept it would never do. Worse still—forgetting what she wanted to say. Frustrated with herself, she turned from the hotel's window and its grand view of snow falling through shafts of golden light onto the gathering crowds below.

Time to look over her speech again. She'd put her extensive notes somewhere in the hotel room when she first arrived, record of a long life of activism. There was a time when Mary hadn't needed notes to give a speech, but lately she feared her mind was becoming increasingly dreamy. The only paper she saw now was the note from her niece, wailing that the promised baby sitter had let her down and she'd be late. Surely the hotel concierge could take care of the problem? In any case, those children were old enough to be trusted on their own for a couple of hours.

Where had she put the notes? Gabriel would've scolded that she hadn't committed them to some form of electronic storage. Of all her offspring, and her offspring's offspring, she'd felt most bonded to this one. In any case, there was something about writing the old-fashioned way with a pen that appealed to her heart.

As if thinking about her grandson called him into existence, the hotel's comm system pinged. Her heart jolted as she read the name of her caller. The small control panel that had appeared urged her to touch a button, and a small hologram of her tall, beautiful grandson, stood on the table before her.

"See, *Abuelita*," Gabriel said, smiling at her. "Modern technology isn't so very awful after all."

"Worth it to see you as well as hear you, my dear."

"I'm so sorry I couldn't get away to be with you—we were working right up to the last minute. I want you to be the first to know."

His expression was joyous, bubbling over. She couldn't make out the room behind him. He was a post-doc at Princeton; she really didn't need to see lab equipment to know that.

She had a sudden thought—maybe he was calling to tell her he was finally engaged? She'd hoped so much to see that!

"Sit down, *Abuelita*. This is astounding news."

"Tell me, Gabe, before I have to rush away."

"Yes, I understand. Such a wonderful honor—you really deserve it."

A slight tap on her door and Catalina looked in. "Mama— We need to be ready in about an hour!"

If her daughter saw who it was, she'd want to talk too, and she wasn't ready to share Gabriel, even with his mother.

"Have you reviewed your notes?" Catalina came into the room.

Agitated, she tried to block Catalina's view of the comm unit and its displayed hologram but succeeded only in knocking the thing off the table onto the floor. The hologram vanished.

"Ah! Now look what I've done!"

"It's not broken, Mama," Catalina said. "Besides you don't have time right now for chatting. Do you need my help with your notes?"

Irritated, she waved Catalina away.

Might as well do something while she waited. Reviewing her notes was a good idea. Where had she put them?

Small lights followed her around the hotel room as she searched. The notes weren't on the coffee table, nor in the drawers of the bedside chest. She opened the suitcase still on the folding stand. Empty. Surely she could do this without notes? Doctor Mary Aragon had plenty of experience, often in the heat of crisis! Yet in many ways, she was still a creature of the twentieth century she'd been born in, only reluctantly giving in to the advances that swept over her, a tidal wave of technology engulfing her stubborn insistence on taking care of herself without help. Yet that was nonsense! Hadn't everything good and useful in the world been accomplished with the support and goodwill of others? Wasn't that to have been the theme of her speech tonight? Surely she could remember enough to give her speech?

Instead of a flood of memories, there was a sudden terrifying blank in her mind. She slumped into a chair that conformed to her contours.

The sensation ebbed slowly.

Nerves jangling, she sat stiffly in the gilded chair by the window. Outside, the street lamps made golden confetti of the snow. Above them, the dark sky glittered with helicars arriving early for the ceremony. How strange to be in this room, in this city, looking back over a long life of dangers overcome and success achieved, love found and taken away too soon, children and grandchildren, given and taken away.

And now, at the last, this great honor.

London, December 1944

When the air raid siren wails, Rosemary wants to switch the bedside lamp on but it's blackout rules. Even a little bit of light seeping through the blackout curtains might be helpful to Jerry, the Air Raid Protection warden says.

Mum pushes the door open. "Come on."

She's carrying the pink dressing gown that used to be Margaret's.

"Come on, dopey!" Margaret is already dressed in a pair of gray slacks with a gray blanket draped over her shoulders.

Rosemary sticks her tongue out at her sister. Margaret, being older, gets to have one of the two proper bedrooms in the flat. Rosemary has to make do with a tiny one that Daddy made out of a space at the top of the house.

Mum makes a big thing of pulling the sleeves the right way around in the pink dressing gown before she hands it to her. She knows this is because Mum's pretending to be calm. Rosemary can spot panic in everybody. She takes her time tying the cord around her waist, adjusting the length of its big tassels. That done, she drags her special little suitcase from under the bed. It's heavy, so many of her best bits and bobs in it.

"Mum!" Margaret shrieks. "Tell her we don't have time for that."

"Now, Margaret," Mum says. "But do hurry up a little bit, Rosemary."

Perhaps she should've left the piece of shrapnel out? No, shrapnel isn't what's weighting it down. It's the big book about England's kings and queens that says PUBLIC LIBRARY inside the cover. She especially likes reading about Queen Elizabeth and looking at the pictures of the queen with her courtiers. The library has been closed for two weeks now, since the blast from a near-miss weakened the walls. And she dare not lose the book because Margaret says they'll come and put her in prison for stealing if she does. Even in wartime, Margaret says, they're strict about things like that.

She holds on tight to her suitcase and lets Mum tug her through the doorway and down the stairs. Mum opens the front door, and Rosemary sees the neighbor, Mrs Banbury, heading into the concrete shelter on Marigold Road. Mrs Banbury holds her horrible stinky cat Tomkins in her arms. The ARP Warden is standing by the shelter's door. He waves a finger at them to hurry up. A dim light shines out from the shelter.

She stares up at the sky, crisscrossed with searchlights. They're supposed to be finding Jerry planes, but so far all they've found is another barrage balloon floating above London. Anti-aircraft guns thump in the distance. She likes to think that could be Daddy fighting Jerries, but Margaret always tells her that's wrong.

"Hurry up. You'll get us all killed!" Margaret says.

One of the bulbs up on the ceiling is out. She has to squint to see anything. Mum pulls her inside and bangs the door shut. It smells of cat pee and mothballs in here. Nasty smell. Margaret goes over to Tomkins and starts petting him and making silly baby noises. The cat closes its huge yellow eyes and purrs.

Two other people who are always there in the shelter, are huddled up in blankets, old ladies who never speak to Rosemary because they don't like children. Rosemary thinks they're witches.

"Here," one of the witches says to Mum. "Have a cup of tea, Mrs Forrest." She holds out a thermos bottle and a tin cup.

"Have a biscuit," the other one says, holding out a battered old tin.

Margaret takes one, but Rosemary shakes her head.

There aren't any other kids in the shelter because all the ones on her street have been evacuated. She doesn't mind. She doesn't want to go to the country anyway. It's full of bats and spiders.

Mum has her knitting out. She's always knitting something or other for the troops.

The muffled *Bang-bang, Bang* of the anti-aircraft guns begins. Then a bigger explosion that shakes the brick walls of the shelter. Brick dust drifts down from the ceiling. Even Rosemary gets scared by this sometimes, but she won't let anyone know. Mrs Banbury's smelly old moggy runs hissing under the bunk bed she's sitting on, its fur standing straight up so it looks like the broom the chimney sweep uses when he comes to their house.

"Close one," Mum says.

Her voice is calm, but her face has faded a bit, so Rosemary knows Mum must be afraid.

The shelter's dim light goes out. One of the witches screeches.

"It's one of them new doodlebugs," the other witch says. "Got no pilot makes them worse."

She isn't sure why not having a pilot makes a bomb worse, but nobody takes the time to explain this.

"I don't know why we bother coming out here," Margaret says in a whiny voice. "We're going to get hit by a buzz bomb sometime anyway."

"Not," she says.

"Are."

"Stop it," Mum says. "Bad enough to have Jerry trying to kill us without you two squabbling."

The light flickers back on again.

"Why can't we stay in our beds, Mum?" Rosemary asks.

"You know why," Mum says. "It's safer here."

"Jimmy Green says people get bombed in the bomb shelters too."

Margaret says, "You believe everything that guttersnipe tells you?"

"Margaret," Mum says. "Mind your language."

"Well, he is," Margaret says.

"Isn't. He's my friend."

"I won't tell you girls again—"

More banging and thumping outside. But it sounds like it's happening under a blanket, so Rosemary knows the bombs aren't falling near them.

The all-clear siren starts up.

English Channel, December 1944

A Yorkshireman gave Harry Forrest a quick tour of U7, the Maunsell Fort in the English Channel he'd been assigned to, home of the First Anti-Aircraft Regiment, Royal Artillery.

He'd seen charts of the fort's floor plans already, a central control unit with six smaller outlying constructions connected by steel mesh bridges, but the reality was stark. The main tower in the fort, central control for all seven, had two floors and housed officers' quarters. The rest of the men were spread out in quarters in each of the other towers; more than a hundred men and the NCOs crowded in the fort all together. Around the central structure, six other rooms housed the guns, four 3.7 inch Browning gun towers, a single tower housing the bigger

Bofors gun, and a searchlight tower. They were joined by flimsy-looking steel cable and wire mesh walkways.

"If'n tha's lucky," the corporal said, "tha might get t' sleep t'night. Sometimes, nowt 'appens, an' even t' crew except for t' watch gets to catch up."

The sleeping quarters were lit by blue bulbs so the men's eyes wouldn't have difficulty adjusting to the dark if they were called on deck for duty. They smelled of sweat and tobacco smoke, and the sharp green smell of the sea coming in through an open window. He had a small framed photo of his daughters at the beach on their last holiday together, Margaret eating an ice cream cone, Rosemary riding a small donkey. His younger daughter had inherited his eye color but was fair-haired like her mother. He put the photo on the narrow shelf that ran the length of his bunk.

He stashed the Enfield rifle he'd been issued against the wall in the corner, wondering if he'd get to use it out here. In basic training in Colchester, he'd become a bit of a sharp-shooter; many's the paper target he'd blown to shreds. Rifles wouldn't be much use against actual aircraft. He was so tired his muscles cramped as he climbed up, yet he couldn't sleep.

Even knowing the towers were firmly anchored to the sea floor, he had the sensation of movement. As soon as his eyes closed he felt the Channel rise and fall under the supply boat again, lulling mere humans with a false sense of security. He came from an island full of sea-going folk, but the closest he'd come to the sea was the family's annual week at the Isle of Wight, and the ritual paddle, trousers rolled to the knees, water lapping mildly at his ankles.

He wondered how they were doing. At least the raids weren't as bad as they'd been at the beginning of the war. *Keep them safe, please....*

And just who was that directed at, he wondered, being that he wasn't a religious man. He remembered his father who'd served in the Great War saying, "No atheists in the trenches." He wished he did believe in a god who could be persuaded to end the war soon.

Through the small square window above the bunk he saw a patch of sky, stars bright against the darkness. The wind that had buffeted the sea earlier had broken up the clouds, leaving a sky through which a Kraut might fly his Junkers or his Dornier up the Thames to target London. If he got the chance, he'd be delighted to blow one of those Kraut bombers to kingdom come. He'd enjoy blasting them out of the sky and watching the fragments crash into the Channel.

Wide awake now, he gave up the attempt to sleep. Nobody on the top deck when he emerged, bundled in a waterproof field jacket, and khaki wool scarf Alice had knitted for him. The air was biting cold with a hint of machine oil. Except for the low hum of the fort's diesel machinery and an occasional splash, a swell breaking against a concrete pillar, or a fish jumping, the night was silent.

Two steps from where he stood, the tower housed a Browning, small but a workhorse. The tower was connected to the central control tower by a tubular steel cable and wire mesh walkway. On the other side of the control tower, another steel bridge led to a tower from which the enormous snout of the big Bofors jutted, and beyond that central tower, radiating out, four more towers like this one. He knew that gun well from his training, knew its sound and its recoil, its strengths and its occasional flaws. He liked the sense of power firing the Bofors gave him, but he could handle the smaller ones too.

"Fired the big one before, have you?"

A man emerged from the shadows against the wall. Tall, slender build, angular face like a half-starved monk. Impossible to tell rank. Harry shrugged, unwilling to commit. You learn fast not to answer questions in the army before you know the reason for asking.

"Might have."

"Name's Frank." The man held out a hand.

The shielded safety lamp overhead gave just enough light for Harry to note the man was only a little younger than himself.

"Only got here a day ago myself. Welcome to Uncle 7. That's our affectionate name for this fort. Maunsell Fort U7's too much of a mouthful."

"Makes sense." He held out his own hand. "Harry Forrest."

An alarm rattled. Searchlights based on one of the towers jumped into the patchwork sky. The alarm cut out, and the Tannoy barked orders. His heart pounded. Out here, on the Channel, they were totally exposed.

"Buzz bombs!" somebody yelled.

A sergeant who had field glasses said, "No. These are the real buggers again."

In the sweeping lights, Harry saw the oncoming planes aiming for the open road of the Thames. He recognized the silhouettes, bombers capable of a screaming dive to drop death on terrified civilians. The very same monsters that had done so much damage to London in the early days of the war. The rumble of big engines filled the air—he felt it like a tidal wave of hatred in his belly.

Then—the deep-throated boom of the Bofors getting a line on its approaching target.

He hadn't been given orders yet so had no idea what he should do. He watched the gunners load shells into the smaller gun. The air filled with reverberations. A sergeant shouted something he couldn't hear. Men scrambled to their positions. One of the Browns chattered angrily from the next tower over, another joined in. He felt the urge to do something, but in the army, doing something without orders was as bad as not doing something when you did have orders.

He squinted up at the approaching horde. Smaller shapes separated from the heavy shapes of the bombers. Messerschmitts, the German fighting dogs that guarded the big boys. The smaller guns would take them on. A round of Bofors 40 mm tracers shot up like a flight of arrows. The big gun boomed again.

A low flying Messerschmitt peeled away, engine whining, smoke pouring out of its engine as it plunged into the water.

"You! Private!" The sergeant appeared beside him and screamed into his ear. "Gunner hit. Take his position on the Browning!"

His ears roared with the sound of the oncoming planes and the answering guns. He raced across the vibrating metal bridge to the control tower, on to the next gun tower, took position on the 3.7, slapped on the earphones. Smoke drifted over the water, a smell like spent matches. Another soldier loaded shells, his face flat in the moonlight.

Radar predictions of the enemy's flight streamed in, orienting the gun. He peered through the range finder and found the target. The gun had to be aimed ahead of the target, where it would be, not where it was now. His hand shook as he reached for the trigger—the Pig's Ear, gunners called it because of its shape. A geyser erupted due west of Uncle 7. Another Kraut not going to make it to London tonight.

As soon as his hand touched the gun he was calm. Streams of calculations he'd learned flowed through his mind—speed of enemy craft, speed of shells, direction. A gunner's greatest problem: prediction. Radar helped, yes, but he had a gunner's native belief the human brain was better. The first of the approaching Junkers was his. He fired. The sound deafened him. He fired again. And again. The gun spat spent shells out by his feet. The bombers kept on coming.

A hail of bullets spattered across the deck. One of the bombers was almost overhead. He hurriedly repositioned the gun and fired again. The Brownings might be small but they were as vicious as bulldogs in a fight. In the confusion of flash and smoke he couldn't see what happened to it. Had he hit it? It headed lopsidedly for the water, engines whining like a giant mosquito. He hadn't missed.

And then—he had no idea how much time had passed— their part in the current battle was over. The remains of the German force headed up the river. Maybe a gunner onshore at the mouth of the estuary would catch them first. He saw flower-like bursts of flame in the distance as the estuary units came into action.

"Stand down," the sergeant ordered.

He had difficulty hearing, deafened by the guns. If he'd been on duty, he would've worn ear-protectors. There hadn't been time to get any. U7 had taken down two fighters and one bomber tonight. He'd made his first kill. There was one casualty. The gunner he'd replaced had taken a bullet in his head.

"Why've they gone back to manned craft, Sarge?" somebody asked.

"Beats me," the sergeant said. "But makes no difference. Kill 'em all anyway."

Once the adrenaline subsided, Harry was knackered. He made his way unsteadily back to his own tower and down the inside stairs to his sleeping quarters. The bunk sagged when he sat on it. His heart still raced, and his skin was damp with cold sweat in the aftermath of the violence he'd taken part in. Drills at the gunnery school, no matter how realistic, were nothing compared to the shock of the real thing.

He'd killed a German pilot. What the hell? That was what war was about, wasn't it? That's what they'd trained him to do. Kill or be killed. One less devil on his way to bomb London.

In the dim blue light, legs dangling over the edge, he pulled out his smokes; his hand shook as he lit the cigarette. Us or them. That was always the way of war, winners and losers. It might've taken the government a while to get to him, but Harry Forrest was going to be one of the winners.

London, December 1944

Next morning, Saturday, Rosemary sets out after breakfast. It's very cold this morning. The sharp smell of wet, charred timber hangs on the air, and small specks of soot and grit drift past the front door. There are few people on the street, but she sees Jimmy Green hurrying in the opposite direction. His dad has a fruit and veg barrow down the market and sometimes Jimmy has to help out. He sticks his tongue out at her. She ignores him and walks right past.

It's a game the kids play after every raid. Whose house is still there? Sometimes, it's *who* is still there, too. She passes a group of three houses that got bombed a month ago and aren't interesting anymore.

There's smoke in the sky, but she can't see where it's coming from; the sky is too cloudy. She turns at the corner where the pub is with the name she's always liked, *Pig and Whistle*. Today it has a new sign on the chalkboard by the open front door. HITLER CAN'T BEAT US! An ARP warden stands in the doorway, talking to the landlord, who's just opened the pub for the morning hours.

She sees a small piece of shrapnel on the road and darts out to collect it. Jimmy Green told her shrapnel comes from Jerry planes that have been blown up in the sky, but Margaret says it's just bits of anti-aircraft shells that have fallen down. Margaret thinks she knows everything.

She finds the new bomb site quickly, halfway down the street, a house just like theirs. It looks as if a giant baby has grown tired of playing with a stack of bricks and flattened them with an angry fist. The chimney is all that's still standing. Three firemen in tall Wellington boots, their faces tired and grimy, are picking through the ashes, and a small group of men in long rubber coats is standing on the rubble arguing over something and waving their arms.

She's missed the most exciting part. No ambulances. No bodies. Or perhaps this wasn't the worst part of the raid last night, and everybody is somewhere else. One good thing is Jimmy Green isn't here to beat her at finding anything—if there's anything to be found. Now she has a new worry. What if he's found somewhere more exciting?

She'd like to get closer, stand on the rubble like the firemen, maybe find some bigger shrapnel. Or maybe something much better. Perhaps a dead body? Or even part of one would be good. A bobby stands guard on the site, which has been cordoned off with tape. An old man with a tin helmet and an armband is pointing to something she can't see. He turns, and she recognizes him, the ARP warden who's always giving them lectures about accidentally sending messages to Jerry because their blackout curtains aren't tight enough. Some women with scarves over their hair curlers lean together discussing what's happened. She recognizes a couple of neighbors. If they see her, she knows they'll tell tales to Mum.

Skirting a fire engine that nobody's paying attention to right now, she picks up a chunk of brick and heaves it. The bobby turns at the thud, and Rosemary ducks under the tape unseen and walks right up to the edge of the rubble. First thing she notices is that the bomb site is still warm and smelly close up. She covers her nose.

She knows the family that live in this house. There's a girl her own age. Rosemary's seen Joan in church. Joan's mum didn't want her to be evacuated either. She tries to feel sorry about what's probably happened to Joan, but it's like her feelings are shut away like the library book locked in the suitcase with the lump of shrapnel.

She waits to see if the firemen will bring out any bodies. She'd like to be able to top Jimmy Green's stories with some of her own.

"What you doing here, little gel? It's too dangerous for kids." The bobby has come up behind her.

"I wanted to see for myself," she says. "Nobody tells me anything. Except Jimmy Green, and he makes stuff up."

The bobby laughs and pats her on the head. She doesn't like it when grownups do that. "Not very pretty, innit? Still, nobody died this time, thank the Lord."

"When's this war going to be over, then?"

The bobby pushes his tall helmet back and scratches a spot on his forehead. "Better find yourself a gypsy if you want an answer to that. Run along now, there's a good gel."

She watches him pick his way back over the rubble, sees him stop to talk to a fireman holding a dripping hose. She stands patiently for a long time, first on one foot, then on the other, but nothing exciting happens, so she turns to go home.

Something small and shiny on the pavement catches her eye, and she bends to retrieve it. A coin. *See a penny pick it up, all the day you'll have good luck.* This coin is only worth half a penny.

She turns the ha'penny over and sees the picture on the back. Sir Francis Drake's ship, the *Golden Hind.* There's a picture of that ship with Sir Francis on it in the library book. She folds the coin carefully into her handkerchief and puts it into her pocket.

English Channel, December 1944

Harry had been deployed to the fort so fast he hadn't had time to write his weekly letter home. An hour before he had to go on night duty—might as well use it.

Not that he could write very much without attracting the censor's penknife. Some of the men in the barracks made a game of seeing what they could find to say that wouldn't attract the censor's sharp blade treatment. The answer was, not much. He picked up a pencil—pens were pretty much useless, too much of a problem getting ink—and began:

Dearest Alice,

I've been relocated since I last wrote—which might explain my lateness in writing—

He broke off. Would that pass the censor? He wasn't saying from where or to where, but you never knew. He decided to leave it in.

I'm still getting settled but doing fine. Our quarters aren't posh, but they'll do.

Prevented by the censors from writing about bringing the Kraut bombers down the other night, he ought to write about things he and Alice shared a liking for. A great flock of shore birds that had passed over looking like a flying shawl—Seabirds would indicate he was on or near the Channel. He decided to leave the birds out.

The afternoon light coming through the square windows jittered across the metal walls, reflecting off a choppy sea. Stone cold day out on the Channel. Two weeks to go before Christmas. The handful of men who were lucky enough to have leave made plans and bartered with their mates for cigarette rations to take home as gifts.

We get a ration of 40 cigs a week, and Woodbines are fourpence for 20. What do you think of that? Not too bad. I'll bring some home on my next leave.

On-shore, the ration hadn't been so generous. Maybe a spy would figure out from that where he was? He left it in. Give the censor something to do.

And one bar of chocolate a week. I'll save them up. Meg and Rosie will like that. He thought for a moment, rubbed it out and wrote *Margaret and Rosemary*. Alice didn't like nicknames, even affectionate ones. The sharp pencil threatened to make a hole in the flimsy paper where he'd erased the names. A memory came of his daughters, snuggled up with him on the settee while he read them a bedtime story, or maybe one of Kipling's poems.

He glanced at his watch. Better hurry this up. There really wasn't much he could say.

The news on the radio in the fort's recreation room indicated that the nightly flood of bombing raids on London that occurred at the beginning of the war had slowed. So that was a comfort. He'd often worried they'd made the wrong choice, not packing the kids off to some farm in the country with the other evacuees.

They don't keep us nose to the grindstone all the time, he wrote. *We have a chance to do all kinds of activities in a special recreation room. We can play darts, have a sing-along around the piano, paint, learn to embroider or knit—*

A couple of the lucky shore-bound men were taking things they'd made in the rec room home as Christmas gifts. Nothing else he could say. Let the censor snip out the bits he didn't like. He signed it, *Your loving husband, Harry.*

"Harry Forrest. Hello." Frank stood in the doorway, his head cocked to one side.

"Haven't seen you around. Started to think maybe—"

"That I'd taken a round?" Frank came fully into the bunk room. "You don't get rid of me so easily. Been occupied. You know how it is in the army."

The man's eyes were an unusual color, a grayish green that his grandmother called "moss on the north side of an elm tree." Bit of a toff, judging by his accent, but probably harmless. Older than himself. The government was really scraping the bottom of the barrel for fighting men these days.

"I didn't catch your surname," he said.

"It's Smith." Frank laughed. "Improbable, really, isn't it?"

"Most common name in the kingdom, I should think." But not a name found much in the gentry. And if it was, they'd have pronounced it *Smythe*.

Frank shrugged. "Come on, I want to show you something."

A bitter wind scoured the deck under a low gray sky. The sea rolled and broke up against the fort's legs. The scent of fish and ozone was strong. The sun disappeared, and night settled fast over the fort.

"See that chap on the Bofors tower?" Frank pointed. "On the platform just below the building? Know what he's doing?"

Harry shook his head.

"He's fishing."

"Why's he doing that?"

"Why does anyone fish? To catch his own dinner, I imagine. A lot of chaps do it when they're off duty and the weather allows."

"Anything worth catching out there?" To be honest, much as he loved a good fry-up of fish and chips, he had the city man's usual lack of knowledge about how it came to be on his plate.

"I'll say! Cod. Halibut—"

"Better than the tinned herring they served last night."

Frank laughed.

Overhead, a vee of planes made its way out to sea. He recognized the shapes in the gathering dusk, American bombers heading to the German rail-yards on the continent. The rumble of their engines drifted down to the men on the fort.

"Did you know that a bomber pilot flies a limited number of missions before his number's up?" Frank asked. "Something like two or three. The odds are stacked against them. They're all young men, too. Rather a waste of life, don't you think?"

"You seem to know a lot about it."

"I like to stay informed. Anyway, it's not classified info."

Maybe not, but he hadn't heard that grim statistic. "With a bit of luck, we might blast the damn Krauts to kingdom come. Finish this bloody war!"

Frank studied his face for a moment. "This Channel has seen a lot of wars. What's the possibility of this being the last?"

"How am I supposed to answer that?"

"Francis Drake defeated the Spanish Armada here, you know."

"Yes."

"He was vastly outnumbered, but he took the victory."

"Every schoolchild knows that!"

Frank gave him an odd, sideways look. "Do they still teach that in school?"

Arrogant twit, assuming a state school couldn't be as good as his aristocratic Public School. "Of course they do!"

Frank looked thoughtful for a moment. "But really, Harry, don't underestimate the Axis powers. A lot of nasty, unsettling things still to come." Then he added, "Just guessing, of course."

Harry glanced at his watch with the luminous hands. "Time for me to report for duty. Assigned to the Bofors tonight."

"Odd thing, war, isn't it?"

"Sorry?"

"We get to find out how what we think we've been fighting for isn't what matters at all."

"I'm afraid you've lost me."

"Getting ahead of myself," Frank said. "I'm turning in for the night. Tally ho!"

Oslo, December 2035

Much of her childhood was now a merciful blur. What she did remember was long evenings with her father after the war, talking about pacifism, his hopes for the newly founded United Nations. Her father's example had made sure she'd grow up on fire to make a difference too. She'd chosen Cambridge to prepare her for work on conflict resolution, a career that had taken her all over the world.

All so long ago!

One day, in her early-thirties, she'd been standing on a barren hill in Sub-Saharan Africa, watching the headman of the local tribe haggle with two German engineers over the best place to prospect for hidden water. Sand stung her cheeks, made its way up her nostrils and into her lungs. The argument had been going on for hours. They were hardly aware she was even there.

As soon as water began to percolate up, the headman turned his attention to fending off the demands of a rival tribe, a quarrel that could easily blow up into bloodshed. This uneasy truce between the water-hungry desert dwellers was only temporary. Hostilities, jealousies, old tribal rivalries, not much had changed in centuries, except for the influx of modern technology that promised to solve some of the problems and at the same time pour fuel on the fire of ancient animosities.

That's where she came in. The pursuit of peaceful solutions on micro as well as macro levels, that's what she'd trained for. Lessons learned from childhood trauma, tragedies to be avoided. It almost always turned out in conflict situations that they needed each other in their fight to survive. If she could bring them to see that before they slaughtered each other and their families and their camels—

"Never changes, does it?" a deep, Spanish-accented voice said. "People always know better than the experts."

She turned to the tall, dark-haired man who'd come up behind her, his solar-powered jeep gleaming in the hot sun a few steps away.

He swept off his sunhat. "Carlos Aragon, at your service."

"Hello. I didn't see you coming. My name is—"

"Mary," he said.

She said frostily, "My name is Doctor Rosemary Forrest."

He gazed at her for a moment. "Mary suits you better. Regal and sacred, both."

"Are you making fun of me, Señor Aragon?"

"My apologies. Doctor Forrest, your reputation among the Tuareg proceeds you."

"Please excuse me, Señor. I have work to do." She turned away.

"As do I," he said smoothly. "These engineers work for my water company."

Hardly a promising beginning.

The next time she encountered Carlos Aragon was in Southeast Asia where conflict seemed endemic and intractable—and two generals seemed determined to eradicate each other and their tribes too. He arrived on a day when she felt so ill she'd begun wondering if she'd finally fallen prey to malaria. He took her immediately to a gleaming new hospital. He'd founded the medical center, a nurse told her, gazing wide-eyed at her rescuer who was chatting with a surgeon.

He was intelligent and thoughtful as well as over-confident. And very rich. He was the rock against which her storms battered without destroying either of them. She was attracted by the their differences, she such a long-term planner, he spontaneous. Before she'd realized what was happening, she was in love.

One day in New York, at the top of the newest and tallest skyscraper—one of his companies had built it—he took her by surprise and proposed. She surprised herself by accepting. They'd married in his family's ancestral home in Barcelona.

Her daughter came into the hotel room, breaking into her memories.

"Time to dress, *Mamá*," Catalina said in her soft voice.

She smoothed the support cobwebs of her mother's undergarment in place, molding them till they were snug, supporting her unreliable joints like an exoskeleton. Over it, she slipped the formal tea-gown, teal gray velvet shot through with midnight blue, a hint of tiny diamonds at neck and wrists.

"You look very distinguished," Catalina said.

"Thank you."

"Are you nervous about the ceremony?"

"No worse than standing between two rival generals spitting blood and broken teeth."

"You deserve the honor, *Mamá*. You've worked so hard."

Her heart had gone out of it when Carlos died. The daily betrayals of her body when she was in the field these last few years hadn't helped. But retirement was out of the question; there was still so much to do. Nowadays, she sat in her gleaming steel and glass office at the top of the Aragon Tower in New York and supervised the work of the foundations they'd built together. Funding schools and hospitals was vital but didn't make her pulse race the way risking everything standing between kings and chiefs whose nations hated each other and probably always would.

"I just wish Gabriel could've made it," she said.

"He really tried to get away." Her grandson's mother hurried to excuse him as usual. "You know how it is."

"Of course I do." She decided not to mention Gabriel's call that she'd accidentally aborted. Still time for him to try and call her again. Gabriel reminded her so much of Carlos, the same passion for his work, the same genius for problem solving.

"His work is so important to science," Catalina said.

She glanced at her daughter, taking in the graying hair, the lines anxiety etched into her forehead. Catalina probably didn't understand what Gabriel was working on any more than she herself did.

Catalina kissed her lightly on the cheek. "Is there anything else I can do?"

She preferred to be alone with her worries. "Dress yourself. We'll go down in a while."

The latest in helpful meds, prescribed for her by a very young doctor far too respectful of her reputation, were on the shelf in the hotel bathroom. She wouldn't take them unless she absolutely had to. She'd come this far in life without chemical crutches and she intended to continue.

She could remember her first meeting with Carlos, but not the speech she wrote yesterday. What else had her fickle mind overlooked? Something lurked, some part of the puzzle was still missing.

Things better left in the past, probably.

London, December 1944

The next time when the siren starts wailing, Rosemary already hears the drone of a buzz bomb through the wail of sirens. Searchlights will be crossing the sky to catch the Jerries. What will they do when they catch one? If they shoot a buzz bomb down, won't it still fall on somebody's house? She decides not to ask Mum those questions.

She sits on the edge of the bed, dangling her feet, rubbing her instep along the rim of the little suitcase.

"Hurry up, Rosemary!" Mum calls outside her closed door.

Sir Francis Drake is standing by her bedroom door.

She knows right away who he is because his picture is in the library book in her suitcase, and for a moment she thinks about taking it out and checking. She decides that would be rude. He's wearing his floppy hat with a feather, just like in the picture where he met the queen. And he has a lace ruff too. He looks a bit cloudy, like a reflection in a puddle, but perhaps that's just the dim blackout light.

It has to be him!

But what's he doing here? When she was little, she often pretended her toys could come to life and talk to her. She doesn't do that so much anymore now that she's nine. So how did he get here? It's like her library book coming to life as she often wishes it could.

"You should do as your mother tells you," he says. He flips one side of his red cloak over his shoulder and nods at her. He's very tall and thin, not like in the library book picture, really, she decides. But the cloak and the hat are the same.

"You need to go down to the shelter," he says.

"In a minute. I'm thinking."

A long time ago when this war started, they all went down to the cellar or the street shelter as soon as it was night. Lately, they've been going to bed in their own rooms and only getting up again if the siren sounds. The bombs have come pretty close, but their house has never been hit. She knows how to work your chances out. First you listen to the whine of the buzz bomb coming closer. If it stops before it gets right overhead, you are the target. You'll get hit. If the motor doesn't turn off until it's right over your house, you're all right. Someone else is going to get bombed. Then you say, "Hallelujah!" But only if Mum isn't around.

"I don't like this war," she says.

"No reason you should," Sir Francis says. "But you will be safe."

"You mean I shan't be bombed?"

"You shall not be bombed."

"Promise?"

"Promise," he replies.

Rosemary stares at him. She's surprised to see him standing in her room, as if he stepped out of the library book, but then she's not really surprised at all. She feels like she's known him a long time.

But he doesn't get a chance to answer. Mum cracks the door open.

"Rosemary. Hurry up!"

"I'm not going out to the shelter," she tells Mum. "It smells in there."

"Now Rosemary—"

"Well, it does. It's that stupid old moggy."

"Tomkins isn't a moggy. He's a very nice cat," Margaret says. She's standing behind Mum—she's probably been there a long time, spying on Rosemary, and of course, she's all ready to go.

"Is not."

"Stop it right now, both of you!" Mother sounds angry this time. "All right then. We'll go to the coal cellar like we used to. But no more arguing."

"I wish we'd leave her up here to get bombed," Margaret mutters, just out of Mum's hearing.

They hurry through the kitchen to the cellar steps. The blackout blinds in the kitchen windows don't quite fit at the edges, so they have to keep the torchlight low. Stripes of bright light from the searchlights in the sky run up and down the wall over the sink. In the cellar that smells of coal dust, Margaret drops her own small bag of precious things on the makeshift bed.

Sir Francis has managed to get there ahead of them. He spreads his red cloak on a concrete ledge across from the family and settles himself. He winks at Rosemary. She looks around at Mum and Margaret, but they don't act as if they can see him at all.

The sound of the anti-aircraft guns comes through the cellar walls, softly, very far away. She picks up one of the emergency candles that Mum has stacked on the shelf over their heads. Some nights the light goes out, but it's never stayed out long enough for them to light the candles yet. She likes candles and wouldn't be sorry if they had to use them.

Margaret reaches over and takes the candle from her, replacing it in the box with the others.

"I don't care if everybody else gets killed," Rosemary says. "I'm not going to be."

She deliberately shoves her suitcase into Margaret's bag so that it falls off the edge of the bed and onto the stone floor where the spiders run in and out of the cracks.

"Don't talk like that," Mum says.

"Oh, don't pay any attention to her, Mum," Margaret says. "She's daft. Did you know she still has an imaginary friend? At her age!"

"Do not," Rosemary says.

"Do too. You talk to your invisible friend. I heard you in your room."

"Did not."

"That's enough," Mum says. "Get settled down now."

Mum does what she always does as soon as they get into the coal cellar during a raid. She reaches into her brown leather handbag and draws out a silver-framed picture of Daddy in his soldier's uniform. She has a sudden thought that maybe she's been stolen away from her real parents, that she's not related to these two in the coal cellar. She wouldn't mind not being Margaret's sister.

Overhead the thudding begins.

"Mum, I want a biscuit."

"Those are emergency rations, in case we get trapped here!" Margaret snaps at her.

She's putting little gobs of spit on each nail in turn, polishing them with the edge of the army blanket. Rosemary watches carefully to see if they will shine in the dim light of the one bulb. Sometimes she even starts to feel sorry for her sister. Mostly, she watches to see which pretend things work and which don't. She decides spit doesn't.

"Well, then, I want a piece of barley sugar."

This is even more outrageous than a biscuit. Barley sugar is what people save for real emergencies. She's often wondered just exactly what sort of hit the Jerries would have to make on their house before Mum would get out the precious honey-colored sweets. Once, a near-miss shook the walls and swung the light in the cellar. And when they went upstairs in the morning, they found all the windows on the street side of the house broken and a lump of shrapnel as large as her fist lying in the hallway. The windows are all boarded up now. Nobody has glass to repair them in wartime, Mum says.

The gun noise gets louder. She can hear the humming sound of a plane flying low on its bombing mission.

"Just give her a biscuit and shut her up," Margaret says.

Listening to the muted thump-thump and the thunder of planes, occasionally made interesting by the whine of a dying plane, Rosemary wonders what the Jerry pilots look like. Do they really have red faces and little black mustaches, like the man on the poster in the library? She nibbles the biscuit to make it last. It's a Peak Frean's oatmeal with chocolate on one side, the kind she likes best. Once, a plane crashed by the fish-and-chip shop, and as soon as the all-clear sounded, all the children came running. She got there just as they loaded a body into an ambulance, and Jimmy Green said it was the pilot. Another boy said it wasn't and Jimmy pushed him, and the boy pushed back. Everybody else stood around thinking about all the awful, exciting things that happen to pilots. A skinny kid said that the pilot's arm was missing, and they all wanted to search for it in the rubble, but the bobbies wouldn't let them get near enough.

"I hope they get shot through the head and crash and burn up and their fingers and toes fall off and get lost so they can't bury them all together," she says as the walls shake, showering dust down on them.

"Rosemary!" Mum says.

"You shouldn't say things like that," Margaret adds. "Even about a Jerry."

"Jimmy Green says if they get broken up into pieces, they won't be able to rest in peace in their graves, and then they have to go wandering around as ghosts forever."

"Lot he knows!" Margaret says scornfully. "Anyway, you wouldn't talk so big if you'd ever seen a dead body."

"I did too, once."

"Fibber."

"Margaret. Rosemary. Stop this immediately."

"When did you ever see a dead person?"

"You didn't say person. You said body. I saw the butcher's moggy lying in the gutter with its stomach hanging out. It got hit by a lorry. It was going to have kittens, too. And I didn't even get sick."

"Mum, make her shut up."

"The butcher said I could've had one of the kittens for Christmas."

"Mum—"

"I would've liked a kitten. But these were squashed and all covered in blood."

Across the coal-dusty floor, she sees Sir Francis frown at her. Perhaps she's gone too far.

"I really worry about what this war is doing to you children," Mum says. "It's turning you into little monsters."

And now there's a sudden screaming, whistling roar through the air above them, like a train gone mad and hurtling down the sky to burrow its way deep in the ground that's shaking and rumbling at its approach. The three of them cower together, heads tucked in their chests as the air raid drill taught, knees drawn up and eyes closed against the light that goes out anyway.

After a while, the walls stop quivering and Rosemary opens her eyes. She can hear Mum fumbling around nearby. Presently, there is a scratchy sound, then a small light blooms in Mum's hand. It shows up the cloud of coal dust that's hanging in the air now.

Sir Francis isn't there anymore. She looks all around the cellar but can't see him.

"That was close," Margaret says in a squeaky voice.

She can tell Margaret's been crying. Her own eyes are wet, but she wipes them before anyone can see. Mum doesn't say anything. When the candle is burning properly in its brass stick, Rosemary looks round. Dust has showered down from the low beams of the ceiling, covering Daddy's picture. Mum takes a hankie out of her handbag and wipes it clean again.

"Your Daddy is a real hero," she says. "All our soldiers are. England always has the very best soldiers. And—make no mistake—they're going to win!" She opens up the thermos and pours a beaker of sweet, milky tea for them to sip.

"Is Sir Francis Drake a hero?" The words are out before she can stop them. She puts her hand over her mouth to prevent more words falling out.

"Of course he was a hero!" Mum says. "Haven't you been reading your history book?"

"He was a pirate too," Margaret mutters.

That's a new thought. She'd like to hear more about it, but instead she asks, "When will the war be over?"

Mum puts her arm around Rosemary and draws her close against her chest. Her nose fills with the smell of the lilac talc Mum uses. "It can't last forever. Then we'll have peace again."

"What's peace like? I don't remember."

Margaret sniffles. "Oh, peace is wonderful. You can have anything to eat at any time you want."

"Even barley sugar?"

And Mum opens up the package and hands them each a small, golden square.

English Channel, December 1944

The wintry sun slipped behind the distant coastline as radar picked up the incoming plane and sent the warning. "Unknown craft approaching."

Harry and the young soldier from Yorkshire tossed the cigarettes they'd been smoking over the rail and assumed their positions at the Browns. All across the platforms, men raced to man the guns. The last two days had seen very little action apart from Yank squadrons flying east to drop their bombs on Germany before returning west to airfields in Essex. Seven planes had gone out early this morning, and five had come back an hour ago. Two lost, apparently, but there'd been worse days. Nothing else all day. The RAF seemed to have moved its operations somewhere else. What the Krauts were up to was anybody's guess.

He shrugged the collar of his jacket up to ward off the cold sea wind and adjusted his ear-protectors. A sergeant came running across the metal walkway toward them. Harry scanned the sky where another half-hour of daylight at best lingered.

"...southwest, 2000 to 3000 feet—" Control's message over the Tannoy was full of static.

Nothing visible to the naked eye yet. The word going around was that Hitler's troops were being pushed back, and he had few left to spare for bombing England. Harry hoped so anyway. This was one of the times he wished he'd been a religious man. He might've prayed for the safety of his family.

"Jus' tha' one?" The Yorkshireman queried.

"Maybe he's a scout, Geordy," Harry suggested.

"Aye. There's tha'."

The searchlights shot up from their separate tower and drew bright lines across the sky. Harry picked up the binoculars and scanned the area the beams were crisscrossing. "There he is, the bastard!"

A last ray of the setting sun flared on the incoming plane. He couldn't make it out well enough against the sun glare to identify its silhouette, but it seemed too big to be a Messerschmitt, which was what he would've expected of a scout. The other gun from Harry's tower and those on the next gun tower over chattered. Harry aimed and fired. The gun thundered, spitting its shell.

"Tha's a canny one!" Geordy yelled. "Tha' almos' got him." He was loading shells into the 3.7 as fast as he could.

Harry fired again. Missed. The big plane was executing clumsy avoidance movements. It kept coming through the streaming light and the shells aimed to destroy it. Definitely bomber, by the size of it, not a fighter plane. A Junkers maybe? Or a Heinkel—

Hold your fire! Hold your fire! the voice in his earphones yelled. *Damn it, gunner. Hold your fire!*

Harry snatched his hand off the Browning. Geordy stared open-mouthed. The other guns fell silent too. The bomber kept coming. It appeared to be listing slightly to one side. Maybe a shell had clipped its wings after all. The searchlights disappeared, but their after-images burned on his eyes for many seconds.

The sergeant had turned away from the guns, holding his earphones close to his ears. Harry couldn't make out what the man was saying—shouting, actually—his own ears were still ringing from his gun's noise in spite of the ear-protectors.

"What just happened?" He stared toward the now-dark line of the coast where the bomber was headed.

"One of ours," the sergeant said, ripping his headphones off. His face showed his disgust. "Trust a Yank to forget to switch on his I.F.F, so our radar could identify him!"

Identification, Friend or Foe. Harry felt the cold rush through his veins. Just as well he'd missed. He might've shot down a Yankee ally a bit late going home after the rest of his squadron. Adrenaline still pumped through his veins, making him shake.

"Stupid bugger!" the sergeant said.

When sarge was out of hearing, Geordy said, "Tha's a champion gunner, by gum!"

"Lucky I missed the target that time."

Bloody mess this war was! Whoever said it was a glorious thing to fight for your country was a fool. Wars were the game played by the powerful, but it was the poor ignorant sod who got to give up his life. He'd always thought Kipling, a soldier himself, had been right about that.

Frank Smith was in the mess when Harry got off duty at dawn, leaning back against one wall. Watery light fell through the windows onto the cook station where they lined up for breakfast. Harry loaded up his plate. Some kind of Shepherd's Pie this time, made from last night's leftovers apparently.

Frank followed him over to an empty table. He listened to Harry's story of the pilot who almost got his plane shot down by friendly fire.

"War is full of unfortunate accidents, mistaken identities, wasted sacrifices," Frank said. "A thing that seems of enormous importance can amount to nothing in the grand sweep of history. And conversely, a little thing can bring down an empire. Many casualties, in either case. And then a few years later, we do it all over again."

"Student of history are you?"

"Parts of it."

Have you news of my boy Jack?—an old Kipling poem he'd had to memorize in school came to Harry's mind. He couldn't remember the rest of it. Something about a father seeking news of his son who'd been at the front in World War I. Not a poem he would've read to his girls!

London, December 1944

The school caretaker is just lighting the gas lamps in Mr Henstridge's classroom, reaching up with his stick that has a hook on the end to the chains hanging from the lamps and pulling them so the flames shoot up. Afternoons get dark early, this close to the Christmas holidays. Mr Henstridge has been teaching them about the midwinter-solstice, and how people in the Very Old History Days they'd been studying used to celebrate. One silly girl with yellow pigtails in the front row asked if Baby Jesus had a party for the solstice, and of course everybody in Class Two fell about in their chairs laughing at her. Rosemary thinks she might ask Sir Francis if Good Queen Bess celebrated the solstice or just Christmas. The library book doesn't mention this. That's her favorite period of history, and she'd like to know for certain.

Rosemary likes to watch the caretaker light the gas. She likes the *pop* the gas makes as it flares. But right now she's handing out pencils because the class is about to start another lesson in handwriting. Mr Henstridge teaches Class Two, second oldest in the school, and he's very strict about the children learning to write neatly. It's important not to give up the things that civilize us, Mr Henstridge says, even if there is a war on.

She's just about to give a pencil to Jimmy Green when the air raid siren starts wailing.

"Boys and girls!" Mr Henstridge claps his hands. "You know what to do. Line up by the door in alphabetical order. Quickly now."

What is she supposed to do with the pencils? If she takes the time to put them back on Mr Henstridge's desk she'll probably end up being out of proper order in the line by the door. "Green" comes right after "Forrest," and Jimmy won't want to let her get in front of him if she doesn't get there first. She looks down at the four pencils still in her hand. These aren't new ones, of course. She hasn't seen a new one in a long time. These are all stubs, sharpened and sharpened again until they're almost all gone, handed out to use and then collected again because pencils are precious. Pencils are needed for the War Effort, Mr Henstridge has explained to them. Rosemary thinks about her daddy using a new pencil to write things down about how to beat Hitler.

"Rosemary Forrest," Mr Henstridge says. "Come along."

She pushes the pencils into the pocket of her jumper. Jimmy Green sticks his tongue out at her as she shoves in front of him. He's a short boy for his age, and she can push him around if she wants to. The line starts moving out the door, down the stairs, across the playground to the bomb shelter built in a corner of the playground. They've used it once in a practice.

The shelter—just like the one in the road in front of her house only bigger—is cold and damp, and there are no old neighbors inside making tea or handing out biscuits. Rosemary's class is the last one inside, and it's already crowded. All the benches along the walls are taken, boys one side, girls the other. Mr Henstridge makes his class squeeze in. Rosemary ends up squashed between an older, Class One girl and a small one from Class Three who'd got there first. It would have been worse last year, Rosemary thinks, before so many children were evacuated to the country, leaving some room for the others. The pencils poke her in the thigh, and she can't get comfortable.

Jimmy leans across the space to her. "What if them doodlebugs fall on this shelter?"

"Never happen," she says. But she's not as sure of this as she pretends. Maybe Sir Francis only means her own house will be all right? She wishes he could be here right now.

"Settle down, boys and girls," Mr Henstridge says. "Find a seat on the benches, or sit on the floor. Keep your arms and legs to yourselves."

It's cold in here; she's glad Mum made her wear her thickest brown cardigan this morning and knee socks. It's stuffy, and smells of wet woollies and boys' socks. Everyone talks at once, especially the younger children. She can smell pee too. That's because the shelter's next door to the brick building where the boys go. Or maybe one of the little kids has wet his trousers. She pinches her nose.

The thumping begins as the anti-aircraft guns try to shoot down the Jerry planes.

"It's like thunder an' lightnin'," Jimmy shouts over the noise. "Count the seconds an' you'll know how far away the Jerries are."

"That's silly," the Class One girl sitting next to Rosemary says. "You have to be able to see a flash first to be able to do that."

"I can see it up 'ere," Jimmy taps his forehead. "You don't know nothin'."

"Anything," the older girl says. "It's 'You don't know anything.' But I'm right, and you're wrong."

"Boys and girls! We're going to sing a song." One of the lady teachers waves her arms in the air. "All together now. There'll be bluebirds over—"

The children roar, "The white cliffs of Dover...."

Rosemary moves her mouth around to make it look like she's singing but doesn't make a sound. It's a stupid song. Everybody knows there's no such thing as bluebirds. Maybe sparrows. Or pigeons. Mum doesn't like pigeons because they make such a dirty mess.

A huge BOOM! and the walls of the shelter shake. The lights go out. Dust pours down.

The children cover their heads with their hands as they've been taught, and they all bend over to their knees.

It seems like a long time before the All-Clear. Some of the younger children are sobbing. She's scared, like everybody else, but she's too big now to show it. Mr Henstridge gets the shelter's door open and a kind of dusty gray light comes in. Everybody stands up. They're very quiet, not like when they came in. Rosemary's quiet too. They file out in the order they came in—last being first now. So that's why Jimmy Green sees it before she does.

"Lookit!" he yells. "Jerry 'it the school!"

The children start pushing and shoving in the doorway.

Rosemary stares at the school's roof. There's a big hole in it at one end, and smoke is coming out. Windows are blown out. Broken glass is everywhere. Bricks and tiles scattered over the playground.

"Blimey, that was a good 'un!" Jimmy says.

He's going to get into trouble for swearing. No way Mr Henstridge didn't hear that. And he's very strict about them not speaking Cockney. But Jimmy's right. It really is wonderful to see the school on fire. She clasps her arms over her chest and stares at the marvelous sight.

She hears the fire engine's two note warning coming closer, and soon there's another one, and a police car swerves onto the playground.

"I'm very much afraid we can't go back into the school," Mr Henstridge says. "Boys and girls, you will just have to go home a bit early today."

Everybody lets out a big cheer, and Rosemary joins in. Nobody else but a teacher would be daft enough to be sad about going home early.

"Have your mothers check with the school tomorrow to see if it's safe to use the building," Mr Henstridge shouts over the noise of everybody laughing and clapping their hands.

The Class One teacher frowns at him. "It's more likely we'll be starting the holidays early."

Mr Henstridge looks at her with his mouth open, shuts it quickly again.

"Coulda bin us, innit?" Jimmy said. "Cor! We coulda bin brown bread."

"We could've been *dead!*" Mr Henstridge said sternly. "Speak proper English, young man."

But Rosemary knows they were never in real danger—at least, *she* wasn't. She trusts Sir Francis.

The children make a dash for the playground gate, pushing and shoving, little ones falling over and crying, even though Mr Henstridge is shouting at them all to walk in proper lines.

The little girl with the pigtails starts wailing. "My new satchel—It's still in the classroom."

Nobody pays her any attention, not even the teachers.

English Channel, December 1944

As he was leaving the mess after breakfast the next day, Geordy put out a hand and stopped him.

"Thee knows I'm tha's mate, Harry—"

"Of course. What's this about?"

The Yorkshireman looked away, embarrassed.

"Out with it, lad."

"When's nowt but t'sea, a man can go daft."

"What're you talking about?"

Geordy, shrugged, obviously embarrassed. "Ah heard thee chuntering on in t'mess t'other morning. An' nowt there but empty dishes."

"You didn't see anybody else?"

"Nay," Geordy said softly.

"You didn't see a tall chap? Looks a bit—foreign. Calls himself Frank Smith."

Geordy shook his head, his expression solemn. "Nowt like that. But mebbe tha's jus' maddled—many a lad cain't take it out here."

"I'm not ready for the funny farm, if that's what you mean."

"Nay, nay! Ah knows tha'. But mebbe thee should try t' rec room?"

"Not a bad idea at that," Harry said. "Cheer up, lad. I won't go bonkers on you."

Geordy's face lit in a big smile. "Champion!"

The men's recreation room on the intermediate floor of the gun tower was busy when he came in, and blue with cigarette smoke. The windows were propped open as far as they'd go, which wasn't much but better than nothing. A soldier wearing a paint-splattered cook's apron over his khakis was painting a vase of flowers. Roses? Or were they meant to be petunias? Two others were playing darts, exclaiming over bulls-eyes and misses in loud voices. Someone else was knitting, swearing each time he dropped a stitch. About the only activity that wasn't offered was a firing range. Harry would've liked to shoot a few targets sometime. Keep his eye sharp and his hand steady.

The bench that interested him housed the model makers and their equipment. A young red-cheeked private looked up as Harry approached.

"Name's Jonesy," he said. "You interested in one o' these?"

"Don't know yet," Harry said. "Maybe a galleon."

"Over there on the wall you'll find all the kits you could want. I'll give you a hand getting started."

He found a kit that would produce a galleon and took it over to the bench. A loud guffaw made him look over his shoulder at the darts players. One of them seemed to be celebrating a victory.

"Those two are our champs," Jonesy said. "Getting ready to challenge Nore again. Big Christmas match this time."

Nore was another Maunsell sea fort, several miles away. "They go over there, or—"

"Nah. They do it over the telephone, innit?"

"Have to be honest then, don't they?"

"Where's the fun else? But those two are good. We're gonna win this one. You might want to put money on it."

Harry shook his head. "I'm skint."

He spent an hour considering the kit, laying out the parts beginning with the galleon's hull. Across the rec room, an amber lump of resin slowly melted in a pot over a Bunsen burner. He could smell the glue's deep, rich incense all the way over here. A memory came—Saturday morning with his father, sorting a lump of resin just the right size from the ironmonger's, getting it weighed. Back home, melting it in one of Mum's old saucepans. He must've been about thirteen at the time.

"The smell of resin's as good as incense for some people, or so I've heard," Frank Smith said behind him.

The man had an annoying habit of showing up when he would've preferred to work without the need for company or conversation. Not that he could expect much privacy on a structure as crowded as U7.

"May I enquire what you're working on?"

No, you may not, he wanted to say, but held it back. "Planning to make a model of the *Golden Hind.*"

"Excellent choice." Frank settled himself on an unoccupied workbench.

Harry thought of his father's war, the Great War, and Kipling's bitter insights into the life of the common soldier, but he didn't want to give this strange man any more ammunition for conversation. He glanced round the room. There were at least eight men here. None of them paid Frank any attention. Come to that, when had he ever seen anyone besides himself interacting with him?

"And the ironic thing," Frank continued, "is that 'the war to end all wars' never does."

He concentrated on the work of laying the parts in their right places for assembly. It was going to be a fairly big model, perhaps two feet long from bowsprit to stern. He wouldn't know how tall until he got the masts upright. The masts— They'd require sails and some research to get the emblems and the symbols right. The stern would require a painted coat of arms too. Anticipation sent a small shiver of excitement up his spine. Almost like a religious feeling, if he'd been religious.

Then he stopped, main mast in hand. "What does that mean, 'the war to end all wars'—"

"Perhaps I'm being cynical," Frank said. "The Great War was supposed to be the last. But now we have this one. What if there's another one?"

"You're talking rubbish!"

"I fear the next war would use weaponry far worse than Jerry's buzz bombs."

"That's why we have to win this one. So there aren't any more."

"It almost makes one question whether meeting violence with violence is the answer, doesn't it?"

Across the room, laughter broke out, cheering. The dart players had a fan club.

For a moment Frank's attention seemed focused on something far away. "Drake should've lost, you know. The Armada was overwhelming."

"But he didn't."

"Quite," Frank said.

"May I ask where this conversation is going? Otherwise, I'm rather busy."

"I see you as an ordinary citizen who happens to be an ace with a gun. I'm wondering which is the real you."

Harry was saved from finding an answer by a muffled thumping that came through the open windows. The section of water framed in the small window roiled, white and angry crests as far as he could see. Far off, he heard the drone of a bomber's engines receding.

"Frying tonight!" someone announced.

The men cheered.

Harry moved over to the window where several of the other off-duty men were crowding. The surface of the water was now covered with astonishing white and silver shapes, as if a gigantic school of fish was swimming on the surface. Only the fish weren't swimming. They were either stunned or dead.

"That returning pilot just jettisoned his remaining payload," Frank explained. "Good for him, and even better for us because the explosion has resulted in quite a quantity of fish."

"How do you know all that?"

Frank shrugged. "You should go on deck and help bring in dinner."

London, December 1944

Rosemary wakes up in her own bed when morning light creeps around the edges of the blackout curtains. They're supposed to shut out all the light in the room from getting outside, but Mum ran out of black cloth when she was making curtains for the flat. Her tiny bedroom has a very small window, so it isn't important as long as she doesn't turn on the light when she goes to bed. If any light does get through, the ARP warden will come knocking on their door. She's found a way around this—she reads under the eiderdown with a torch.

She doesn't remember going to the cellar or the bomb shelter last night when the sirens went off. She doesn't remember any sirens either. Always sirens when there's a raid.

Mum opens the door. "Breakfast is ready."

"Why was I in my own bed this morning?" she wants to know when she comes into the kitchen. It's warmer in here because Mum has the hob on to make the porridge. "Didn't we go to the shelter?"

"No raids last night," Margaret says.

"Why not?"

"Just be glad we were lucky to get a good night's sleep for once."

She doesn't like porridge. "Can I have raisins in it?"

"Raisins? Where did you get an idea like that, young lady?" Mum says. "I haven't seen raisins in the market for months now."

"She doesn't even remember what raisins are," Margaret says. "She's making it up."

"Am not."

"Are too."

Mum sighs and ladles out a small heap of porridge into Rosemary's favorite bowl.

"But I did get a treat for you girls when I went to the shops yesterday." Mum holds out a small green tin with gold writing and a lion's picture on it. "You like Golden Syrup. I think it must come from somewhere far away, like Australia."

She carefully scoops out a small teaspoonful of the syrup, twirls the spoon to catch all the drips, and holds it over Rosemary's porridge.

"That must have taken a whole hundred coupons," Rosemary says.

"Don't be daft!" Margaret says. "Nothing takes that many coupons."

"Some things do."

"Bet you can't name one."

"A roast of beef," Rosemary says.

"You can't get beef anymore!"

"Get on with your breakfast," Mum says.

She swirls the syrup into the gray porridge before Mum pours milk on it for her. The smell of bread burning fills the kitchen because Mum is making her own breakfast—one slice of bread toasted on a wire rack over the gas flames. A piece of toast with something on it would be much nicer than porridge, even with Golden Syrup.

"'Better than butter,'" she reads off the syrup tin.

"Anything's better than National Butter," Margaret complains.

"I like National Butter."

"That's because you don't remember the taste of real butter without margarine mixed in."

"Do too."

"No you don't."

"Girls!" Mother says sharply. "I won't put up with this today. Eat your breakfast, Rosemary, because I want you to start doing some lessons at home."

"Why do I have to do lessons? I don't have to go to school anymore because it isn't open."

"That's exactly why," Mum says. "I can't have you turning into an ignoramus. Whatever will Daddy say if he comes home after the war is over and finds you've turned into an ignoramus?"

"A what?"

"She means stupid," Margaret says.

She knows Margaret's just jealous because her secondary school didn't get bombed. She's not happy about doing lessons at home. It's not fair.

"We're going to start with reading," Mum says as they go into the sitting-room where Daddy's bookcase is.

That's all right with Rosemary, who loves reading.

Mum spoils it. "And not one of your own books, because I want you to learn something."

"I could read *Swallows and Amazons* again. I could learn about sailing."

"Baby stuff," Margaret says, peeking round the door.

"Do your hair in pigtails before you go to school, young lady," Mum says. "You need to be dressed properly, even in wartime. Do you have your liberty bodice on under your school blouse? You'll need the extra warmth."

"Mum!"

"And you're going to need gloves. It's cold enough to snow today."

Margaret bangs the door behind her.

"It never snows in London," Rosemary says, wishing it did.

"Certainly it does," Mum says. "Sometimes."

Mum's pulling books off the shelves, flipping through the pages and putting them back. These are some of Daddy's schoolbooks that he read when he was a boy. Rosemary squints at the titles. A lot of poetry. But also, on the bottom shelf, a pile of magazines with an exciting title: *Thrilling Wonder Stories*.

"Can I read one of these?"

"I want you to read something educational," Mum says. "Here. Read this one." She holds out a book with a faded green cover and gold writing on the spine.

"What's it about?"

"Read it and find out," Mum says.

By this she knows that Mum has never read it herself. She decides to come back for the magazines with the exciting title later.

Oslo, December 2035

"Gabriel used to joke that his great-grandfather was England's version of Mahatma Gandhi minus the loincloth," Mary said.

Hairbrush in hand, Catalina closed the door behind her. "*Abuelo* did very valuable work."

"Yes. No argument." The family respected Harry Forrest's post-war activism against nuclear proliferation. "It's a mercy he had the chance to do it. But I wonder sometimes…"

She broke off, not sure herself where she was going with this.

"Why you survived the war?"

Surprised by this unusual insight, she glanced at her daughter. "I suppose so."

"I have a theory," Catalina began.

She waited, but her daughter obviously thought better of it. Silence stretched itself in the room.

"Sit down, and I'll arrange your hair," Catalina said, and Mary obeyed. Catalina lifted the fine hair gently and began to brush and arrange it. After a while, she put the brush down and held out a mirror.

She studied herself in the mirror. Silver hair, smoothed till it shone and piled artfully on her head, covering the parts where it grew so thinly she was almost bald. Catalina's handiwork was excellent. Catalina and Gabriel. All that were left to her now. Time raced away from her, and night advanced like a tide that couldn't be stopped. So much she'd made out of a life that almost might not have been, if the Fates had decided otherwise.

She would never have had the great joy of knowing her first grandbaby, Catalina's only child, Gabriel.

I'm thinking of reading physics at Princeton when I leave school, Abuelita. Did you know Einstein was once there? They'd been walking along the Embankment, the trees aflame with October, the Thames sparking in autumn sunshine. What a handsome young man Gabriel was growing up to be! He'd inherited Carlos's dark Catalan looks and his family's green eyes. *I wish you'd choose a university here at home, Gabriel,* she'd said. She remembered the light touch of his lips on her cheek as he kissed her. *I promise I'll come and visit you instead, Abuelita.*

There. Again, that tiny bit of shadow lurking at the back of her mind. Something she needed to think about. Something that had not yet come to fruition. She waited, but nothing surfaced. Her daughter, hairbrush in hand, was looking at her curiously.

"I never told you about a strange thing that happened in my childhood, Catalina," she began.

Catalina sighed. "Mamá—"

But even as she started to speak about the memory now rising in her mind like a dark whale, the absurdity of it tied her tongue. Instead, she asked, "Do you suppose the world without me would've been different or mostly the same? Better, or worse?"

Catalina looked away, uncomfortable with such speculation.

Mary thought of Gabriel, the plane trees along the Embankment dappling his young face with shadow, his enthusiasm for following in Einstein's footsteps. Of all her little family, Gabriel was the child she most cherished, the one she'd always felt closest to—and most worried about. Ironies abounded. She remembered he'd wanted to talk about Time's one way arrow; illusion, Einstein had called it, Gabriel said. He wanted to learn all about it. She remembered his fresh, young animal smell as she hugged him.

"The committee has provided us with handsome escorts," Catalina said, breaking into her memories. "I caught sight of them waiting in the hotel foyer. Young men, too."

"Are they afraid I can't walk up to the stage by myself?"

"Oh! I'm sure that's not right. You're very strong...."

"For my age, you want to say."

The committee probably preferred to give the prize to older candidates. It prevented the indignity of laureates living long enough to embarrass them.

English Channel, December 1944

The fish, mostly fat sea bass, coated in a light batter and served with malt vinegar, was delicious. They got precious little fresh food out here, and that only when the supply boat docked. Sometimes, there wasn't any meat; dinner often meant tinned sardines or tinned Spam. Occasionally there were eggs if the chickens around the Thames Estuary were getting enough of the right things to eat to encourage them to lay. Some of the men had suggested they keep hens here on the fort. They already had a place where carrots and potatoes grew in boxes. Not enough sun this late in the year to grow much else, but chickens probably wouldn't care as long as they were fed. So far, they hadn't been given permission to try that experiment.

He was off duty this morning. Chilly, typical December weather, not cold enough for snow, ice-blue sky and pale sun, fog low on the water. The sea black and crawling beneath the concrete spider-legs of the towers, an occasional glitter from the breaking swells, the air heavy with the smell of seaweed, the wind starting to rise. No sounds from the fort, not even the thrum of the four diesels in the engine room that powered everything, though he felt their vibration through his boots. Earlier, he'd watched a squadron of American bombers heading for the continent and wished them luck. Many of them wouldn't make it back. Young men whose parents would mourn for them. As they had in countless wars throughout human history.

"Have you news of my boy Jack?"

Not this tide....

Rudyard Kipling, the soldier's poet. The words he'd learned in the classroom came to life out here on the water. Or came to death.

"When do you think that he'll come back?"

Not with this wind blowing, and this tide.

He'd never forget London in those early, dark days of the Blitz, the rubble, the smoke, the little parish church where he and Alice had been married—flattened. The Krauts deserved anything and everything the Allies could dish out. It had been a relief when the government, fresh out of young men, called him up to be a soldier. They'd trained him to be a killer, and kill was what he'd do, every time he was given the chance.

Maybe it was easier to do when the enemy's face was hidden inside several tons of metal.

The tower itself seemed to rock silently as the tide passed under it, the sands on which it stood sliding imperceptibly. In the past, without sonic depth finders, navigators measured depth by dropping a leaded line over the side of their ship, a task that pretty well had to be continuously repeated in the neighborhood of these sandbars and shifting sands. Well-named, Shivering Sands. He scanned the surface of the water. Easy to think about death and ghosts, if a chap was superstitious. Come to that, England was full of ghosts. His own grandmother claimed to have seen several. There was something cozy about ghosts in thatched cottages in an English village. Out here, not so much.

He leaned against the rail and checked his pockets for the pack of Woodbines, took out the last one, struck a match and cupped the cigarette. It caught after a second, and he sucked in, tasting the sharp, slightly sour flavor of the cheap tobacco. Better than nothing.

Breathing in the tobacco smoke, he gazed at the low Kent coast, barely visible. He couldn't see the mouth of the Thames—foggier along the coast—but knew it was there as surely as any German pilot aiming for London. Though there hadn't been much action lately since the Yanks had started their heavy bombardment of railway lines and factories on the continent. The Krauts had sent another batch of clumsy, unmanned planes armed with bombs a couple of nights ago. They'd shot down a couple. He might even have hit one of them himself. Hard to tell when everyone was blazing away like Errol Flynn in the American movie they'd watched in the recreation room last night. Yanks winning the war without any help from the Tommies. But it was entertaining, and the men had cheered in all the right places.

It felt good to knock down unmanned planes.

Word was, half of the buzz bombs crashed short of any target. He couldn't see how they were an advance over sending manned bombers, but it was good to know Hitler could be a blithering idiot too.

His throat tightened at the memory of home. Things had to improve now that the Yanks had come into the war. Yet there was something about this idea of a quick end to hostilities that he didn't quite accept. He was inclined to suspect Frank Smith was right. Maybe Hitler had some tricks left up his sleeve.

It was the Kipling poem that had brought the mood on. He laid a hand on the metal railing, damp from the creeping fog, feeling the vibration from the fort's diesel engines. He sensed the strong run of current though he couldn't see it. If he fell in right now, no one would hear him shout for help. Even if he reached the concrete leg of the fort, he'd be far from the little dock or the iron ladder up. Each tower had a lifeboat, but he'd have to have more than a little luck to locate it and clamber in. Fat lot of good the swimming lessons in the pool at Colchester barracks would do him.

For what is sunk will hardly swim.

A sudden sense of being surrounded by death, invisible and patiently biding its time, chilled him. He rubbed his arms against the cold, but it didn't help. The darkness was inside as well as out. He recognized the problem for what it was: homesickness, especially now, with Christmas fast approaching. And no letter from home on the supply boat yesterday.

There was a sound, far off. The bell on a buoy placed to warn mariners off the sandbar clanged with the rise and fall of the swell. The bell only deepened his sense of isolation. Easy enough to hallucinate the presence of enemy boats out there. He raised his field glasses.

Some kind of disturbance out there under the water.

Big fish? Maybe even a seal. He'd seen a few of those out here. Impossible to see under the tower because he couldn't lean far enough out. He raised the glasses again and scanned the grayness.

A splash. Lot of big birds' nests down there on the towers' legs.

Yesterday, one of the younger men on U7 had been sent ashore. Couldn't take the strain of isolation and danger out here anymore. The sergeant had found him trying to climb down into the rubber lifeboat. He had to go. Danger to everybody else if he went off at the wrong time. Harry sympathized with the young lad's distress, but it wasn't a choice to abandon one's mates. That wasn't just military code of ethics either. It was what had made humans out of apes.

He pinched off the lit end of the cigarette and stuck it back into the empty packet. At the briefing yesterday, the lieutenant told them to keep a lookout for U-boats picking up or dropping off spies. If a U-boat surfaced in this growing fog, nobody would see it. The fort's radar watched the sky, not the waves.

There.

Something—a darker bit in the dark, shifting water. Something moving He slammed the field glasses up to his eyes again, but they revealed nothing. Unaided, his eyes were actually better in these conditions. Most likely a seal.

Maybe he should give the alarm anyway.

And then say what, exactly?

London, December 1944

It's supposed to be Margaret's job to scrub the front doorstep, not Rosemary's. Every day when she doesn't have school like today, a Saturday, and it isn't raining. War or no war, Mum says. Like all the other mothers along Marigold Road, Mum takes pride in having a clean marble doorstep. It's the grandest thing about their house. And every time there's a raid somewhere, there's ash and soot all over everything. Not that the step stays clean for long after it's been scrubbed, but it's important to keep up appearances, Mum says. Even in wartime.

Rosemary's stupid sister has managed to twist her ankle running home from school, and now Mum says she has to rest it.

"Can she do my jobs for me, then?" she asks.

Mum is tying her hair up in a head-scarf without looking in the mirror over the kitchen sink. How does she manage to do this without looking? It's an old scarf that Mum uses to go down the market. She does this whenever it's safe with no air raids because they have to eat. She likes to go shopping. There'll be a couple of barrows with potatoes and cabbage, probably carrots. Maybe even some apples. Coxes, this late in the year. Jimmy Green's family owns one of the barrows in the market. Sometimes, he even gets to work on it, loading stuff from the boxes to display on the barrow. Sometimes he gives her a little apple when his dad isn't paying attention. He shouldn't do this, of course, because everything's on the ration book these days.

"No," Mum says when she's finished tying the scarf properly. "She has to stay quiet with her foot up."

"It's going to rain anyway, and the step will get all mucky again. Maybe it'll even snow."

"If you don't stop whining, young lady, I'll find some more work for you to do."

And Rosemary knows she's lost that battle.

"Put a thick cardigan on," Mum says as she opens the front door. "It's cold enough for snow today."

When Mum's gone, she puts on Mum's big apron over her ugly brown cardigan. She gets the pail from under the sink and fills it with warm water. The old brush with half its bristles missing and the other half worn down and leaning sideways, comes next, and the tin of Vim scrubbing powder.

"Make sure you do a good job!" Margaret calls from the sitting room where she has her foot up on the pouffe.

She wouldn't dream of admitting this, but it's actually fun to scrub the step. She's done it a couple of times. First she pours a bit of water over it, then she shakes the Vim. After that she scrubs as hard as she can, back and forth till her wrist aches. It's a good idea to work fast because that way she doesn't feel how cold it is today. Sometimes she puts the brush in her left hand to give her right one a rest, but that's slower, and the work takes longer. The water is quite cold already.

The marble step used to be pure white, with little streaks of yellow and brown in it. It's old, maybe a hundred years by now, Margaret says, because that's how old this row of houses down Marigold Road is, and it never comes properly white anymore. There's also a worn-away dip in the middle where the scrubbing-water puddles.

Down the street, she sees the milkman putting his bottles on a doorstep. He's wearing that same old torn cloth cap he always wears. Moth-eaten, Mum calls it. She'd better get this job finished so it can dry before he gets to her door. She scrubs a bit harder at a stubborn spot of dirt. Doing the front step is better than going to school anyway.

"Quite the industrious young lady."

She stops scrubbing and looks up. Sir Francis is leaning on the lamppost outside their door. She's worked out that he only talks to her when she's alone, he doesn't want other people to know. It's their secret. She likes secrets. Today, he's pulled his brown hat with a long feather down over his ears to keep out the cold. It looks wrong, not like the picture in the library book.

"You keep on using words that are too big!" she complains.

He bows. "I humbly beg your pardon."

"Now you're making fun of me."

"Not at all. Carry on."

Still annoyed, she says, "And you're wearing your hat crooked. That's not the way it is in the picture in my library book."

He frowns at her but puts a hand up and straightens his hat. That makes it better, but still not quite right.

She finishes scrubbing and pours the rest of the water over the step to rinse it off.

"You promise I will get to grow up?" She's asked him this several times, but it's always a comfort to hear the answer.

"You will get to grow up, Rosemary."

"Why?"

He makes a puzzled face. "Why?"

"Yes. Why shall I be safe and other people in London get bombed?"

"You ask too many questions!" But she won't take the question back. He says, "You wouldn't understand the answer even if I gave it to you."

"Try me. I'm the smartest kid in my class. My teacher said so." Mr Henstridge also said she talked too much and didn't listen, but he didn't need to know that.

"Perhaps the laws of the universe need you to be safe."

She knows what the universe is. "The universe is just stars. It isn't a person."

He sighs. "I can't explain it to you."

Then she remembers the bobby's advice. "Are you a gypsy?"

"I'm afraid I don't quite follow—"

"A bobby told me. Gypsies know the future. But they always want you to do something—cross their palms with silver or something."

Sir Francis thinks about this for a moment. "Sometimes big things matter, Rosemary, and sometimes it's the little things. And sometimes people have to be around because—" He breaks off just like she herself does when she can't find the right words. "Well, just because. Do you understand that?"

"No."

She glares at him, daring him to argue with her. He isn't smiling. He looks a bit like Mr Henstridge when he's talking about everybody doing their duty to England and the King. Maybe that's what Sir Francis is talking about too. Then she remembers what Margaret called him. A pirate.

"I don't trust you!"

He looks startled. "I'm sorry to hear that—"

"Rosie! Rosie!" Jimmy Green comes running up the street "See what I got."

He skids to a stop almost on top of her and holds his hand out, palm up. Something white is lying on it like a small twig.

"What's that supposed to be?"

"It's a bone—a finger bone from a spy—a Jerry, innit?"

"Is not."

"Is! I jus' foun' it, din't I?"

"Fibber. It's a chicken bone."

"Where'd I get a chicken bone? Ain't any in the market. Look, I'll take you. It's jus' over a coupla streets."

"Mum says—"

"Aw, come on, Rosie. We can find some more."

She wants to do this so much it makes her stomach hurt. Nobody will know if she goes with Jimmy. Mum always takes her time down the market, talking to the other women.

She looks up to see if Sir Francis has an opinion, but he isn't there now.

No time to get her coat. She pulls Mum's apron off and runs after Jimmy.

English Channel, December 1944

"Looking for someone?"

Frank Smith leaned against the rail of the central building of the control tower. He was smoking, the glowing cigarette cupped in the shelter of his corded hands. The scent of rich tobacco drifted on the foggy night air, as Harry emerged from the stairwell.

"You're a spy," Harry said.

Frank chuckled. "I've been called worse. But what makes you think that?"

"Something was out there a while ago. I heard it splash."

"Remarkable how fast I got out of the lifeboat and climbed up here, isn't it? Brr! That water was cold." Frank took another deep pull on his cigarette and tossed it over the rail. "It's the fog. And the Channel itself. Puts strange ideas into a chap's head."

Sobranie, by the smell. He hadn't smelled those since before the war. The man had expensive tastes. Where did he get
them? Not from the little store on the fort. "What are you
doing here on U7?"

"The same thing you're doing. Playing my part in a war
not of my choosing. But listen, one of the chaps has some rum
down there, in the rec room. Coast Guard very kindly brought
it over from one of the navy forts up the coast. Knock John,
I think it's called. Quaint name! Early Christmas gift and all
that. Maybe you should pop down for a quick nip? Chase the
cold out of your veins."

Every word out of the man's mouth deepened Harry's unease. "You could've been on the landing dock, signaling with
a torch—"

"Good Lord! It usually takes more than your few weeks
out here for a soldier to start hallucinating. Maybe you'd better
have a word with the medical corpsman?"

In the silence, the sandbar's warning bell boomed again.
He heard the sound of voices from one of the fort's other
towers, muffled and indistinct, the watch changing. No sign
another sentry had noticed anything amiss out there on the
black water.

"Forrest!"

The sergeant's bark snapped him out of his thoughts. He
came to attention even though he wasn't on duty.

"Sarge?"

"Check the new duty roster. Going to need you."

"Right, Sarge."

"Carry on." The sergeant disappeared back into the fog
from which he'd emerged.

Harry turned away from the door to the fort's interior. On the side that faced the low coastline of England—invisible under blackout rules, but he had it memorized—he paused, overcome by a deep longing. Not so far in terms of miles, but tonight a world away. And further upriver, where his little family lived—a lost paradise where enemy raids and suspicious characters didn't intrude. Then it hit him.

"He didn't see you." The sergeant must have walked right past him.

Frank spread his arms in a gesture of defeat. "I don't know how to explain it."

"Try me."

"Remember Einstein? The one way arrow of Time is an illusion. But play it wrong, and you upset the universe."

"For God's sake, man! You're not making sense."

"I've said too much already." Frank moved away from the wall and stretched as if his muscles were stiff from the cold. "Are you sure I can't tempt you to sample the rum? No? Well, I'm turning in. Good night.

London, December 1944

Jimmy was telling lies when he said the interesting thing was just a couple of streets over. It's much farther than that. Mum will be angry if she finds out how far from their street Jimmy is taking her. But Jimmy's her best friend, even if he is a boy. She's thought about letting Jimmy in on her secret visitor. He'd be jealous that she gets to talk to Sir Francis Drake! But she's decided not to just yet, not before Jimmy shows her some real dead person's bones.

"How much farther?"

"Jus' round this corner," Jimmy says.

"If you're telling me fibs, Jimmy Green—"

"Can't you smell it?"

She's smelling something. Something very odd. A thick smell. Sweet, at first, it's sort of like when Mum perspires on a hot day in the summer. But this smell makes her stomach shiver. It sort of reminds her of the time Nan was cooking and accidentally let a pan full of meat catch on fire.

"What is it?"

"Bodies," Jimmy announces proudly as if he'd thrown them on the fire himself. "Jerry pilot bodies. They stink worsen anythin'!"

He skids to a stop just as he rounds a corner into a dead-end street that backs up to the railway lines, and she almost bumps into him. They can't go any farther because the bobbies have put a barrier across the street to stop people. Now she notices gray smoke curling up from a large building that must've been bombed last night. A lot of men are standing around, pointing and waving their arms.

A fireman goes through a brick archway that's still standing, into the ruined building. The arch seems big enough for a lorry to go through. Another fireman comes out. She can see police cars and an ambulance, a fire engine and firemen still sloshing around in their wellies, carrying dripping fire-hoses, But there aren't any flames anymore, just a lot of ash and grit drifting in the air like clouds of flies. And this horrible smell. It makes her sneeze. She has no idea what the building that got bombed might have been.

"What is it?" she asks.

Jimmy shrugs. "There's prob'ly bodies inside."

"You don't know that for sure, do you? You haven't been inside." The nasty smell is much worse here. She pinches her nose against it. "Pooh! It smells like sick!"

"That's the smell of evil Jerries, I tell ya."

"I'm going to tell on you for all the fibs, Jimmy Green!"

Of course, she can't do that because she's not supposed to be here. And maybe, just for once, he's right, and there really are bodies. She doesn't know what dead people bodies smell like—she's only seen the butcher's dead cat. If that's true, she wants to see the ambulance men carry one out. A real dead person would be much more exciting than a dead moggy.

Nobody seems to take any notice of them, so they huddle against a brick wall and keep watching. Now that they've stopped running, and nothing seems to be happening, she's feeling cold again. She's shivering because her cardigan isn't warm enough for outside. And the smell is making her sick.

One of the firemen comes out of the burned building and stands talking to a bobby. A big black car drives fast down the street toward the building. It stops so suddenly it looks for a moment as if the top is going to rock right off the wheels.

"Crikey!" Jimmy whispers in her ear. "That mus' be the landlord."

"How can you tell?"

"'Cause it's a rich geezer's car, innit? A Rolls Royce."

The man who jumps out of the Rolls Royce doesn't look rich to Rosemary. He's wearing a wool scarf and a cloth cap, just like the milkman. They're too far away to hear what's being said. The bobby holds up one hand as if he's going to stop the man in the cap, but the landlord—if Jimmy's right about him—ignores the bobby and goes through the archway into what's left of the building. The bobby and the firemen follow.

This is interesting, but not nearly enough to keep her there, shivering in the ashy cold and the horrible smell. There are no Jerries here, dead or alive, she's certain.

Another man runs out of the same brick archway and straight up the street toward them. His face is streaked with dirt. When he gets closer, she's astonished to see tears making tracks down his cheeks. The man doesn't see them and almost runs right into Jimmy.

"Sorry! Sorry!" the man says. It comes out like a grunt.

"Please, sir," she begins in a very small voice. "Can we do anything to help?"

The man is sobbing now. She doesn't know what to do. She hasn't seen many grown-ups cry, and never a man. Perhaps he knows somebody in that bombed building? She's been hoping to find dead people in the ruins, but this is different.

"Lose somefink, Guv?" Jimmy asks. His voice is shaking too.

The man suddenly collapses at their feet, back to the wall. "Brownie—I lost Brownie."

Rosemary looks at Jimmy, but he just looks back. Neither of them can sort this.

She pulls a hankie out of her sleeve and offers it to the man. The terrible smell is all over his clothes. He takes the hankie and wipes his eyes. The result is worse because now his cheeks are striped with black and gray like some horrible clown in a picture book.

"Lost yer mate, 'ave yer, Guv?" Jimmy says. "This Brownie's yer mate?"

The man stops crying and looks up at them. "Not my mate. My horse. Brownie was the best carthorse I've ever had."

This is hard to understand. Now she can see that under all that grime he's their coalman. She can't remember his name, but she knows Brownie. She's a big brown horse with a white patch on her nose and little brass medals like a long necklace down her front. She pulls the coal-cart down the streets. Sometimes, when the coalman comes to their house, she gets to give Brownie a carrot. She remembers how the big horse takes it so gently off the palm of her hand. What's happened to Brownie? Did she run away?

A hand touches her on the shoulder, and she looks up into the face of one of the bobbies.

"You kids better run along home now," he says. "We'll take care of Mr Hopkins here."

"His horse," she says, in a very small voice. "Please, what's happened to his horse?"

The bobby looks at them for a moment as if he's deciding whether they can understand what he's going to say.

"Give it to us, Guv," Jimmy says, almost in a whisper.

"This was a stable that was bombed last night," the bobby says. "Stable's mostly for the brewery's horses, but some of the coalmen keep their horses here too because it backs up to the railway lines. It went up fast—all that hay. A few of the horses managed to get out. Hopkins's horse didn't."

Perhaps something happened to her ears. She must not have heard this properly. The policeman sounds ever so far away. Perhaps she only thought he said that? Horrible things like horses getting killed by bombs didn't really happen, did they?

"Run along now," the bobby says again.

Tears come to her eyes too. Horses aren't supposed to get killed. Jimmy takes hold of her hand and they walk away, leaving Mr Hopkins and the bobby talking behind them.

"I don't want to play this game anymore, Jimmy," she says. "It's a bad one."

"Don' like it too much meself," he says.

English Channel, December 1944

In the mess, Harry chewed his corned beef fritter without tasting it. The mess hall was noisy and stuffy, but he shut it out to think. Accusations about another soldier without proof were not well received in the Royal Artillery, anymore than they would be in civilian life. Sometimes he wondered whether Britain would ever be the same after all this was over, and if it wouldn't, what were they fighting for?

He was fighting for Alice and his girls. He'd kill to keep them safe.

Einstein, Frank had said. What did that mean? The masters hadn't got very far in their science instruction before he'd had to leave school. But he'd always been a reader, especially pulp magazines. *Thrilling Wonder Stories* from America had a lot about physics in them. Nothing came immediately to him, but his mind had a habit of working on things when he wasn't thinking about them and offering solutions much later.

Mid-afternoon, but it was already twilight out. The mess was muggy from the warmth of so many bodies, and clouds of cigarette smoke hung over the occupants, though the windows were open. The other men were making bets on the outcome of the over-the-phone darts match later that evening with Nore Fort.

The lights were cheerful enough, draped in lacy paper cut-outs. Somebody had strung festive paper chains along one wall. Somebody else had put up a small artificial Christmas tree and decorated it with tinfoil they'd saved from cigarette packets. The hall echoed with shouted challenges and insults. Much laughter. He tried to block the noise out, not joining the wagering, friendly though it seemed. Every man supported the U7 team, obviously, but the challenge was to predict the score by which they were going to win.

The general merriment didn't distract him from his worries for long. What proof did he have? Frank Smith kept turning up wherever Harry was. He didn't look English. He seemed to know too much. And none of the other chaps reacted to him, as if they weren't able to see him.

Tell Sarge that, and he'd be sent off to the funny farm.

Yet he couldn't shake the feeling that there was something decidedly wrong here. Smith would have to give himself away sooner or later.

He got up to pour himself another mug of tea, and Geordy touched his arm.

"Some folks reckon there's U-boats int' water," Geordy said.

"Not surprising, is it? Channel's probably full of them."

"Tha knows ah hate 'em! Nazis!"

He knew how personally the young man had taken the bombing attacks on his beloved York Minster. "We all do, Geordy."

"Cap'n said t'keep a lookout."

Farmer's son, he'd told Harry. Sheep on the moors. Solid C of E upbringing. Good kid, one of England's finest, even if he did lapse into almost unintelligible Northern dialect from time to time.

"Radar'll spot 'em, Geordy. Don't worry about it. And we've got the big guns—"

"Nay," the younger man said. "Summat's up. Tha's goin' ta invade us, tha Nazis. Reckon ah'll kill a few iffen tha comes here."

"I doubt they'll get very far."

There was little confidence behind his words, but the York-shireman nodded and went away.

The harsh sound of the Tannoy broke his thoughts. "Diver! Diver!"

The mess hall turned in an instant from a gathering of men ready for a friendly competition to a hive of activity as they ran to assume battle stations. He stood up too—he wasn't on duty, but that didn't hold during a raid. He went up to the top deck where the guns were already in action. The tower shook under his feet. The air smelled of rotting kelp and gunpowder.

"Something different about this one, Harry."

He turned to see who had shouted in his ear over the thunder of the Bofors. Frank Smith. He felt the skin crawl on the back of his neck.

Frank pressed field glasses into his hands and gestured at the sky to the northeast.

Something coming fast. Very fast. At least half a dozen somethings. At different heights—going to make it tough for the gunners. Something about their shape was wrong. They had to be bombers, but the silhouettes he was seeing were *wrong*.

"Forrest!" Sarge yelled as the Bofors roared again. "Tell Jenkins to take the Browning. I want you on the Bofors."

"What the hell are they, Sarge?"

But Sarge had already disappeared. Harry raced over the vibrating metal bridge to the big gun's base and laid a hand on Jenkins's shoulder. The man understood immediately—Harry was the best gunner on the fort—and quickly gave up his seat. Harry seized the earphones.

He settled himself in control of the Bofors. The air was full of thundering guns and smoke.

"Rockets," Frank shouted in his ear. "Your guns are little use against them. Too fast."

"What?" he shouted back, not taking his eyes off the sky.

The man made no show of doing anything to help out. "V2s. Big improvement over the V1s—" He stopped abruptly.

Harry turned to him, earphones pushed back over one ear, all his suspicions returning. "How do you know that?"

"I pay attention to the briefings that come down from Command, just like any soldier should do. Rockets. Scientist name of Von Braun builds them for Hitler, but they're from an American—Goddard's design. Of course, the Russian Tsiolkovsky—"

No, Harry's mind objected. *No, any soldier wouldn't know this!* This wasn't in the briefings.

Then the Bofors thundered and shuddered under him. He'd fired it automatically as he'd been trained. The flock of V2s whined overhead so fast their sound trailed after them. The smaller Browning guns stuttered in fury.

There was no way any of the guns were fast enough to catch rockets.

Oslo, December 2035

Had Carlos ever understood what troubled her about her childhood?

She stood at the hotel window staring out at the quiet dark, all the helicars landed now, their passengers taking their seats in the fabled hall. She'd told him some of her story, not understanding most of it herself. A jigsaw puzzle with key parts missing. Even after all these years, she still wasn't sure what the picture really was. He'd folded her in his arms. "You're here now, that's what really matters," he'd said. She'd started to tell

Gabriel one time—the family had been at Princeton for his graduation. But the timing had been wrong, and the subject too difficult anyway, so she'd given up the attempt.

She waited the final minutes, till the knock would come and the escorts—*handsome, provided by the committee*—and remembered a yacht, the *Halcyon*. Long ago, when Catalina and her now-dead brother had both been quite young.

The yacht had rocked at anchor in the Aegean, white pillars of her turbo sails gleaming, the sky above the water an unrelenting hot sapphire, the air heavy and laden with the smell of fish. Carlos came on deck in swimming trunks.

"There's something I want to show you, Mary." He brought out the scuba gear he'd hidden behind his back. She took it, and he helped her put it on and adjust the gauges.

He was always eager to show her something—an ancient city hidden for thousands of years in the Chinese mountains, older than civilization itself; enormous, unexplored vistas of moonlike landscapes on the Steppes; the Aurora Borealis over a glacier near the North Pole; a wrinkled old man in the Australian Outback playing an instrument straight out of prehistory. Sometime, perhaps in the near future, tourist visits to the moon would be possible, and she knew he'd want to show her that too. How eager he always was to give her the world! His hair was graying now, and his cheeks a little jowly, but his enthusiasm for life hadn't changed. Nor had her love for him.

The young Greek *au pair* they'd hired took the children below to fix their tea.

Carlos stepped backwards off the swim deck of the *Halcyon*. She prepared to follow him. Bobbing in the swells, Carlos pointed to his ear, reminding her to make sure she was ready to communicate.

Wine-dark, Homer had described the water of the Mediterranean, but clear as glass and soft as velvet. She slipped below the surface, enchanted by the schools of small fish like silver coins darting away from her outstretched hands, the columns of sunlight falling through the cool water as if she floated in an underwater cathedral.

Come on, his voice said in her head. *It's not far.*

She followed him, swimming deeper, past gaping fish, bright coral and the occasional curious dolphin, until the bottom came in sight. Swirling sand clouded the water as bottom dwellers scurried to safety as they arrived, but she could make out shapes, mounds, covered in barnacles.

Look there, Carlos sent.

What am I looking at?

He swam closer to one of the larger mounds and began brushing sand off. At first his movements only added to the swirling cloud that hung over the mound like a curtain. Slowly, as the sand settled back to the seabed, a shape began to emerge.

What is it?

She sensed rather than heard his chuckle. *What does it look like to you?*

Surely that was the side of a boat—a rather large one. And that part sticking up there, a mast? *It looks like a boat.*

Roman. A trireme. Marine archaeologists have done a lot of work in this part of the Mediterranean, but so far they've missed this beauty.

For the next thirty minutes they swam through the wreck. It hardly seemed damaged by the passage of more than two thousand years, and she almost expected to see a toga-clad Roman come out of a cabin to demand to know their business on his ship. She lost count of the number of carved statues, metal boxes, the unbroken amphoras that seemed to promise they'd kept their contents safe, the tumble of swords and shields, anchored by kelp and home to schools of fish, the tragedy of lost lives they spoke of muted by the passing of so many centuries.

I feel like a time traveler! she sent.

Too soon, Carlos tapped his watch, and they began the slow rise to the surface. Afterwards, they sat on deck of the *Halcyon* and watched the sun set over the Greek islands. The children's voices drifted up from the cabin where they prepared for bed.

"Easy to imagine that beautiful trireme sailing past the Pillars of Hercules at Gibraltar," she said, sipping her chilled Pineus. Carlos could afford any wine in the world, but he drank only Spanish wine.

"Think of the effect it would have had on those blue-painted natives of Britain as it emerged from the fog in the channel!" Carlos said, laughing.

"Yes," she said. "It might as well have been a spaceship."

He took her hand. "Something's troubling you, *cara*."

"Sometimes that shocking clash of new technology with old culture does great damage, Carlos," she said slowly, working it out. "The Romans built their astonishing roads and walls, and often all that was left for the older ways of doing things was to shrivel up and die."

"History has many tales to tell us about that," he agreed. "Not all of them happy ones."

"Think of the mischief a time traveler could cause."

He bent closer, looking into her eyes as if he could read the thoughts behind them. "What puts these odd ideas into your head?"

She thought of those stories she'd read during the war, hiding her father's science fiction magazines behind the covers of the school book she was supposed to be reading. And the strange fantasy she'd had about a man who dressed like Sir Francis Drake—if fantasy was all it had been.

"My childhood visitor. I don't think that story is complete just yet."

He nodded. "Perhaps not."

"I keep thinking there must've been a good reason for the visit."

"I can't answer that, *cara.*" He smiled at her. "But we have a saying in my family: *Asi la marea sube, la marea cae.*"

And now they were dead—her father and mother, her sister, Carlos. Even her son. So much sadness! Yet Carlos had been certain that everything balances out in the end, like a tide rising and falling.

The uniformed soldier waiting outside her hotel room was in fact quite lovely, with a skin as polished and dark as the Black Madonna in the monastery who'd blessed their marriage. The young man took her arm with great courtesy. Her daughter with her own young escort fell in behind.

London, December 1944

Mum is waiting for her on the door step when she gets home. The pail with the Vim and the brush is where Rosemary left it.

"And just where have you been, young lady?" Mum demands. "You're filthy. Look at your cardigan—streaked with dirt. Is that soot? And—are those tears?"

"No!" She swats at the tears on her cheeks. "I got something in my eye."

"Good heavens, child! What is that terrible smell on you?"

"Brownie got bombed last night, Mum."

"Who?"

"Brownie—Mr Hopkins's horse. The one that pulls the coal-cart—" Only, of course, Brownie wouldn't be pulling any more loads of coal up their street.

"Oh, sweetheart!" Mum pulls Rosemary close. "I'm so sorry."

She jerks away and runs up the stairs to her tiny bedroom. Inside her room, she slams the door shut.

She flings herself on the bed—and she doesn't care if she's getting soot all over her eiderdown either. What good is it if she gets to be safe but horses like Brownie don't? It's all going wrong.

A moment later, Mum opens the door. "Rosemary?"

"Don't want to talk about it!" She buries her face in her pillow and sobs.

After a while, her tears stop. She rubs her eyes on an edge of the eiderdown and sees the black smudge of dirt this leaves. She sits up.

Sir Francis is sitting cross-legged on the floor. His red cloak has slipped off his shoulders, his hat is in one hand. He looks as old as her grandpa right now.

"You promised everything was going to be all right!"

"I can't take care of everything," he says irritably. "Do try to be reasonable. Not that I expect you to understand."

He's right. She doesn't understand a word of it. But it's not important anyway. "Why did Brownie have to die? It's not fair."

"Life isn't about being fair, It just *is*."

"Well, it shouldn't be! Brownie didn't deserve to be bombed. She was just a horse."

She slams her way out of her tiny bedroom.

When she reaches the kitchen, Mum grabs her hand as she goes to sit at the kitchen table. "Wash first, please, sweetheart. And you need some Dettol in the bowl. No telling all the nasty stuff you got into."

She helps Rosemary out of her grimy cardigan, then pours the Dettol in the water. The yellow liquid turns the water white like milk. She scrubs her hands.

It's baked beans on a piece of toast tonight, with a cup of tea. She isn't hungry. She doesn't want to think about that stable and poor Brownie in it. All the flames! But the thought just won't stay out of her head. She pushes some beans onto her toast and tries to get the fork up to her mouth.

"She still stinks, Mum," Margaret says, pinching her nose.

Rosemary drops the fork, splattering beans and tomato sauce all over the table cloth. For a moment she stares at it. The sobs start again, and now she can't stop.

Sir Francis keeps saying she'll be safe. But why wasn't Brownie safe too? Don't horses matter?

It's like Mr Henstridge teaching something big. You understand it's important, but you can't understand what it is.

And perhaps you wouldn't like it if you did.

English Channel, December 1944

Afterwards, Harry sat on his bunk, a small writing pad on his knee, pencil in hand. His Enfield leaned unsteadily against the lower bunk—something Sarge would fly into a rage over if he saw it like that. But Sarge was busy elsewhere. The new wave of flying bombs had caused something of an uproar in command circles. They were rocket propelled bombs, faster than anything Hitler had thrown at them before. Hard to shoot down.

The distant clang of the bell buoy drifted through the window, bringing with it the ever-present cold smell of the sea. He pushed the window shut and returned to his problem.

What was that business of nobody else seeing Smith? How could he possibly go to command with a tale of an invisible man? They'd think he was hallucinating. And perhaps he was. The sense of isolation out here on the Channel wreaked havoc with the nerves.

Two days ago he'd posted Christmas cards, one for Alice and one for the girls to share. He would've sent them one each, but the small display offered in the recreation room only had two designs to choose from. Well, it was wartime. Even children had to learn to share.

But today his heart hammered, his entire body, bones and all, ached with an urgent need to send a letter to his wife.

Dearest Alice—

The supply boat was due to dock in half an hour with a quick turnaround. Just time enough to take a sack of mail.

His hand was shaking with the urgency he felt and he nearly put a hole through the flimsy paper.

Something very strange's going on—I'm not sure what, but—

Scrub that. It would never get past the censor.

Get right to the message. *Get yourself and the girls out of London. Now!*

That wouldn't work. Without an explanation, she wouldn't do it. They were Londoners. They didn't desert London in her hour of need. Even the king and queen were still in London. But he couldn't explain any more than that even if he'd known what was going on.

Please, at least let them evacuate the girls. Or take them to their Nan in Cheltenham—

What could he say to persuade her? Nothing the censor would let through. He could only hope Alice would catch his urgency and take herself and the children to the relative safety of the countryside.

"Ah there you are."

Frank Smith came into the sleeping quarters as if they were his own.

"I'm busy. I have to get this letter to the post."

"Well, carry on, then. I'll just sit here and wait."

Frank climbed up on a lower bunk opposite. If it had been difficult to find the words before the man interrupted him, it was now almost impossible.

I have some leave coming at the end of next month. I can hardly wait for the joy of holding you all in my arms.

He glanced up to find the man's eyes on him. Frank smiled. Harry put the pencil down on the bunk beside the pad.

"Right. I've had enough. Now you're going to tell me just what you're up to. Why you hang around me."

"If I told you, you wouldn't understand."

"Rubbish! I may not be one of your Old Boys from Harrow or Eton, but I'm not a stupid man—"

"Of course not, Harry. I'm well aware of that."

He launched himself off the bunk and seized the other man by the collar, dragging him to the floor. In his rage he would've killed him. But the door to the sleeping quarters opened, and another soldier came in.

Reluctantly, he let go of Frank and pulled back.

The newcomer looked from one to the other of them. "Too much aggro around here!" the man grumbled. He went off to his own bunk at the far end of the room, leaving them to it.

"He saw you. Others don't see you. Explain yourself."

"How does one prove a negative?" Frank said. "This may surprise you, but I'm not interested in who wins this war. That's already been decided."

"That's *what?*"

"I'm more concerned with what follows. It's a dilemma, Harry, seeing the danger but not daring to interfere. The technology for time travel exists in the future. But it's rather like walking a tightrope. That's the risk I'm taking."

"Is it absolutely impossible for you to give me a straight answer?"

Frank gazed at him for a second. "Yes," he said.

London, December 1944

The day before Christmas Eve, but it doesn't feel like it. This morning, Rosemary has been helping Margaret tear up pieces of old newspaper, braiding them and pasting them in loops to make paper chains. Mum is stringing the finished chains up so they crisscross the kitchen. There's only enough coal left to light one fire, and the kitchen is easier to keep warm than the sitting-room. There won't be any more coal deliveries for a while, until Mr. Hopkins gets another horse.

She doesn't want to think about Brownie because she'll start crying if she does.

The kitchen's fireplace has a smoky chimney, and it's making her cough. It reminds her of the stable that burned down too. Tears come anyway. She rubs them away before Mum or Margaret can see what a crybaby she is.

The newspaper chains don't really look right for Christmas. Real Christmas decorations are supposed to be red and green or silver. She can't remember ever having seen any like that because she was too little when the war started. But today two cards came from Daddy, one for Mum and one for her and Margaret to share, with a picture of a real Christmas tree on it. She's disappointed he didn't write anything except *Happy Christmas from your loving Daddy*, but Mum explained the censor would've cut it out if he had. She wonders if Daddy wrote more words to Mum, but she tucked her card away in her handbag and didn't show it to them.

Sometimes there's silver paper, wrapped around a biscuit or a sweet or something precious, but Mum says they can't use that for decorations. They have to squeeze it into one big ball and save it for the war effort. There won't be Christmas cake either, because Mum says the shops don't have what it takes to make one. And she wouldn't have enough ration coupons to buy the things even if they did. Only a ragged old fake tree that stands on the table, waiting to be decorated with fake ornaments. Mum says Nan will come up from Cheltenham if the trains are running.

Will there be any presents? She doesn't believe in Father Christmas anymore, but it would be nice to have presents, even very little ones. Margaret has been making a small potholder for Mum, out of old scraps left over when Mum cut up one of her own dresses to make one for Rosemary, who's growing so fast that they never have enough coupons. The pattern looks better as a potholder than it does as Rosemary's dress. Mum will probably pretend the potholder is exactly what she wanted. She's started to make a bookmark with a bit of cardboard cut from an empty box of tea, covering it with a crayon drawing of trees on the blank side. Mum won't mind the picture of a cup and saucer that was on the other side, even if she's had to cut some of the saucer away to make it the right size.

She wanders off to her bedroom, restless and irritable. She doesn't feel like finishing the bookmark. She'd rather go out and look at the shops down the market. Some of her friends might be out shopping, so close to Christmas. Even Jimmy Green will be better than nothing. Anyway, Mum isn't as keen on reading as Daddy is, so there's no point finishing the bookmark.

In her bedroom, she sees that Sir Francis is back, legs crossed on the little stool.

"Quite finished with decorating for the festivities?" he asks.

Rosemary frowns. "Not going to be festivities—whatever they are! There's a war on." Jimmy Green would say she's off her rocker for talking to him. What does Jimmy Green know, anyway.

"May I suggest a shopping excursion?"

"A what?"

"Something to relieve your boredom. A trip to the shops."

That's exactly what she'd been thinking of doing, but she's annoyed with him for trying to put ideas into her head. "I'm going to read my daddy's magazines. They make more sense than you do."

"If only you knew, child!" he says with a sigh. "But come now, surely you'd like to look around the shops?"

She makes her decision. "No. I don't want to go out."

"But you like to go shopping!" Sir Francis says. He looks startled. "You like looking at the stalls and the people."

"Perhaps I do, and perhaps I don't. But I don't want to go today. So there!"

He fiddles with the feather on his hat. She knows by this that he's thinking hard.

"Rosemary," he says, "I must insist that you go."

Astonished, she gapes at him. "You can't tell me what to do!"

"Please, child. It's important."

"It's what?"

"I can't explain it to you. You need to trust me."

She glares at him. "I haven't any money, only the ha'penny I found."

He looks puzzled for a moment, the way he does when he doesn't understand something that any baby would know. "Show it to me."

She fishes in her pocket then holds it out on the palm of her hand, with the side showing the *Golden Hind* up.

"Drake's ship," he says. "A good omen! It's all you'll need."

Rosemary shakes her head. "I want to decorate the tree even if it isn't real. It's important that we keep appearances up, Mum says, even if it's wartime."

"I can't believe I'm having this argument!" Sir Francis says. "I'm doing you a great favor, child."

"You're not really Sir Francis, are you? Who are you? Why are you here in my house?"

He stares at her as if he's trying to decide what to say. "Because it's important to us both, that's why," he says. "Now go!"

She slams the door behind her and goes to find Mum.

"Can I go out and see if there are any shops open, Mum?"

"What do you want with the shops?" Margaret says. She's sitting with her bad foot propped on another chair as she makes chains. "You don't have any money saved to buy presents even if they are open."

"Do too have money."

"Show me."

She brings out the lucky ha'penny. "There."

Margaret shrieks with laughter.

"I hate you! I wish you weren't my sister!"

And without waiting for permission from Mum, Rosemary grabs her dark blue coat from the peg behind the front door and goes out.

It's very cold outside, the sky is full of low, gray clouds, but at least the air isn't as smoky as the kitchen. Everything's going wrong. It's not fair. There isn't going to be Christmas cake with icing on it. There aren't going to be presents under the silly old fake tree. She doesn't really have enough money to buy anything more than a couple of sweets with her ha'penny—but she doesn't have any coupons anyway. And Daddy isn't coming home for Christmas.

There aren't very many people on the street, or at the market when she reaches it. The barrows that sell fruit and vegetables are half empty. She knows enough about wartime now to know they probably weren't even full this morning. She'd had a bright idea about buying an orange. One of the costermongers—Jimmy Green's dad, probably—would take pity on her and sell her one small orange for a ha'penny, wouldn't he? Even if she doesn't have the coupons? She'd like to give that to Mum for Christmas. Small oranges were all they had these days, anyway, when they had any at all. Mum says that's because of the long way they have to come across the Channel where all the U-boats are. But today neither Mr Green or his barrow are here. She doesn't know any of the other costers well enough to ask.

Half the shops aren't open today, either. Woolworths and Boots-the-Chemist have signs up saying they'll be open tomorrow, Christmas Eve, for only a couple of hours. The butcher's shop is open, and two women with baskets on their arms are going inside. But all he has hanging in the window is one string of sausages that don't look anymore tasty than the paper chains she was making earlier. There's a Methodist church at the end of the street where the market is, but it got bombed a few weeks ago. Someone's put a sign outside the church door that says, *Bombed not beaten. Christmas Eve services.*

It's one thing for Sir Francis to promise her she's going to be all right when the war's over, but right now she feels miserable, and it looks like the war is going on and on forever.

Something touches her face. Something cold, and wet. She looks up. It's snowing. She puts her tongue out and catches two more snowflakes, and her coat has tinsel sparkles all over it. It's like the lacy white curtain in Nan's sitting room, only prettier, just drifting down to the street and hiding all the dirt. She doesn't remember if it snowed last winter, but it couldn't have been prettier than this Christmas snow.

Laughing, she turns around to go home and tell Mum and Margaret the good news.

The air raid siren starts wailing.

And then—a terrible, loud whining noise like nothing she's ever heard before fills her ears. She squats down low on the pavement and covers her ears with her hands, but there's no shutting this noise out. She peers through the falling snow at the sky, but the clouds are too low to see anything.

People are shouting at her—she can see their mouths moving. An Air Raid Warden appears— She understands he's telling her to get to a shelter. But where? The noise is dreadful!

A huge BOOM!—and a blast of hot air knocks her over. Then she's in the gutter, several feet away. Thick clouds of dust are billowing around. And the smell of burning.

Her ears are ringing, and her arm hurts where she fell on it. It feels like a lot of time going by. It feels like no time at all.

"You all right, li'l gel?" A woman, her face streaked in grime holds out a hand to her. "Where d'you live, darlin'?"

She has trouble hearing. And she can't get the name of her street past her lips, so she points. It's two streets over, just past the *Pig and Whistle.*

"Oh no, luv," the woman says, "I don't think we better go near there!"

The siren is still wailing. Warning of attack. A bit late now! The bomb—it has to have been a bomb to make that much noise—has dropped somewhere already.

"Where's this child come from?" A warden, hands on hips, is standing behind the woman now. "Who're you, young lady, out all by yourself when there's a raid on?"

"Says she lives up that way." The woman points just like Rosemary did.

"Blimey!" the warden says, peering down at her. "You've been a very lucky little gel."

The siren stops. She can hear the fire engines coming. The sound is muffled, like the voices of the people talking to her. Her ears hurt. Her heart is pounding, making her chest hurt too. She can't think very fast. Her head feels like it's underwater.

It's snowing hard now.

"Here. I'll take you to the Women's Auxiliary ladies," the warden says. The all-clear is sounding now. Raid over. "They'll make you a nice cuppa."

But she doesn't want a cup of tea. She wants to go home. She pulls her hand out of the warden's grasp and runs through the snow, which is already turning to slush on the pavement. Her left arm aches badly. One of her ankles seems to be hurt too, and it's difficult to run without falling over.

The falling snow is mixed with ash so she can hardly see where she's going. There are fire engines and ambulances racing down Marigold Road. Bricks and rubble all over the road and the pavement make her stumble. The air is smoky. And a lot of muddled noise that she can't make out clearly because her ears are still plugged from the blast. Nobody seems to notice her, so she pushes through a jumble of people.

What she sees doesn't make sense.

The smelly old air raid shelter is a flat pile of rubble—bricks scattered over the road. Smoke and soot everywhere.

There's a big space on the road where some of the houses had been.

Her house isn't there.

Only the chimney is still standing. Smoke pours out of it in a thick stream as if the fire in the kitchen is still lit. Maybe it's not her house?

She sees the marble front step, all by itself now, and knows it is.

"Very lucky you weren't home when the bleedin' rocket hit," Mrs Banbury says. She's holding tight to her old cat. Tomkins is yowling.

How could her house get bombed?

"You promised," she whispers.

All the noise around her and the smell and the gritty clouds of cinders mixed in the snow make it too hard to think straight about his words. But Sir Francis—whoever he is—told her the truth. She's alive.

He never said anything about saving anybody else.

English Channel, December 1944

"Summat real mardy happenin' up thy way," Geordy said. Gloomy-faced, Enfield in hand, the Yorkshireman came to stand by Harry at the rail.

Harry had been staring at the low coastline of Essex and Kent, the gaping, shadowy mouth of the Thames between them, for an hour now. He was at a loose end, not on duty, not ready to celebrate the season. Christmas Eve, the forecast promised, would bring, if not fair weather, at least no storms. Last night, the wind had blustered past the fort carrying snow flurries to land, but that had turned out to be more drama than anything and had long since blown away. The sea below was calm at the turn of the tide. The sharp, gray-green smell of kelp filled his nose.

"Has tha no heard the radio sin tha bin up here?"

Harry turned to the younger man who was on guard duty this afternoon. "What happened?"

"London's bin hit. Hard. Heard it on the BBC."

"That's not news. Jerry's been hitting us hard for a while now—" He broke off, thinking of the furious swarms of rockets that defied their guns last night.

Geordy tilted his chin toward the door. "Tha's about done wi' the Christmas rum down there. Better get a sup while ye can. Do ye good."

From the men's mess on a lower floor a babble of voices reached them—laughter, some singing. Cigarette smoke rose up the stairs in a blue cloud.

"You go ahead." He wasn't in the mood for putting a silly newspaper hat on his head and swigging rum with the men— all of them probably half-drunk already.

"Nay, lad." Geordy settled the Enfield on his right shoulder. "I'm on watch."

Christmas Eve. Birthday of the Prince of Peace. He didn't believe in fairy tales. The enormity of it crept over him. The horror, the sheer stupidity, the absurdity of thinking they were making a difference in any way. A hundred and sixty men on a series of rickety platforms in the channel trying to shoot down the most fiendish weapon ever. Multiply that by all the other forts up and down the coast. And all of them sitting ducks for enemy bombers. The kid who'd gone daft and had to be taken off the fort had understood better than any of them the absolute futility of it all.

Something splashed below.

He reached for his Enfield—reflex action—but he didn't have it with him; he wasn't on duty. He leaned out far over the rail and scrutinized the sea running between the fort's spidery legs. Nothing. Had to have been a seabird fishing.

He heard it again, followed this time by another sound he couldn't identify.

"Geordy. Did you hear that?"

The younger man joined him at the rail. A large bird flapped up from below and swept past, wings beating angrily. Then another. Both birds circled overhead. Something out there, disturbing the birds.

"Lookit!" Geordy whispered.

Harry stared at a spot where whitecaps erupted. A gray conning tower. A mast sticking up from the tower. Waves breaking over the tower as it rose. No markings. Not more than twenty feet away.

"Harry?" Geordy whispered. "Tha's a U-boat. What'll we'un do?"

"Stay here, Geordy. Keep an eye on it. I'm going to raise the alarm."

"Not so fast." Frank Smith stood behind them. "Give them a moment."

Harry turned to Geordy and saw the young man drop his shoulder and pull the sling holding his Enfield, raising the rifle into position.

Frank saw it too. "Put that down, my young friend. It's not needed."

"I dinna take orders from—"

"Wait, Geordy," Harry said. "You can see this man?"

"Aye," Geordy said hesitantly. He lowered the rifle.

Harry turned back to Frank. "How do you do that? This time, you're going to explain."

"Nanomaterial with a negative index of refraction. You might think of it as an invisibility cloak. The technology's almost due to be discovered."

Harry glanced at the rising conning tower, water sheeting off it. He should sound the alarm. But he had to know. "Tell me the truth."

"Think of it as a paradox, Harry. You used to read the comics."

"You don't belong in this time," he said.

"Harry." Geordy tugged at his sleeve. "Look! There's summat on tha boat."

A long, sleek grayness stood out above the churning water, and a man in a seaman's cap peered out from the open tower.

"We maun go down t' the dock!" Geordy slung the rifle over his shoulder and turned to the iron steps that led down to the floating dock.

Frank made no move to follow. He watched Harry as if there was much to say and little time to say it. Or perhaps, Harry thought, no way to say things that made sense.

"Why have you come here, Smith?" he demanded. "Why now? Why this fort?"

"Because you need to understand your options—and I'm afraid you're headed toward the wrong choice!"

Harry followed Geordie down to the dock. Frank's footsteps on the iron sounded behind him. The steps were slippery from sea spray. Help from the drunken revelers was very far away; their voices floated thinly down to him—they were murdering "Silent Night" now—mixed with the agitated calling of seabirds. He felt as if he were the butt of some stupid joke. An urge to do something pulsed through him. But what?

"I know what you're thinking," Frank shouted into the noise of the waves and the wind. "I'd be examining my options about now too."

The dock, moored to a leg of the fort, rose and fell with the commotion in the water that the surfacing U-boat caused. A wave washed over the narrow platform and soaked Harry's legs. The sharp smell of salt and kelp were overwhelming. And something else—diesel, leaking from the U-boat. Unsafe to make any fast movements. He stared at the U-boat. A man climbed out from the conning tower. He appeared to be attaching a flag to what Harry had thought at first might be a communications mast but now saw was a flagpole. A man in a white dress uniform and an officer's cap came to stand beside the first seaman. Waves splashed over his boots.

The flag hanging listlessly from the mast was white.

"They're surrendering."

"Indeed they are," Frank said. "It used to be the custom to forgive your enemies at Yuletide."

In his father's war, the troops in the trenches exchanged cigarettes and chocolate with the enemy, and sang carols. Surely, this war was different?

"Kill 'em now!" Geordy tugged his rifle off his shoulder again. He seemed to be having trouble getting it free in his agitation. "Afore they kill us!"

"Geordy—Wait—" The nervous state the lad was in, any of them could get shot by accident.

"The outcome of this small piece of the conflict has already taken place, Harry," Frank said. "We're not going to change that. Lower that gun, Geordy before you hurt somebody!"

Geordy's face matched the gray tops of the troubled water. He was shaking visibly. He took a step towards Frank, his foot sliding on the wet planks. Harry motioned with his hand—*Stay back!*

But the young man was too worked up to pay attention. "Tha's the enemy, Harry!" Geordie yelled. "Tha's invadin' ussen!"

Geordy brought the Enfield up to the low-ready position and squinted through the sights, lining the back with the front sight. He flipped the safety off.

"Give me your rifle, Geordy!" Harry yelled over the sea noise. "Come on! I'm a better shot than you. Give it to me!"

The white-uniformed figure standing on the U-boat was joined now by two others in regular German navy attire. The submarine seemed hardly more stable in the water than the fort's loading dock, which bucked up and down, making it difficult to keep his footing. The U-boat appeared to have developed a small but significant list to starboard that seemed likely to be the reason for the surrender. The Germans had a problem.

"You'll never hit them, Geordy. Give me your rifle."

"That's General Klaus Hausmann," Frank said. "A very evil man who has his fingers all over the V2 rocket program."

"Harry! Thissun's a traitor!" Geordy turned toward Frank, the butt of the Enfield braced against his side, pinned by his elbow.

He took an awkward step forward across the heaving deck.

Harry tried to grab him. But the boy lost his footing and slipped beyond Harry's reach. He flailed, trying to recover his balance, and the Enfield dropped out of his hands and slid along the wet deck. Harry lunged toward him but was powerless to prevent him from toppling over the edge—and down into the waves.

He needed a life-preserver—a rope—anything! There had to be something—

Nothing. The inflatable lifeboat was moored against one of the fort's spindly legs but impossible to reach in water that bucked like a mule. He leaned over, stretched to catch the mooring line, almost fell in. For a second, he thought he saw a hand above the waves. Then gone.

A shock wave of grief washed over him as he scrambled back to his knees on the heaving deck.

"I didn't mean for that to happen," Frank said. He stooped and retrieved Geordy's rifle.

"If you come from the future—" Harry screamed over the noise of the waves breaking against the tower and the faint cries of the men on the U-boat. "Why come to me?"

Frank edged cautiously toward the edge of the wet dock where tendrils of fog were climbing aboard. "Look. The general's waving—wants to make sure we know he has no surprises up his sleeve. His submarine is damaged. They'd never make it back to home port. This is his only chance." He held Geordy's rifle out. "Do you want to shoot him, Harry?"

"Why're you doing this?"

"Because I want you to make the right choice—for your own future as well as mine! That man in the white uniform, that good-looking blond specimen of the Aryan race, he played a part in the development of the rocket weapons at Peenemunde."

Someone on the U-boat yelled at them, a stream of words that might've been German and might've been English. Harry had no chance of understanding them in the noisy slap and gurgle of the disturbed water.

"Listen to me," Frank said. "Yesterday, a flock of those V2s passed over this fort. Remember that? Your guns couldn't knock any of them down. They went on to London."

Summat real mardy happenin'....

"One of them made a direct hit on a house on Marigold Road."

The words took a second to penetrate. His house—bombed? Alice killed? His daughters too? That couldn't be right. He'd told them to evacuate—

But not soon enough. The letter hadn't had time to reach them.

Rage overwhelmed him. He lunged at Frank, slipping on the wet dock, but managing to grab hold of the rifle in Frank's hand. In the blackness that descended over him, the urge to kill someone rose up like bile in his throat—Alice. Margaret. And Rosemary. Dead— The man in the dress uniform was a Nazi who'd killed his family.

The U-boat listed badly now, waves breaking over her. More German sailors had come out to stand on her spine. One, hardly more than a boy, stood beside the general. He sensed their desperation. The white flag they'd hoisted flapped listlessly in the slight breeze. It would be an impossible shot even for him, with the deck moving under his feet. His fingers on the Enfield tingled.

"Where's the end to it all if revenge rules?" Frank shouted to him. "Is there no better way for humanity? For you, Harry Forrest? For *us*?"

He turned back to face the man who was making him face this choice, Enfield lined up parallel to the deck, aimed at the man's heart.

Frank raised his arms in surrender. "That's the chance I'm taking, that you'll kill me. Do you understand? Hausmann doesn't matter—he's going to die anyway. He has cancer. Take your revenge, if it'll make you feel better. It won't change anything today. Do you remember the Grandfather Paradox? The decision you make will change our future."

One of the German sailors tossed something in their direction. Something heavy, clumsily wrapped in a sheet of paper. A surrender message, perhaps. It fell short of its mark with a splash. The water was racing now with the force of the winter high tide forcing its way up the narrow throat of the Thames.

For a fleeting moment, Harry saw Geordy's face superimposed on the German boy's. And behind the boy—rows and rows of soldiers and civilians in endless wars—hardly more than boys, most of them. English and German and American and Drake's Sea Dogs—all the way back to the Romans. It didn't even stop there.

But it could stop here. He didn't have to be a killer. He lowered the Enfield.

When he looked back, Frank was gone.

London, January 1945

The tide was out. Gulls, terns, and an occasional heron, picked over the mud exposed along the river's banks. It was a mild day but sunless. The smell of the mud flats was rich and earthy, not unpleasant.

A man and a little girl sat on a stone bench beside the Thames, not speaking, watching the birds. The little girl's left arm was folded across her chest in a white sling. People strolled past along the river walk. Couples arm in arm. Mothers pushing infants in prams. Children roller-skating. Londoners, exhibiting their determination to keep their customs and their society alive in the face of the worst the enemy could do.

The child looked up at him. "What will we do now, Daddy?"

The man thought for a while before answering. When the Red Cross told him the news he already knew, he'd immediately thought about the house, totally gone. But the kind lady told him, his youngest was still alive; her Nan had come up from Cheltenham to care for her temporarily. The army granted him compassionate leave to take care of business at home, even though he no longer had one.

The wound was still too raw for him to answer the child.

She fingered the edge of the white sling. "He promised me. I never thought he meant—"

She'd told him about the visitor who'd wanted her out of the house so urgently.

"Nobody else saw him, did they, sweetheart?"

"How did you know that, Daddy?"

Somewhere in the city, a church bell chimed the hour in the midst of the bomb damage all around it—a bell that hadn't been silenced by the blitz or the subsequent rocket attacks.

"I want to know the truth," she said when he didn't answer. "I'm old enough."

"You understand that man, whoever he was, was not the real Sir Francis Drake?"

"'Course I do! I'm not a baby."

"No, sweetheart, you're not."

There'd been no enquiry after the U-boat surrendered. "Frank Smith" didn't show up on any rosters anyway. Geordy's body was never recovered from the sea, just another casualty of war. *Not with this wind blowing, and this tide.* He'd volunteered to be the one who carried the sad news up to Yorkshire, as soon as he'd taken care of his own child.

The German U-boat's crew was turned over to military intelligence. The man who called himself Frank Smith had saved this child from a bomb. But he hadn't saved her mother or her sister. Paradox, Smith had called it. Einstein's arrow. He understood why the man had come, but who he might have been was only now coming into focus.

They watched the birds digging out worms and small crustaceans from the mud.

"We won't always be at war," he said. "We're winning. Mr. Churchill says so. And we trust Mr Churchill, don't we? We'll have the whole future ahead of us."

A shiver ran over his skin—*a crow walking over your grave!*—his grandmother would've called it.

"Will there be another war?" the child asked.

"We'll have to try very hard to prevent that," he said.

He glanced up at the sky, half expecting the sun to be out now. It wasn't. But the clouds radiated a mild light that seemed to promise 1945 would be a better year.

She looked at the seat beside her where a charred library book lay. Its bright pictures of kings and queens were dark with soot and tattered now. It was the only thing the firemen had been able to retrieve from the bombed house. It smelled of smoke.

"I don't need this anymore," she said. "Can you do it?"

He took the book from her and heaved it in a great arc far out into the Thames, pages fluttering, where it floated out to sea on the outgoing tide.

Oslo, December 2035

The helicar settled gracefully onto the roof of Oslo's City Hall where they were greeted by a guard of honor carrying flares to brighten the darkness of the winter afternoon. Several awkward steps to the elevator, and she began to worry that perhaps she should have given in to Catalina's urging and accepted a mobichair. Soon the spidery undergarments kicked in again—a soft, silky feeling of being cradled in a fairy's armor. She walked proudly, her velvet tea gown rustling around her knees.

"Madam!" A tall man in a dark snow parka ran toward them.

She felt rather than saw her escort's instinctive stiffening.

"Doctor Forrest," the man said. He held something out to her on the palm of his hand. She recognized the new technology that gave her so much trouble.

The escorts stepped forward immediately, alert to danger.

"It's all right," she said, and they fell back.

Alone now, outside the magnificent City Hall where the ceremony waited for her, in the floodlit falling snow, she watched the man activate the comm unit. The tiny holo appeared.

Abuelita! Gabriel's image greeted her. *I have something to celebrate too. Do you have time? I must tell you!*

Later, she marveled that she hadn't fallen to her knees.

In the hall, a blur of sensations overwhelmed her. Bright murals—the assembled members of the committee—the fashionable crowd standing in respect—the trumpet salute. The Secretary, white-haired but younger than she, walked beside her to her place on the dais.

More trumpets. The royal party arriving, elegant but understated. The middle-aged king was handsome. She'd expected the queen at least to wear a tiara. Little thoughts, light as dandelion fluff, distracted her mind from Gabriel's message.

The Master of Ceremonies, a tall blond man in a smartly cut suit and blue tie, began his introduction. "Your Majesty, your royal highnesses, excellencies, ladies, and gentlemen—"

Her little finger was twitching. She made a fist to control it. Normal reaction, she reassured herself. All recipients of the Nobel Peace Prize are nervous at the ceremony.

She could do this. She had spent a lifetime talking, planning, collaborating with Carlos to advance her father's dream of world peace. This would be no different. She would talk about how that necessary work must continue, even though her father and Carlos were dead and she would be too someday soon. Had it made a difference? The world seemed to lurch between good and bad outcomes even now, in spite of her work. She had to believe there was a purpose to life.

Another musical interlude. The program informed her it was a medley of English folk songs in her honor. She didn't recognize them.

Thunder of applause—And then it was her turn to speak.

"Doctor Rosemary Forrest Aragon," the Master of Ceremonies said crisply.

She stood. Secretary Eriksen, perhaps catching a moment's hesitation, offered her his arm. In the face of crisis, she'd always found her way. This was no different. She could do this.

I apologize that I couldn't come to this celebration, Abuelita, Gabriel's holo had said.

Behind him, a Princeton courtyard where Einstein had once walked. Dark Catalan face, green eyes he'd inherited from Carlos's family. A door in her past swung open and something dark surged in. A sense of a puzzle being made complete. *I've made a big breakthrough—Actually, of course, my team and I!*

She was aware of the secretary gazing at her in concern, the audience murmuring behind their hands at her delay. To gain time and her composure, she pretended to cough and sought a non-existent handkerchief. An elderly female member of the Nobel committee hurried up to her with a tissue. Deep in her past lay things she'd not understood until now.

We've broken through the barrier. The one-way arrow of time is only an illusion.

She thought of the sunken Roman trireme, its menace to those not ready for it. But surely the breakthrough was inevitable—if not Gabriel, then another. "The tide comes in, the tide goes out," Carlos's voice said in her memory. Life was like that, a river flowing from past to future—and maybe backwards too. We only do the best we can. Horses get killed even though they are innocent.

The man from the future had made sure she was not there when the bomb came for her family. She understood now that it was because he had no choice.

She stepped up to the podium and began to speak.

About the Author

Sheila Finch was born and raised in London, UK. Because most of the schools were closed for the duration of World War II, she didn't get a lot of normal education before her tenth birthday—which was probably a blessing in disguise, as she got to spend a lot of time reading books beyond her grade level. Her undergraduate career started at Bishop Otter College, an Anglican women's college in Sussex that has now morphed into the co-ed University of Chichester. Upon graduation, she taught for one year in a primary school in London's docklands, a slum in those days, but now home to multimillionaires with yachts. After marriage to an American, she lived in Indiana for five years, doing graduate work in Medieval Literature and Linguistics at Indiana University. Moving to San Luis Obispo in the sixties, she found life on the West Coast to her liking and—except for two years spent living in Bavaria—has stayed in California ever since. She taught creative writing and the literature of science fiction at El Camino College for thirty years. She's retired now and lives in Long Beach with two cats. She has three daughters, eight grandchildren, and one great-grandchild.

Sheila is the author of eight science fiction novels. Numerous short stories have appeared in *Fantasy & Science Fiction*, *Amazing, Asimov's, Fantasy Book*, and many anthologies. A collection of the "lingster" stories about the young men and women trained as translators and interpreters to aliens appeared as *The Guild of Xenolinguists*; one of them, "Reading The Bones," won a Nebula. She has also published non-fiction about writing and science fiction.

Her musings can be found on Facebook, and her website is at: www.sff.net/people/sheila-finch/.